The Banana Skin Tango

Martin Pilcher

Copyright © 2005 Martin Pilcher

The right of Martin Pilcher to be identified as the author of this work has been asserted in accordance with the Standard Copyright License (US)

All rights reserved. No part of this publication may be reproduced, stored in a retrieval system, or transmitted, in any form or by any means, electronic, mechanical, photocopying, recording or otherwise, without the prior permission of the copyright owner.

This book is a work of fiction. Names, characters, places and incidents either are a product of the author's imagination or are used fictitiously, and any resemblance to actual persons living or dead, events or locales is purely coincidental.

ISBN 978-0-9556819-1-2

AADVARK-ZAP PUBLISHING (UK)

For Missoo

1

'You're staring at me again,' said Samantha, her eyes widening in resentment.

Melvin ignored her and continued shredding his beer mat. Eventually she came over.

'Okay, is it the usual or are you driving?'

'I'm always driving, so it's the usual, as usual.'

She poured him a double vodka on the rocks with a separate glass of water on the side. It was possible to be that specific in the Buster Keaton club. He pushed a fiver across. She managed a half smile. There was a temporary truce. After the kind of week he'd just had, he was grateful for any manner of break.

He settled himself on a bar stool and eyed her sideways across the top of his glass. It was Friday night and she was wearing a gossamer thin blouse that had as much practicality as a spider's web on a tennis court. His defences were low and as far as he was concerned she looked like a knickerbocker glory on heat and the fine line between sexual harassment and socially acceptable cordiality lay somewhere between enlightened breeding and utter filth. And that was that.

He took a slug on his drink and relished the moment when the fire hit his stomach. A sup of water afterwards reminded him that contrast was one of the simpler pleasures in life. Unlike sex. In a way it was difficult to comprehend, but the fact was, ever since Outi, his brooding Finnish wife had booked herself into an alcoholic's recovery clinic, he had been shagging Samantha practically every night for the last week or so. And her boyfriend Russell didn't seem inclined to do anything about it, even though it must have been patently obvious what was going on. That was the trouble with bisexual blokes. You never knew which way they were going to swing next. And Russell was notorious for swinging with a particularly lethal pair of diamond studded knuckle dusters.

As owner of the club, he felt it was his right to express his distaste for unwelcome customers in whatever manner pleased him.

'Christina was asking after you,' said Samantha, in a tone that suggested the truce was still holding up.

He groaned inwardly. Christina was a bore but he had to bear in mind that she was also his wife's closest colleague and it was only from her that he had learnt the truth behind Outi's resignation as company accountant.

'She'll find me in due course,' he replied, peering into the gloom of the jaded West End drinking club where somewhere the usual gang from Ahus Ericsson Ltd were kicking the shit out of it. It was no surprise to him that Outi had resigned. He had seen it coming a mile off, just like all the other stormy exits that had piled up at such an alarming rate over the last two or three years. This time, however, he had an awful sense of foreboding. As far as their financial position was concerned, it was as welcome as a needle up a camel's sphincter. As for their marriage, well, it had been holed below the water line for longer than he cared to admit and now there was his affair with Samantha to consider. God knows where that was heading.

Christina emerged from amongst the throng of drunken revellers and moved towards him in her precise, controlled sort of way. She was a Swede of the cool detached type and it had never ceased to amaze him what it was that Outi, the quintessential fiery Finn, had seen in her that drew them so close together. As far as he was concerned, there were two types of Swedes. There were the neurotic, off-the-wall types who stayed up all night discussing suicide and the size of their genitals, and there were the others, who were so cautious and correct, that they needed to know the specific gravity of the floor they stood on before putting the next foot forward.

'I must say something about Outi,' said Christina, fixing him earnestly with her pale blue eyes.

'Oh yes?' he replied, in his best drawing room politeness.

'You know about today, obviously.'

'Oh yes.'

Well of course he knew about today, he paid daily visits to the hospital and she knew that as well as he did. Her attitude annoyed him intensely. She treated him like some kind of retarded buffoon who was incapable of coming to any conclusions about anything. Sometimes he felt the bond between Christina and Outi was so strong as to exclude him altogether. As it was, she had somehow managed to visit Outi whilst she was still on the de-tox programme and that was supposed to be against the rules of the game which needless to say he had dutifully observed.

'Outi has been very upset.'

'Yes I know, I spoke to Virginia her counsellor about it.'

'I think she will need your support.'

'Well yes.'

'And you must give it.'

'Yes, of course.'

Bloody Nora, who did this stupid bitch think he had been married to for the last fifteen years, Nanook of the North? Perhaps she thought he slept in the chauffeur's lodge, or something? Hadn't it entered the frozen tundra of her mind that he might just know more about Outi's state of mind than all the consultants, doctors, nurses, counsellors and the entire administration of the Friends of Florence Nightingale Hospital put together? He grappled with his temper.

'I'm serious about this, Melvin,' she continued.

'Yes, yes.'

'She is putting on a very brave face now, but tomorrow will be different.'

'Yes, I know.'

'Of course you do, but this time it will need greater understanding.'

'Greater than what?'

'Greater than you may have given her before.'

'May!'

He was practically apoplectic. What more was he supposed to do that he hadn't done already?

'You must understand her more deeply.'

'Yes, I think we've got most of Ingmar Bergmann on video.'

'Please listen Melvin, I'm being serious now. I realise that you too must be under some stress.'

'Well, yes, some.'

'So you can talk to me later if you wish.'

'Thanks,' it occurred to him that he'd rather do something creative with an ice pick, 'I'm listening carefully to the advice of specialists.'

He took another slug of vodka whilst she sipped delicately on her Dubonnet as if it were poison. With any luck she might get the message and bugger off.

'Outi said you might be joining the Co-dependants therapy group.'

Christina seldom got the message.

'I'm considering it.'

'Good, I think it will be useful and so does Outi.'

'Oh I see, you've discussed it together have you?'

'Well of course we have, you know we discuss everything together.'

She gave him a look of benign patronage. He felt like a two year old that had just been given an abacus to play with. He knew that the chances of a normal conversation were receding fast and he figured his best bet was to bale out before he said something he might later regret. A quick nip to the gents should do the trick.

'Well, if you'll excuse me,' he said, 'I'm just going to milk the lizard.'

She accepted the disengagement without comment.

For reasons known only to Russell, and they were no doubt pretty sick ones, the mirror in the gents had been positioned above 'me stainless steel piss trough' and Melvin, like every other man, was obliged to consider his image whilst emptying his bladder. There was something horribly narcissistic about the process as the electronic eye triggered the flushing mechanism for something like ten seconds.

He inspected his dishevelled demeanour. In spite of the galvanising effect that his intense love making with Samantha was having on him, he harboured the fear that matters were flying inexorably out of control. Perhaps everything *was* his fault after all? Mind you, being married to a brilliant but complex woman, who was also a manic depressive and an alcoholic, had nothing whatsoever to do with his inability to stop lusting after other women. On the other hand, how can you tango with a bottle of vodka and a bucket of guilt?

He had known for a long time that when it came to understanding the nature of her illness, he was way out of his depth. Her obsessive nature affected her every action, and not surprisingly, her quest for perfection became the benchmark by which she judged every one of his. She was impossible to please and so in the end he simply gave up trying. If the knives and forks didn't sparkle, so be it. As far as he was concerned, it was an accurate reflection of their life and if it really were such an important issue then hopefully some of their friends would take notice and come to his rescue. The trouble was, they didn't have many friends. Loads of spongers and freewheelers who were always ready to pig out on one of Outi's extravagantly sumptuous feasts. Or was that his bitter perception? But as her drinking sapped her energy and withered away her enthusiasm, their socialising contracted accordingly. Everything was too much bother, including conversation.

He had tried to justify the situation to himself by concluding that Outi had never been a natural listener in the first place. However, on the one occasion when he'd sought to challenge her on that point, she had retorted that she knew what he was going to say anyway, so why bother? In the end he had taken her advice. The galling thing was, it didn't seem to matter. She would talk *at* him and he would listen but not hear. For a while it seemed quite an agreeable arrangement but eventually all they seemed to do was spend their weekends getting pissed and falling asleep in front of the telly.

On one memorable Saturday however, the sheer aridity or their situation had caused him to have a sudden outburst.

'This is hardly an uplifting experience!' he had yelled. Outi had glowered at him through a maze of bottles and a mountain of cigarette ash.

'Why bother to lift yourself up,' she had said falteringly, 'when you've only got to fall down again?' and had then promptly crashed out on the sofa where she had remained until midday the following morning. This was the stuff of their life and now it looked as if it were going to get worse.

After Outi's resignation, events fell into a familiar pattern. She spent her days lying around the house, her ear glued to the telephone in deep depression mode anguishing endlessly with her sister in Finland. Yet again the bills would be astronomical. The equivalent of at least ten crates of vodka. It had occurred to Melvin that since half the population were probably alcoholics anyway if they did but know it, British Telecom could do no worse than advertise their call rates in fluid measure equivalents. 'Say happy birthday to your mother in law, for less than a litre of vodka' he intoned. Melvin's mother in law lived in northern Finland and couldn't speak a word of English. It was a God-send.

He zipped up his flies and took one final glance at his pallid features. He was pissed and knackered. Swaying unsteadily, he tried to convince himself that all this was just a dodgy phase that he was going through. Things would be fine in the end. Deep down though, if he was really honest with himself, which he seldom was, he knew that his life had about as much value in it as a fag-end in a urinal. He lurched out of the gents and fumbled his way along the gloomy corridor.

At the end of the passageway he sensed another presence and sure enough, amid the cloying odour of stale farts and hoovers, were two men, locked in epiglottal embrace. And one of them was Russell. A well-cut Armani suit couldn't disguise his bouncer's physique. He was confident and strong and his clean-shaven face boasted Stanley Knife nicks. With his steely grey eyes and fashion cropped hair, there was no denying he had charisma. Like Goldfinger on D-Day. Melvin did an abrupt about turn, it was amazing how some things sobered you up, and tip toed back to the bar via another labyrinthine route.

Russell's bi-sexuality was widely known, and in the early days, when Melvin was always with Outi, it had nearly ruined his fantasies about Samantha. Eventually, however, when he realised that his imagination need not be concerned with such intrusions, the fecundity of his cerebral letching settled down as happily as before. Tonight, however, for reasons he couldn't quite put his finger on, he saw things in a different perspective. Did it mean that Samantha was a bit kinky? Well, not in the moralistic sense. He was never one to get too judgemental. Whichever way you want to swing, fine, as long as we all know the right steps. No good having a pile up on the dance floor is there? The point was though, all this arse-about-face with partners just wasn't fair.

Back at the bar he took a deep slurp of water promptly followed by a slug of vodka. Things had quietened down a bit so Samantha settled herself opposite him behind the bar. It was a clear signal that their earlier clash was a trivial thing of the past.

'You're a real poser, aren't you?' she said teasingly.

'No I'm not, it's a great way to drink vodka, Outi's dad introduced me to it.'

'Yeah, so now you're a fearless Finn from the forest, eh?'

He was trying to think of a witty repost when his stomach rumbled noisily -

'Oh, 'scuse me, is there any food on tonight?'

She was about to say no when Russell emerged from a shadowy doorway. He gave Samantha a controlling bear hug.

'Alright, flower?'

'Ouch, don't do that,' said Samantha, her eyes watering as she attempted to push him away as a kitten would a brick wall. He released her but kept his arms outstretched with obvious menace. He turned to Melvin in a way that seemed to invite collaboration but Melvin pretended to be absorbed with chasing his ice cubes.

'So, how's 'er indoors, then?' said Russell.

'Not too bright, I'm afraid.'

'Well, I gotta nice hi-tech watch if she fancies it. Even gotta barometer so she knows when's a good time to 'ave a depression.'

He fixed Melvin with a look that dared him to voice objection at his deliberately insensitive remark.

'Oh, thanks very much . . . can I buy you a drink?'

'Not tonight.'

Russell had this disconcerting habit of switching from being friendly to being cold at the drop of a hat. One minute 'mine host', the next, a psychotic criminal.

Just as things were becoming a shade uncomfortable, a tall man with a creased up jacket and nondescript tie entered the bar. You could tell he was CID a mile off.

'Brian, my boy,' said Russell, suddenly becoming the soul of amiability.

'Russ,' acknowledged Brian, stubbing his fag out with big nicotine stained fingers.

'You may as well push off, flower,' said Russell sarcastically, throwing Samantha a pointed glance as he started to pull Brian a pint, 'no point being an overhead all night.'

And with that, he turned his back on her and joined Brian in a chin close tête-à-tête down the other end of the bar. She looked at Melvin and gave a disconsolate shrug.

'Probably for the best,' said Melvin softly.

'No doubt about that,' she replied, and then cautiously 'I'll see you outside.'

Melvin took one last slug and then sloped off towards the exit.

Samantha joined him outside and they settled into the front seats of the car without comment. As they began to gather some sort of speed along Oxford Street, Melvin said:

'D'you mind if I have some music on?'

'No, go ahead.'

'It's Radio 3'

'Whatever.'

He pressed the button and was relieved to hear the gentle strains of Dvorak floating through the air. Couldn't be better. At that time of night you could never be sure what the BBC eggheads were going to serve you up with. Usually, it was a toss up between Classic FM's umpteenth repeat of Bolero or some esoteric opus for Chinese gong and tuba.

They neither of them spoke for the remainder of the journey, preferring instead to let the sublime melody permeate their souls. Eventually, he pulled to a halt outside her flat in Notting Hill Gate. As he turned to face her he was quite taken aback to see a tear drop streaking her cheek. Was the music really that potent? He didn't know what to do. He fished out a tissue from somewhere. She took it and dried her eyes.

'I'm sorry,' she whimpered.

'There's no need to apologise.'

She composed herself a little.

'It's just that in all the two years I've been with Russell, he's never once offered to take me home, it's either call a cab or piss off.'

The music finished. Melvin turned off the radio and silenced the engine. Obviously some tender loving care was called for and idling engines somehow gave out the wrong signals. Just as he was wondering what to say next, his stomach stepped in with a long gurgling grumble.

'Oh, 'scuse me again.'

'Come on,' said Samantha, pulling herself together with a smile, 'let's have some pasta.'

The Trattoria Trevi was just across the street and as they stepped off the kerb she slipped her hand in his arm. Well, dang my old willy, he thought to himself, as her gentle perfume suffused the night air. Here we go again. A gangster's moll and a plate of garlic. And the weekend had only just started. By the time they emerged it was nearing two o'clock in the morning.

Samantha's flat was a vast one-room studio affair. The centre of attention in the high-slung ceiling was an enormous Chinese lantern whose gold and crimson tassels hung heavily like a mare's tail dipped in wood sap. The fact that they were about to make love was a forgone conclusion.

Samantha switched on a bedside lamp and dimmed the main light until it was no more than an eerie pagoda suspended in the night. They undressed silently. She pulled back the bedclothes and dropped naked onto her back. As he moved in beside her she grabbed his erect penis. She parted her thighs and thrust his hand urgently into the very centre of her wetness. Their desire for each other was rampant. Their simultaneous orgasm nearly breaking the bed.

Afterwards, they lay motionless and glistening, only stirring occasionally to caress each other with tender strokes and a delicate brushing of the lips. In the street outside, somebody kicked a bottle which rattled and clattered across the pavement until it crashed and tinkled in the gutter.

He drank in the beauty of her naked body in an aura of sexual contentment. He was at peace with the world until a blood soaked image of his genitals skewered on the end of a splintered Becks destroyed the moment forever.

Somewhere, he thought he heard Russell laughing.

2

Ajit rolled up the iron shutters of his off-licence and observed the pulsating grot that framed the patina of the day. In his opinion, half way between Arnos Grove and Whetstone was a good place to be. He was a happy man with a penchant for brilliant silk shirts and a range of turbans so dazzling that they made Barbara Cartland look like a forty-watt light bulb on a dimmer switch.

He unhooked the shutter pole and stood in the doorway. It was only ten o'clock but he enjoyed stacking the shelves for the Saturday bonanza. Across the main road which was already buzzing with traffic, he saw the trades vehicles parked on the shredded grass verge whilst their drivers nipped into the Diamond Cafe for a cup of tea and a bacon sarnie. Above the cafe were the windows of Melvin and Outi's flat. The curtains, as always at this time of day, securely drawn. And there next door, peering out onto the world in her pink nylon housecoat was Gladys, her car boot binoculars ever at the ready. She would be across the road soon for her Daily Mirror and bottle of bleach. And not long after that he could expect a call from Melvin. Outi and Melvin were good customers. They drank a lot. A minimum of twelve Pils lagers a day and at least a litre bottle of vodka by Sunday lunch time. They didn't always have the necessary cash but he wasn't concerned. They would run up a slate and it would always get paid in full at some stage or other. Mind you, since Outi had taken her sabbatical, or whatever it was that Melvin had said, their consumption had gone down a bit.

He hadn't seen Outi for two weekends now and he couldn't but help notice that the light in their lounge window didn't seem to be on as much as it used to. Even Gladys hadn't got anything new on the situation, although she was adamant that Melvin had been keeping some very peculiar hours of late, and Missoo, their cat, was often to be seen at the kitchen window crying for her tea. Whatever the case, it was Saturday and that was good for business. Melvin owed him forty-eight pounds sixty and he had no doubt it would be settled before it reached fifty, as was usually the case.

Unfamiliar sounds greeted Melvin in the morning. There was an absence of throaty diesel engines and the bang and clatter of shopkeepers opening up for business. In their place was the gentle gurgle and slurp of a coffee machine. He was still in Samantha's bed. His watch told him it was gone ten o'clock. Some enchanted evening.

'Morning Romeo,' said Samantha, appearing at his side. He was lost for words. She was wearing jeans and a loose smock. Her face was unpainted. She was fresh and alive whereas he felt rather nauseous and crumpled.

'Coffee?'
'Please.'
'Black or white?'
'Black, thank you, one sugar.'
Their day had started.
'Toast?'
'Maybe later.'
'You can have a shower if you like.'
'I probably need one.'
He pulled himself up and rubbed his eyes. She returned with a mug of coffee.

'I'm sorry about this,' he said sheepishly.
'About what?'
'Well, for crashing out.'
'That's okay, ' she gave him a cheery smile, 'you gave your all last night. Help yourself to the bathroom when you're ready.'

She busied herself in the kitchen. It was strange to see her in her own setting. She was no longer obliged to put on an act. Even the quality of her smile appeared different, more natural, less defensive. He began to observe his surroundings. It was the first time he had seen them in daylight. The studio area seemed much larger than last time and there appeared to be doorways leading off to other places. The furnishings were classy and comfortable. She had taste and style, no doubt about that.

The shower had multi selections and he chose the strongest blast. Three prongs of hot steamy water juddered across his cranium and splattered down his spine. He squirted away with a posh looking gel that produced a heavenly scent and a divine foam. He revelled in the sheer luxury of it.
'Better?' she said afterwards, when he reappeared gleaming and steaming.
'You bet.'
'Would you like some toast now?'
'Yes please.'
He wasn't used to this kind of attention. Normally he would be skulking about trying not to disturb Outi. The difference was appealing.
'I have to feed Missoo,' he said, sinking his teeth into the warm buttery toast.
'Miss Who?'
'Missoo, the cat, she'll be expecting me.'
Samantha nodded. He thought he detected a slight air of disappointment. Perhaps she wanted him to kick around for a bit? What did she normally do on a Saturday? The Buster Keaton was only a weekday operation. Did she do mundane things like shopping? He couldn't imagine Russell pushing a supermarket trolley.

'Penny for your thoughts,' said Samantha.

'Oh, nothing much, it's just that I have to get back, there's all sorts of things I have to do.'

He was relieved when she didn't say 'like what?' In fact, she didn't say anything. He munched his way through the toast wondering if there was going to be a sullen silence, but it never came. She seemed to accept the situation as it was. There was a calmness about her which he hadn't been aware of before. She just seemed to be content to exist for the moment and he was drawn into her aura of stillness. Surely he wasn't falling in love with her? And then she kissed him lightly on the forehead.

'Are you seeing Outi today?'

'No, she's in some sort of therapy.'

He tried to unclutter his mind. If only he could hang on to the essence of the morning, enjoy it for what it was instead of his usual habit of fretting and worrying. Unable to sort out the significant from the inconsequential. Always there was a feeling of too much. Too much of what he did not know but all sorts of things became issues which grew into complications and finally matured into angst ridden scenarios from which there was no escape. Jesus Christ, perhaps he needed treatment too? But treatment for what?

'Samantha, do you think I'm neurotic?' he suddenly blurted out. She laughed with surprising gusto. It was a big, throaty laugh, almost masculine.

'I don't see what's so funny, it was a serious question.'

'You're just tense, you must learn to relax a bit more.'

'There's not much to relax about.'

'Why can't you relax with me?'

The possibility hadn't even occurred to him. He was cheating on his wife and half expected Russell to crash through the front door at any moment and sever his balls with a Stanley Knife.

'I've got a lot of things on my mind,' he said.

She said nothing. Again that silence.

'I admit that I'm scared shitless about Russell though.'

There, he had bared his soul, but he didn't feel any the better for it.

'He's no problem,' she replied, in a strange tone of voice.
'How d'you mean?'
'Just think about it Melvin.'

She lit up a cigarette and moved to the window. He noticed that it was raining quite heavily. How could Russell not be a problem? He didn't respect the sanctity of human flesh. Reasonable discussion was not his way of doing things. Violence was his credo. It made him shudder to think about it. He couldn't imagine Russell saying 'well done my old sunshine, Sam's a lovely fuck, wodja drinkin' then?' If there was a grain of consolation, then at least it lay in the fact that Russell *was* bisexual so perhaps the macho male possessiveness wouldn't apply? From what he had learnt so far, it was obvious that he didn't really care about her. 'Just something the punters like to see around' was what he had once said to her. The cold, callous bastard. He had bought her the flat, given her a job and on the odd occasion when his deviant dick had twitched in a different way, she had satisfied him.

And then a weird notion crossed his mind. It sent a shiver through his whole body. Together with Outi, he had frequented the Buster Keaton club for nearly eighteen months during which time he had observed at close quarters how Russell reacted to people he did not like. Particularly the men. They seldom made more than two or three visits and then they were gone, regardless of who they were or how much money they spent. And yet he had become a welcome regular. Somebody entitled to the odd free drink and only one of a handful permitted to run up a slate at the bar. Even his own wristwatch, albeit a birthday present from Outi, had been supplied by Russell. She had told him much later that he had virtually given it to her - 'that's alright my love, can't have Melvin wearing substandard tackle.' And now there was the Mercedes Benz situation.

Melvin loved to trundle around in his old Beetle but now that he had been made Regional Change Manager, it seemed that his car had to change too. Ever since his appointment,

Nigel Denmark the Director of Personnel, had been sending out clear signals for an urgent adjustment to his image.

As far as Melvin was concerned the Cultural Change Management Project sucked. It was just a cynical, paper-thin exercise to facilitate a massive redundancy programme. To make matters worse, he had only been appointed on 'an attachment basis'. This meant he got no extra money and had to carry on with his existing duties as an Area Administration Manager. It was all part of a plot hatched by his boss Fred Brannigan who wanted to get rid of him. Brannigan, (who in Melvin's eyes was a Mafia slob), was banking on the fact that Melvin would probably crack up under the strain of two executive positions. He was pretty near the edge already. Just one last shove.

Outi had mentioned to Russell about Melvin's fascination with Mercedes Benz. It was something to do with his first trip to Helsinki all those years ago. He had stepped off the plane into an indigo winter sunset of minus eighteen degrees centigrade and there at the far end of the tarmac was a row of Mercedes Benz taxis all purring away, their exhausts throbbing regularly in the dry cold air.

Very poetic, I shall make enquiries, was Russell's response. And needless to say, before long, Melvin had found himself foolishly signing a dodgy agreement without even seeing so much as a gleaming bumper. Instinctively he knew it was tantamount to making a pact with the devil but he had reached the point where he no longer cared what direction his life would blunder into. Besides which, what alternative was there? A poxy company Ford Scorpio? No thank you. He would show the bloody philistines what style was all about. Let's face it, when all was said and done, Russell had been most obliging.

'Jesus Christ, you're not saying he fancies me, are you?'

It was his second blurt of the morning. Samantha blew a long line of cigarette smoke at the window pane. It curled up and over before slowly dissipating in the air. She remained with her back towards him.

'Would you like some more coffee?'

The rain had become a deluge by the time he turned the latch on the front door of No.2 Ascension House, his flat above the Diamond Cafe. Damp and despondent, he felt he was not so much ascending and descending.

Missoo whined and complained and demanded his full attention. She biffed his chin with her paw as he bent to scoop up the bills and junk mail from the doormat. She didn't relent until he had placed a bowl of Whiskas selected beef cuts in front of her. She was spoilt and could not understand that it did no harm to experience a dose of neglect even though it was for only one night.

He took a can of Pils lager from the fridge and slumped onto the sofa. Lightning and thunder snaked and crashed outside and the rain dropped with such force that it bounced upwards from the pavement by at least a foot before joining the cascades of water churning and frothing around the gasping drain holes. Such was the scale of the cacophony that Melvin rose from the sofa to observe it at first hand. Mother Nature emptying her bladder and crapping on the earth. Was it a diabolical sign? Russell loves Melvin. Any second now a giant turd could drop from the sky. Fuck you, Chicken Licken. Crash, bang, wallop, zap, everyone jump in the gutter.

When the storm eased slightly and the rain no longer reminded him of Samantha's shower, he played some Mahler on the stereo (he loved the neurotic angst) and poured a second Pils; he detested drinking straight from the can. Outi disliked orchestral music, preferring instead the likes of Dory Previn, Edith Piaf and a rather fat Finn called Jaako Teppo whose strangulated tenor must surely have been formed on the crossbar of a bicycle.

Listening without earphones was quite a novelty so he dragged the sofa across the floor until it was equidistant from the speakers. Missoo climbed onto his lap, she was trembling quite a bit so he stroked her lovingly. Neither of them fell asleep. By the time the symphony had ended the storm had abated so he nipped across the road for a saveloy and chips.

There was loads of food in the fridge but he couldn't be bothered to prepare anything. Neither could he be bothered to tidy the flat or clear the kitchen. Why should he? No one was coming round. Why shouldn't he have a break from routine?

He split open another can of Pils and flicked through the mail. He lived in fear of the telephone bills but the dreaded BT logo was not to be seen. Why didn't somebody write him a nice letter? Y'know, a nice, ordinary, newsy, chatty type of thing. Just one page of blithering niceness would be nice.

He went to the loo. His urine was a lighter shade of Sarson's malt vinegar. Could he face looking himself in the mirror?? At Samantha's he had looked pretty ghastly and not much had happened since then to improve his appearance. But he looked all the same. Not a bad stubble. Could this be a new image? Would the clean-shaven Russell approve? Ha ha ha. Oh very butch, squire. Maybe Russell could give him a second Mercedes Benz as a Christmas prezzie? How about a 1960's 190D with those little fins and a radiator like a gothic mantelpiece? Yeah. And a cream steering wheel and red leather upholstery just like the Maltese taxi drivers had.

Back into the lounge and finish the lager. No telephone call from Outi. Well, bollocks, he wasn't expecting one anyway. Time for another Pils. Piss off Missoo.

Melvin kicked a cushion across the floor and it landed on the telephone dislodging the receiver, but he did not notice. He had decided to play his complete LP set of Berlioz' The Trojans. He needed to feel heroic. He needed taking out of himself.

After all, he'd been shagging Samantha without a condom.

3

Sunday was better. The skies were blue and diesel fumes were at a tolerable level. As yet, the pushing and shoving that so typified people's behaviour on Saturdays was not apparent. Things usually changed after midday in the queues for fags and newspapers.

An hour later would see the jostling for parking spaces in the pub car parks and this would herald the start of a rampant automotive meat parade. Four wheeled drive vehicles with ludicrously fat tyres, half a ton of ironmongery up front, and garish stripes and flashes down the side seemed to imply that today's modern driver was some kind of blundering persona, destined to cavort across the world's stage with all the crude abandon of a pantomime dame exposing her lurid bloomers in some grotesque finale.

Melvin felt contented that his rusting Beetle signified a subculture whose origins were forged in the days when the market place was where you bought sausages and sauerkraut and young boys joined the Hitler youth movement for a decent whistle and flute.

By ten o'clock, Missoo was demanding her breakfast; she had her life to lead, the same as anybody else. She prodded Melvin's stubbled chin until he awoke. For a minute, he did not know where he was. His last recollection was of standing in front of the open fridge munching his way through a packet of olives and a large kabanos. This had been followed by a slice of marmite toast and a stick of celery lashed with sea salt. Everything else was rather vague. The Trojan march had transported him into another world, and a dozen lagers had convinced him that he was an OK guy with chunky muscular thighs and an oily bronze torso.

In the bathtub, things were decidedly different. His hands were shaking so badly he could not shave, so he just lay in the hot sudsy water and contemplated his big toe. Three coffees later he was confident that his jugular would remain intact and so, with commendable concentration, he drove the double blades of his Sensor like a Citroen across his face. Things were beginning to shape up.

In the lounge, he discovered the telephone off the hook. He had no recollection of how this happened either. What if Outi had tried to ring him? Melvin had arranged to join Outi at the Friends of Florence Nightingale for lunch. She wanted him to form an opinion, first hand, of the cuisine, so he would know just how to pitch a letter of complaint that she was seriously contemplating.

As he sat in the restaurant eating a spicy cannelloni as good as anything you could get in Garfunkle's, he broached the subject of his new job. Apparently, Nigel Denmark had met some smart-arse Training Consultant at the IPD conference in Harrogate and naturally, being the Director of Personnel, was incapable of making any sound judgement of character. As a consequence, he had been plied with liquor and, in an advanced state of inebriation, had agreed to subject Melvin and the Project Team to a so-called Cultural Awareness Workshop in some remote hotel in Norfolk.

'What's all that about?' said Outi, after he had just finished explaining what it was all about. He tried again.

'It'll mean I won't be able to start with those co-dependent sessions that Virginia was talking about but that can't be helped.'

Outi looked sour and dejected. As it was, Melvin never seemed to have enough time to visit her regularly and all because of a lame excuse like pressure of work. The way his company went about managing things just beggared belief. Why put somebody on a training course after they had already been thrown in at the deep end? And how on earth could you do anything properly when you were supposed to be in two places at once?

'I don't see how you can be expected to do two responsible jobs simultaneously,' she said.

'I've been given a team of forced volunteers.'

'You should demand more money.'

'We've been through all that last week when I showed you my letter of appointment, it's classed as an attachment, not even a secondment, and I've got no chance.'

'Have you signed anything yet?'

She had a point. He had not but it wasn't quite as straightforward as that. Personnel Admin were always two weeks behind with everything and even then they rarely got it right. He tried to explain the political situation too, the need for large organisations to flatten their structure to survive, the advance of new technology, the threat from the Pacific rim, the global market place, the history and culture of British industry. But it was to no avail.

'From what I can see of British industry,' said Outi, her accent thickening with anger, 'it's run by a load of wankers who don't know their arse from their elbows.'

He sighed wearily. She was right, of course, but all the same, perhaps a crème caramel might not be a bad idea?

'And what's more, they get paid ten times more than you do.'

'I'm hardly a leader of industry,' he pleaded.

'No, but you never get thanked for anything, somebody else always gets the credit.'

He felt a lump rising in his throat. It was the first time in ages that she had paid him any kind of compliment, or even acknowledged that he worked bloody hard and had a position of responsibility.

'Don't sign it and don't turn up at that hotel, or whatever it is, then just see what they do.'

There was an awkward silence. He poured himself a mineral water.

'D'you fancy a crème caramel?'

It was a rhetorical question. He fiddled around with his napkin and then, when it was obvious she had nothing more to say, he sloped disconsolately to the sweet trolley like a bloodhound admonished for slobbering.

All he really wanted was for Outi to get better and be happy. He wanted to see her smile again. She had a lovely smile. It was almost child-like in its openness. Her whole face would light up in a wide grin, her eyes would sparkle and her Slavic cheeks would beam with the radiance of a sunflower. It used to be a constant source of pleasure to him and he longed for its return. He almost wanted it more than he wanted sexual satisfaction. But he couldn't turn the clock back. This was the here and now and he had to make the most of it. He decided to change the subject.

'How are you getting along with your life history?'

She seemed to perk up. When she had first told him that all the patients had been asked to write about their lives and then receive critiques from one another, it had struck him as a rather odd thing to do, given that most of them couldn't focus on anything more demanding than opening a bottle. But Outi was different. It was another task. Another challenge. And she had plenty to tell.

'I've been writing non-stop all day and now I've run out of paper. Can you get me some spare from work?'

'Sure, we're rolling in the stuff.'

After an admirable cup of coffee they returned to her room and she showed him what she had written so far. He was accustomed to her scrawling, misshapen script, the tailing of word endings into an impatient tadpole strim. He couldn't absorb the text but he could see that it was going to be a labour of love. And love her he did. In spite of everything. She was difficult and demanding, but brilliant and talented. An obsessive personality who tortured herself on the rack of perfection. And what was he? An adulterer? An avoider of the truth? A sentimental idealist? Theirs was a marriage made in heaven and pickled in Smirnoff (the Stolichnaya came later when he had accepted the argument for quality).

'What do you think?' she said, as he tried to read it whilst she told him all that was in it.

'Sounds like it's going to be an epic.'

'Well, there's no point leaving things out if they want to know all about you.'

Her logic was unassailable. He was pleased that she seemed to be putting her trust in Virginia even though she was at odds with the hospital administration.

'I'll try and ring you during the week but I'm not sure how my timetable will be,' he said, as they kissed each other on the lips at the lift entrance, 'hang on in.'

On the way down, he had to choke back his tears. To his relief, Mrs Galapagos, who had the charisma of a lizard, was not on duty. There was something unsettling about the dry bitchy way she spoke to him, plus the fact that she held total sway over the comings and goings of all who entered the building.

He hurried across the lilac carpet and out into the pleasant autumn sunshine. He wandered aimlessly up and down the Euston Road for about an hour, finally straying into Charing Cross Road where he watched a gaggle of Japanese girls chatting animatedly in their 'Les Miserables' tee shirts. Somehow their purposeful joy made him feel aimless and depressed. If he went home there was nothing to do except clean the flat and avoid Gladys. In the end, he decided to ring Samantha.

'Will you take my number?' she had said yesterday, as he teetered on her doorway, reeling from the urgency of the kiss she had given him just as he was about to make a dash through the rain. It had been a strange parting. There were disturbing undercurrents. Was he really part of a ménage a trois?

The line crackled and then connected. He didn't know what he was going to say. 'Hello again, how are you? I think I've strained my Achilles heel. Fancy a drink?'

He was horrified when Russell answered. He froze. He couldn't ring off because Russell might get all shirty and psychotic and beat her up. After a few agonising seconds he just said 'hello'. Russell leapt into form straightaway.

"Ello Melv, now there's a funny thing, I've just been trying to contact you.'

'Oh really, well, I've been visiting Outi.'

'Yeah, Sam told me.'

'Oh?'

'Where are you now?'

'Somewhere in the West End.'

Christ, was this it? Was this where he was kept talking until some unsavoury hood materialised to splatter his brains across the pavement?

'Couldn't be better, squire, now can you make it over to Kings Cross, I've got a little something for you to look at?'

'How d'you mean?'

'Now don't be fucking obtuse Melvin, I'm talking three litres here, automatic, eight track stereo, full air conditioning and leather upholstery. Used to belong to an Arab Sheik who sprayed it the colour of camel shit, but we won't get upset about that, now will we?'

'Er, no, of course not.'

'Right then, my old ray of sunshine, up the side of Kings Cross, York Way, go north and take the turn-off for Butler's Wharf.'

'But my car's parked miles away.'

'Well, get a fucking cab then.'

'Yes, well okay.'

'We'll see you in half an hour.'

The line went dead before he could ask who 'we' was. Presumably, he was bringing Samantha along for the ride?

The taxi driver knew exactly where to go and twenty minutes later Melvin was standing alone in a dilapidated area with pot-holed roads and weather beaten buildings. Clearly, the funds had long since run out on this particular inner city regeneration project. Ad hoc parking lots contained battered vans and mud splattered lorries. At the bottom of a rusting iron fire escape which clung precariously to the side of a brick wall for two flights until its rickety platform met a faded wooden door, was a crude hand-painted sign on a sheet of cardboard saying - 'OTT Productions - Auditions'. Somewhere, he thought he heard a goods train rattling across a series of points, but apart from that, there was nothing. There wasn't another soul in sight and he felt distinctly uneasy.

He glanced at his watch. It had stopped. Even a dog wouldn't hang around any longer. As anxiety turned to panic, a dark blue Jaguar XJ6 rose and dipped across the uneven tarmac, the driver's window swishing downwards as it came to a halt beside him.

'What's up Melv? you look as if you're about to be ethnically cleansed.'

It was Russell. He was wearing a black cashmere polo neck sweater with a heavy Grecian gold necklace over the top of it.

'Hop in then.'

He noticed Samantha sitting in the front seat. She was wearing sun glasses which somehow made their rendezvous seem even more sinister. He sunk into the back seat. She didn't speak to him.

'We're only going round the corner,' said Russell breezily, as the car pulled away. And sure enough, a hundred yards round a pock marked bend, they drew up in front of a massive pair of heavy metal doors sunk into an archway that looked as if it had been some kind of loading bay when the old warehouse was in its heyday.

'Follow me, Aladdin,' said Russell, switching off the engine and climbing out. Melvin wished he would stop clowning around, it only made him feel more tense. He did as he was told and watched silently as Russell inserted a complex looking key into the chunky padlock and swung the hasp free.

'This is going to make your weekend, I promise you,' he said, putting his bouncer's shoulders behind the leading door as it swung outwards causing Melvin to stumble backwards to avoid it, 'whoopsa daisy, mind the puddle.'

Melvin recovered his balance as the daylight streamed into the bay and there, gleaming and majestic, was a large Mercedes Benz with a short, vertical, chromium plated rod on its nearside wing which had obviously once supported a small diplomatic flag.

'Now, is that impressive, or is that impressive?' said Russell, his eyes glinting as he watched Melvin closely for his first reaction. Melvin's anxiety disappeared as the sheer beauty of the bodywork glistened in the pale autumn sunshine. Admittedly, it was a very odd colour, not quite as vulgar as camel dung, more a kind of wet Sahara. Nevertheless, it exuded power, status and luxury. And he knew he must have it.

'Take it for a spin,' said Russell, offering him the ignition keys which were contained inside an expensive looking leather wallet embossed with gold Arabic lettering. He hesitated. Mephistopheles was watching, 'go on prat, it ain't booby trapped.'

He unlocked the driver's door and sank into the cream covered leather upholstery. He checked the gear shift for neutral and could have sworn that the numbered figures were laid in gold. The engine started with an imperceptible purr. He had always dreamed of a throbbing diesel but this silent power was intoxicating. Russell slipped in beside him, his face an evil grin. He had unusually small teeth, white, neat and even. He turned on the stereo and they were engulfed in perfect all round sound. A Haydn string quartet, no less. It had obviously been pre-set to Radio 3. Russell's little teeth sparkled again. He knew that he had captured Melvin.

'Forward Macduff, as they say,' the purr became a soft throaty growl as they emerged into full daylight, 'wait for Sam,' said Russell, as they drew parallel to the Jaguar, 'hop in petal, we're going for a spin.'

Samantha obeyed without comment. As she slipped into the back seat, Melvin searched for eye contact in the rear view mirror, but it was met with the implacability of her dark glasses and then the turning away of her head. Something wasn't quite right but there was nothing he could do about it. He kept his eyes on the road and concentrated on his driving.

His hand hovered over the gear shift until he remembered that it was fully automatic. The easy life awaited him.

'Where shall we go?' he asked.

'Anywhere, you're driving.'

He swung left and cruised effortlessly up the shallow hill. A sheik, his minder, and their mistress. Pretty spooky. Melvin made a few left and right turns without regard to where they were actually going, but it didn't bother him as the sheer pleasure of driving took over. After a while, Russell said -

'Well, wodja fink?'

'It's beautiful.'

'It's all yours.'

He didn't consider it wise to enquire about the previous owner. Such details were of little consequence in a transaction of this nature, besides which, he'd already signed an agreement in principle so there was no backing off now.

'Thank you very much,' was his only reply.

Samantha remained mute as Russell gave him a friendly little punch on the shoulder.

'I knew you'd approve Melv, I've always said you were a man of discernment. You can drive it away today, if you like, we'll sort out the details later.'

'I can't, I've still got my Beetle parked near the hospital.'

'Christ, you don't wanna bother about that heap anymore, you're in another league now.'

'Well, I can't just abandon it where it is.'

'I'm not suggesting you should, we all care about the environment, don't we? Listen, I'll give you two hundred smackeroos against your deposit and one of my associates will take care of it tonight, now what's the problem?'

Melvin was too embarrassed to admit that he still had some sentimental attachment to the rotting old heap, but two hundred quid was cheaper than paying someone to tow it away.

'Okay, done.'

'Excellent, a wise decision, even though I say so myself.'

'I've got some personal effects I'll need to pick up.'

'No problem. Do a right turn past this ice cream van and let's get our arses into gear.'

Melvin wasn't sure whether there was some kind of sexual innuendo within the coarseness of the message, but it had fled from his mind by the time he had cleared out the Beetle and handed Russell the keys.

'I'll see you at the club sometime,' said Russell, passing the keys to Samantha, who had finally taken her sunglasses off, 'stick those in yer handbag, luv, I don't wanna spoil the pockets of me trousers.'

'Er, I'm not sure when that will be, things are getting a bit hectic and I may have to go to Norfolk soon.'

'Don't worry about it Melv, Christ, you do make life complicated, don't yer? Enjoy the motor. Lovely drive to Norfolk, what could be better?'

And with that, he shook Melvin's hand vigorously and pulled him close in an arm hug, 'always nice to do business with a gentleman. Ciao, amigo.'

For one dreadful moment Melvin thought he was going to be kissed. He forced a smile and then shot a glance at Samantha over Russell's shoulder.

'Have a nice time in Norfolk.' was all she said.

He hadn't told her he might be going away.

4

'Morning, Dog's Bollocks.'

'Yo, Fart Features.'

It was Monday morning at the office and the ritual greeting between Melvin and Jack Mathews had just occurred. This time, however, Jack was in a disagreeable mood and launched straight in with the source of his discontent.

'I've just had a ten minute bollocking from the Tottenham Shop Stewards about a twelve percent loss of earnings all directly attributable to the arbitrary actions of that beer swilling, fag wheezing, drunken toss pot of a payroll supervisor of yours, Sid fucking Wyatt Earp or whatever the wanker's name is, and I want to know what the bloody hell you're going to do about it.'

Melvin buried his head in his hands to signify concern. As Service Manager, Jack Matthews had a tough job and he was also Melvin's closest ally, so some kind of corrective action had to be taken. All the same, right now he needed payroll problems like a hole in the head.

'Okay, just sit down for a few minutes and talk me through it.'

'I don't want a seat, snot face, I just want these fucking shop stewards off my back, so the sooner you sort that disagreeable piss artist out the better. I'll leave you with it. You have my full support, now good fucking day, dear boy.'

And without more ado, Jack pushed his big loping frame through the doorway. Although Melvin was accustomed to Jack's vulgarity and forthright approach he had this nagging suspicion that of late, Jack had become jealous of his appointment as Regional Change Manager. Jack was ambitious but had been passed over on two occasions for jobs that most people thought he was sure to get. As one organisational plan superseded another and yet more emphasis was placed on reducing manpower budgets, big company politics were becoming more ruthless. Alas, although Jack was a political animal, he had failed to recognise that his colourful personality was no longer in favour. The two of them had stuck close together in the face of Fred Brannigan's bullying but when it was clear that Brannigan was angling to rid himself of Melvin, the survival instinct had woven a strand of mistrust into their relationship.

Brannigan had first told Melvin that he was only nominating him for the new position but then, a week later, at a heads of department meeting, he had rubber stamped the agreement in a manner that left Melvin little option but to accept. Melvin had become tired of the way in which Brannigan had fashioned his management meetings into a kind of blood sport, baiting and bollocking his team and daring them to take him on. The idea of another set of responsibilities that might just put some distance between them had a certain appeal, but when Brannigan made his announcement, Jack threw him a 'you poor sod' sort of look and the rest of his colleagues averted their eyes as if he were a sacrificial lamb that they would rather not see slaughtered.

After the meeting, they had trouped out of Brannigan's office like a bunch of schoolboys. Half way down the corridor, Melvin nudged Jack.

'A quick chin wag, if you don't mind?'

'Are you sure you don't need the bog first?' retorted Jack, giving a jeer rather than a smile.

'Yeah, very funny - have a pew - I drifted off.'

'We noticed dear boy, we noticed. Well, if you're going to get to the end of the year with your nuts intact, you'd better stay alert and streetwise because this is now open season and you are in line to get shafted.'

'Thanks pal.'

'I'm sorry mate, but this Change Manager's role is not an accolade, it's out on a raft time and kiss goodbye to dry land.'

'It's not the first time he's tried to isolate me, for Chrissake. I can survive that.'

'It's more than that, you dick head. Can't you see that that sadistic bastard is lining you up to walk the ship's plank and that's assuming he doesn't try to keel haul you first.'

Melvin slumped in his chair and fell silent.

'Look,' said Jack, in softer tones, realising that he had wound Melvin up enough, 'the writing is on the wall. My guess is that he's already done some kind of deal with Nigel Denmark. Any other time, whoopee, big ego trip, great opportunity, enviable secondment, but in reality you'll be out of sight and out of mind when the permanent jobs are being handed out. Now do you bloody savvy or don't you?'

All of a sudden, the prospect of a balanced day, let alone a balanced life, seemed as remote as an igloo on Mars. Melvin grimaced and twiddled his fingers.

'But surely it will be pretty high profile, won't it?'

'Oh yeah, like a fucking leper with aids. Don't kid yourself that anyone will care a toss for what you'll be doing. It'll be crocodile smiles and lip service and 'piss off plonker we've got a business to run' - and where's that going to leave you?'

Melvin's face signalled realisation.

'Precisely,' said Jack, 'up shit creek without a paddle.'

The two men looked at each other earnestly. It seemed as if the halcyon days of comradeship and fun were about to become history. And now, three weeks later, Jack appeared to be making as issue of Melvin's administration. There was nothing new in payroll problems, they happened all the time and were easily sorted. Melvin would usually meet Sid Wyatt his Payroll Supervisor in the pub and after they had both got pissed, Melvin would sign Sid's excessive personal mileage claim and that would be the end of that. Melvin could never understand what Sid was talking about anyway because figures were not his bag, so to speak. The telephone rang.

'Good morning, and how is my leader?'

It was Zelda.

'Well, Jack's in a foul mood and that's only the first conversation of the day.'

'You should be so lucky, I've had three arguments already and I haven't even sat down yet.'

'Right now I feel as if I need help just to stand up.'

'Okay, I'll bring up a bottle with the post.'

This was how thing always went with Zelda. She was his total support system. Officially in charge of word processing, faxes, telexes and that sort of thing, she had, by sheer dint of efficiency and personality, not mention a dollop of Jewish sassiness, become his PA and the focal point for everybody. Without her, he was lost.

For the last year at least, Melvin had been on auto-pilot. It had never ceased to amaze him that in spite of the odd cock up or two, say every other day, the vast bureaucratic ship that he was charged with keeping afloat had somehow managed to pitch and roll majestically through the worst of storms and yet everyone on board had seemed to remain happy. As Outi's condition had worsened and he had become unable to leave his emotional baggage at home, Zelda had proved to be an absolute rock. It was she who had really kept things moving and he would merely sling his anchor overboard in time to alight on the rock and sign this or that piece of paper that somehow or other caused something to take effect. It was quite amazing really. The accounts more or less balanced out and his reputation as an efficient and caring manager remained intact. But now everything was about to change.

'Is there anything urgent?' enquired Melvin.

'Not really, but Harold Hogger wanted to know if you could see him at the Training College this afternoon, it sounded important so I told him that in theory you were free and I would ring him back after I'd spoken to you.'

'Thanks, I'll give him a buzz in a minute.'

'Okay, I'll speak to you later.'

A call from Harold Hogger was usually a signal of some political skulduggery afoot. Harold was the Training and Development Manager and, as such, was considered to be a Personnel man through and through. The reality was somewhat different. Nevertheless, Nigel Denmark had ensured that as far as the Change Management Project was concerned, Melvin Powell would report directly to Harold. It was his way of keeping rein on a loose canon. From an operational point of view, Brannigan could do what he liked with Melvin but the change programme was *his* baby and *his* passport to a secure future in the new world order. The trouble was that Brannigan seemed to be in cahoots with Gerald MacNab the Director Finance and that made him feel distinctly uneasy. In management circles everybody knew that the two Directors were sworn enemies and MacNab had a network of spies everywhere. One of them was Rupert Selwyn Smythe, a management trainee from Audit whom Brannigan had agreed 'would provide the necessary administrative support to ensure that area operations were not adversely affected by Mr Powell's additional responsibilities'. It was Brannigan's way of acknowledging that his Administration Manager's creative accounting methods were fast becoming a source of embarrassment.

Accepting Gerald MacNab's offer to second Rupert Selwyn-Smythe struck Brannigan as an inspired choice particularly as Rupert had ferreted out a number of policy misdemeanours during a routine audit on the sales commission scheme. He had been unable to pin anything specific on Melvin but Brannigan had been impressed by his weasel like methods, not to mention his castigation of Melvin in the final report - 'the Administration Manager's rather droll and eccentric memoranda do nothing to mitigate his cavalier attitude towards the company's Financial Instructions and Directives'. Brannigan had no such facility with words preferring instead to bludgeon his managers with immortal phrases like 'if you can't see the bloody dust when I'm coming for you that's your problem not mine'.

Melvin and Zelda had certainly foreseen the problem with Rupert Selwyn-Smythe. Zelda was very well connected and there wasn't much that her intelligence sources couldn't find out. For a start, she was friends with Heather, Nigel Denmark's secretary, and what with her expertise in interrogating SNOG, the company's Email system, it hadn't taken her long to uncover Rupert's formal letter of appointment, Personnel Admin. having forgotten to apply a security bar anyway. Rupert would report direct to Melvin and operationally speaking, that meant her. Even so, they knew that Rupert had another agenda and that was the one controlled by Gerald MacNab. Notwithstanding all that, when his name was first mentioned it had definitely spoilt their day.

'Oh Christ, not that slimy brain on a stick,' exclaimed Melvin.

'Yup,' replied Zelda, 'that's the one, our double first from Cambridge who poured French dressing on his chips and then formally complained that you were running an ergonomically dysfunctional salad bar.'

'The little shit, we'll bury him.'

And on day one of his appointment they had literally done just that. Much to the chagrin of Zelda's staff, all fabulous girls that Melvin referred to as his 'Sabre Dancers', Rupert's ego had been stroked by placing him behind an enormous desk at the front of the office. He had then been buried under copies of every conceivable directive, procedure and formal company instruction they could lay their hands on, with the brief to give a current status report.

'That'll teach the little sod to slag me off in Audit Reports,' sniggered Melvin, 'now he can learn what operational reality is all about. Let's see how long it takes him to implement one of his own ridiculous recommendations.'

As a productive triumvirate of happy administrators the situation did not augur well. Melvin looked at the state of his own office. In spite of Zelda's ability to divert unnecessary paperwork elsewhere, he was still cursed with the stuff in ever increasing proportions. The introduction of computers was supposed to have heralded a paper free environment but some people, notably Brannigan's secretary Claudia, hadn't quite grasped that principle and continued to bombard him with reams of hard copy screen prints.

'Stupid fat bitch' he muttered to himself, as he kicked the latest batch under a side table. It was time to do something constructive. He punched Harold Hogger's number at the Training college. It was a good connection for once and Harold was as clear as a bell.

'Harold Hogger, good morning.'

'You called O Wise One.'

The voice at the other end immediately dropped the charade of politeness in favour of avuncular self-mocking concern.

'My stout fellow, what a delight to hear your golden tones, I simply must see you as soon as possible to impart matters of great importance.'

'Would the word 'change' be part of this great intellectual gathering of minds?' quaffed Melvin, warming to their traditional buffoonery.

'Indeed it would, but I am sworn to secrecy on matters of high state.'

'In that case I shall summon my magic carpet and fly hither to your palace.'

'A truly excellent decision, I shall recycle a tea bag in honour of your arrival at two of the noon.'

'Plus a choccy biccy, I hope?'

'On a silver platter, no less.'

'Thank you so much, 'til then, goodbye.'

'Tootle pip.'

They rang off. It was little interactions like these that kept Melvin sane. Harold was one of the few old school managers whose advice and guidance he actually valued. Having Harold as his boss on the Change Management project was the only good thing in what was fast becoming a deepening spiral of regret. After all, why *did* Brannigan want to be rid of him? What had he done? More to the point, what had he *not* done?

During his last performance appraisal Brannigan had said to him, with customary bluntness, 'the trouble with you is that you're too honest for your own good.' Well, what the hell was he supposed to do with that, start lying? Already, his career thus far had been littered with a liberality of lies and yet apparently it was not enough.

He was not so naive as to realise that the forthcoming reorganisation was going to be a major bone marrow extraction job. The flesh and fat had already been peeled back two years ago and this time they would be hanging out the skeletons to dry. No doubt there would be some ludicrous testing of frames to establish who would be strong enough to carry the new mantle of image and efficiency. Past achievements would be like so much urine in a sluice.

Nigel Denmark and his ilk would be administering some complex form of x-ray designed to reveal the slightest deviation from the new corporate DNA profile. Suspect gene carriers would be isolated and then dunked in formaldehyde under the guise of constructive interview feed back. They would be left to crack and disintegrate like so much canker in the toe nails of the company until, when the numbers game was settled and all the shits and sycophants had found their swimming positions in the pulsing new arteries, they would be scraped up and deposited unceremoniously into the nearest trash can. The company called it natural wastage. Personnel called it voluntary redundancy. The victims would call it the sack.

Melvin decided that whatever the outcome of the final solution, he was going to remain a full-blooded human being and have some fun. And with that uplifting notion in mind he left his desk to stroll along the corridor for a quick slash. Unfortunately, this passing happiness was soon dissipated as the awesome mass of Claudia appeared like an ocean liner through the swing doors.

'Good morning, Melvin,' she said, with the merest hint of condescension, 'Mr Brannigan was wondering whether you had completed last month's Energy Conservation Report yet? I couldn't raise you on the telephone last Friday so I sent you a SNOG message which you may not have seen yet. I don't think there's any real hurry.'

It was her way of saying 'I can't stand people like you who never submit their reports on time so I've deliberately dropped you in it'. Melvin countered this with an air of semi-bumbling joviality which denied her the satisfaction she craved. It was yet another example of a twisted human interaction that the current company culture seemed to have bred.

'Oh righto,' he said breezily, 'as a matter of fact I was putting the finishing touches to it last night so I'll whistle it along sometime today.'

'Thanks Melvin, fancy you working on a Sunday, anyway I'll tell Mr Brannigan to expect it.'

And with that, she wafted past him like the QE2. 'Yeah, I bet you will,' he thought to himself, ' you two-faced cow'.

He was surrounded by poison. He knew damned well that Brannigan couldn't care a toss about energy conservation and the only reason he knew that the monthly report was overdue was because Claudia had reminded him. Her whole existence thrived on dropping the management team in it. One by one, she had systematically undermined their credibility whilst smiling outwardly with all the innocence of a Botticelli baby. A weakness for chocolate and cream buns had blessed her cherubic face with several wobbly chins and what with her predilection for steak and kidney pudding and fish and chips, she sported a more than generous girth. Most of the management team deferred to her but she knew that Jack and Melvin called her 'Fat Arse'.

'Malignant bitch' muttered Melvin as he pushed open the door of the gents. Some people needed pissing on. For a few brief moments he imagined she was staked to the ground in the middle of the car park and he was driving a steamroller over her. He would flatten her tree trunk legs and as the force moved upwards, her barrage balloon thighs would swell and split and her bloated belly would strain and roll like some grotesque hippopotamus about to give birth. Then she would explode in a flatulent peroration whose gaseous cloud would finally smother her cries of 'but I was only doing what Mr Brannigan asked me to'. And then she would be dead. He would instruct his po-faced maintenance supervisor to lever her off the tarmac with a giant sized sardine can key and then stack her upright like a totem pole in a skip, ready for incineration. That would do wonders for energy conservation.

The evacuation of urine and bile being over, he zipped up his flies and moved to the sink. Without thinking, he blasted his trousers with a fine spray jet from the energy conservation adjusted water taps. Sod it. Another unproductive five minutes with his leg dog-cocked underneath the hand drier.

Then back into the brave new world with his anger state contained as effectively as the head of Medusa under a hair net.

5

'Okay Fred,' said Gerald MacNab, with false bonhomie, 'we'll keep in touch.'

He rang off and reflected on recent events with smug satisfaction. So far he had out manoeuvred everyone. He had allowed Nigel Denmark, an insufferable twit by anyone's standards, to think that his nincompoops in Employee Relations had solved a problem by agreeing to Rupert Selwyn-Smythe's secondment to Fred Brannigan. In reality, however, they had allowed his most lethal mole right inside Nigel Denmark's pet project.

Already, after a mere three weeks in post, Rupert had used his auditor's nose to sniff out some juicy titbits. One of the most interesting developments was Nigel Denmark's signing up of an external Consultant. 'I think he's breached the Sole Supplier Agreement' were Rupert's words during one of his covert telephone calls, 'and he's allocated the cost to a dummy project number which I'm currently running a search on'. As expected, nay, hoped and prayed for, the temporary loss of Rupert to Fred Brannigan was beginning to realise some potentially explosive dividends. Admittedly, in order not to arouse too much suspicion, Gerald had put up a token screen of resistance which he had then carefully backed away from by feigning a false overdose of comradeship with Fred. In a funny way though, he had a grudging respect for the pugnacious sod.

Fred was a rough and tumble street fighter whose performance in the political arena had as much finesse as a rhinoceros in Swan Lake. Like most bullies he had only mastered one tactic and that was the full frontal charge, nevertheless, with careful handling he could be primed, aimed and fired to devastating effect. Somehow the prospect of a scud missile blasting the heart out of Nigel Denmark's Change Management Project was a temptation he couldn't resist. When the dust finally settled he would come up smelling of roses. There would be a top job for him in the re-organisation and naturally, in the new world order, the bottom line results would reign supreme. The new company could at last be run as a proper business where all those wet, psycho babbling fools who wasted everyone's time with their pathetic prattle about people issues but who couldn't even read a profit and loss statement would be consigned to the dustbin forever. Chartered Accountants would be the only cats to taste the cream. He buzzed his secretary.

'Yes Gerald.'

'Gloria, see if you can track down young Rupert and tell him I'd like a word with him as soon as possible.'

'Yes, okay.'

The line went dead and Gerald MacNab pondered a range of blue touch papers which were available for the lighting thereof. He would caution Rupert not to be too over zealous for the time being. Brannigan was no fool and would be watching developments closely. Meanwhile, he needed to know where Melvin Powell's allegiances lay. That was an area of risk he would prefer not to have. He would need to brief Rupert carefully. So, things were beginning to take shape. Perhaps a call to that music hall diplomat Harold Hogger might not go amiss?

'Bloody bastard!' hissed Nigel Denmark.

His lower lip trembled with fury as he slung the memorandum across the desk. It fluttered in a convoluted bluster before landing on the floor. So, this was it, was it? Knives were out. Vendettas were being launched. Now what precisely was at risk? His personal reputation? The Employee Relations Mission Statement? The status quo? None of them. It was pure politics. Well, he could play dirty with the best of them. After all, he hadn't got where he was today by being nice.

By rights he would never have seen the memo, but when you've got an electronic mailing system people do sometimes press the wrong button by mistake. In this case, the wrong button pusher had been Gerald MacNab, the Director of Finance. From the text of the memo, which was addressed to his Chief Accountant, it was obvious that he had caught wind of Nigel's plan to plunder the Chairman's slush fund to finance the Change Management Project. Well, it wasn't the first time he'd crossed swords with the poisonous little shit and this time he might just have a few aces up his sleeve. Morale in Finance was now arguably lower than that in Customer Service and not every Accountant felt obliged to keep their lips tightly buttoned up. Indeed, only last week he had heard something fishy about the Business in the Community Budget, so MacNab was not squeaky clean himself. Somewhere there was a mole in the department but he was buggered if he knew who it was. His secretary Heather was as professional as they come and it was she who had actually received the memo by chance and had printed off a hard copy for his personal reading folder. As for his direct reporting managers, he had deliberately hand picked them to ensure his own position would remain unassailable. Why should he worry if other people thought they were a bunch of sycophantic wets? He was safe and that was all that mattered. He could delegate most of his work and just attend the swanky meetings in London and it still left him time to wander around John Lewis's once or twice a week. Anyone who sought to query his judgement would soon find themselves buried in a quagmire of policies and procedures.

He had formulated his survival policy five years ago after he'd been caught in an office stockroom with a feather duster down the front of the cleaning supervisor's knickers. As a result he had been promoted to national Headquarters where he had managed to ingratiate himself to the ruling elite to the point where they felt he was the natural candidate to front the company's human resources down sizing programme in one of the Regions.

So, out he was sent and with his team of rats, had fashioned a programme of change that, on the face of it, was the most caring, supportive and people oriented project ever to gain unanimous acceptance by the Board. In reality, it was the start of the most cynical and ruthless slashing of the workforce in the entire history of the company. Inwardly, he knew that nobody in the Personnel Directorate had either the backbone or experience to front the project, besides which, if it ran into trouble, he needed to ensure his own empire was free of the flying brown smelly stuff.

Heather tapped on the door before entering. She was mindful of his insufferable ego and such gestures served to satisfy his status conscious appetite. They also went some way to ensuring that he treated her with at least some modicum of decency and respect. Privately she loathed him. She thought he was an odious turd with no moral principles whatsoever, however, as a professional secretary of the highest calibre, she kept her opinions to herself. When she heard him curse she was already prepared with a plate of chocolate biscuits and black coffee served in an elegant bone china cup.

'Ah, thank you Heather.'

They exchanged smiles and Nigel stuffed the first biscuit in his mouth as Heather made her exit.

'Let me just attempt to summarise,' said Melvin, dunking his chocolate Bon-Bon in a large mug of Earl Grey tea, (Harold was a whizz at brews on the side). He had managed to get through the morning without any more cock-ups and apart from being nearly crushed to death on the M25 had swung his gleaming Mercedes Benz into a quiet corner at the back of the company's Training College.

'You have my undivided attention and indeed the greatest of sympathy,' said Harold piss-takingly.

Melvin was relieved that Harold was at least to hand. He was quite an astute egghead who never imposed his views on anyone. His physical head was rather small, like the whole of his stature, and he was bald with beady black eyes and the ears of a gnome. He would not look out of place on a toadstool. Soberly and neatly dressed and smoking like a chimney whenever he could get one on, he was a pencil of mischief.

Melvin was very fond of him. He was the only male in the entire putrefying company who had any wit. And in spite of being divorced and coping with an ancient mother suffering from senile dementia, he retained a spirit of enjoyment. His feet, little tap dancers that they were, were undoubtedly placed on terra firma.

Melvin began in a mood of cynical supplication.

'Next week, I have to pretend that I am fully briefed and ready to move this epic so-called cultural change management project into so-called go-live status.'

'Yes.'

'And that will entail some masterly explanation as to why the entire project team, including myself, are shacked up at the Flint Shingles Three Star Country Club Hotel in Norfolk, being subjected to five days bullshit from one of Nigel Denmark's brown-nosing, wanker, consultant piss heads that he got rat-arsed with at the IPD conference in Harrogate.'

'So far, so good.'

'After which, I am deemed fit to change the human face of the company whilst the corporate cleansing department, i.e. Employee Relations, to say nothing of the remainder of Personnel, fills its hoses with undiluted sulphuric acid in readiness to squirt it up the renal orifice of the first poor bugger who dares to question the sanity of the whole bloody process.'

'That is indeed an accurate interpretation of events thus far.'

'I am so glad we agree, and needless to say, in keeping with this organisation's enviable reputation for broadcasting all the right signals with the utmost of clarity, they have blessed the project part-time status in the shape of yours fucking truly who is also expected to perform his existing duties without the slightest drop in productivity or level of service.'

'With the inestimable help of Mr Selwyn-Smythe, who, as we know, is our brightest management trainee.'

'And also a spy for MacNab.'

'Precisely.'

The enormity of the pit now opening before Melvin undoubtedly belonged to Satan.

'I need your help Harold.'

'My dear chap, I give it to you whole-heartedly and without the slightest hint of ungraciousness or rancour.'

'No seriously Harold, I do not need to be caught in the mach two cross fan of executive excreta at this stage of my non career.'

Harold looked at Melvin kindly. He knew that Melvin was the sacrificial lamb and what's more, that Nigel Denmark, his functional Director, had appointed him to ensure that Melvin's ritualistic barbecue would reach its optimum temperature at precisely the right moment.

'Just go with the flow,' said Harold, with genuine sincerity, 'and when we see which way the wind is blowing, we can choose our next card carefully.'

The two men looked at each other earnestly. They both knew that they were pawns in a highly dangerous game and their survival would depend on their ability to maintain their mutual trust and respect for one another.

Melvin slumped in his chair like a dispossessed slug. Perhaps the time had come to take a bout of long-term sickness? After all, he was hardly at peak performance. A desperately ill wife, a perilous affair, and a growing intake of alcohol did not exactly constitute the seeds of success. The truth of the matter was that apart from the sublime but transient pleasure of shagging Samantha, he could see no real reason for getting up in the morning. Life had become a monumental saga of disappointment and regret. Somehow his spirit had been sucked dry.

'Cheer up, old chap,' said Harold kindly, 'I've got some good news for you.'

'Oh yippee, may I dance the light fantastic in anticipation.'

'Lisa Joplin your project team leader is now available to commence her duties.'

'Three weeks too bloody late but I suppose when somebody else has appointed my own team the whole question of human resources is purely academic. Anyway, which category does she come under? Misfit, incompetent, appalling sickness record, bungled disciplinary victim or just plain bloody bored?'

'None of those, which is why her local manager has been less than fully co-operative in agreeing her release date.'

'One is surprised.

'She's a very energetic and capable young woman,' Harold twinkled in mischief, 'just what you need, and I'm sure you'll enjoy meeting her at the Flint Shingles Country Club Hotel next week.'

'Well if she's so crucial to my survival, how come I must wait until then?'

'She's on holiday in Majorca'

'Bloody typical.'

'Well try looking at it this way, my dear chap, she'll have a nice tan, she'll be relaxed, and you can enjoy the comfort of the hotel, an admirable way to start a fulfilling professional relationship.'

'You're taking the piss, of course.'

'Well, Nigel Denmark's esteemed consultant Julian Weekes will also be there.'

'Bloody Nora, what does *he* list as his hobbies, fell walking and invoicing?'

Harold realised that he could do little to dispel Melvin's prevailing cynicism but it was not something that bothered him unduly. He had seen Melvin like this many times before; it was a kind of defence mechanism before his natural zealous enthusiasm kicked in. If there was an area of doubt it was the fact that this time the political agenda was being controlled by national forces and that was something he could not influence. He was at the end of his career anyway, so it didn't really matter, nevertheless he would not wish to jeopardise his severance package if it could be avoided. This was going to be the Mother of all reorganisations.

The two men swapped a few more jokes and concluded their business. It did not take them long because they both had an intrinsic grasp of what was expected of them. Everything and nothing. Harold's brief was to keep the lid on things whilst Melvin's was to pedal the propaganda. There was little point in asking for further guidance as none would be forthcoming. Everybody would be looking over their shoulder and protecting their own back. In management circles the project had already been nicknamed 'DED' for dog eat dog and the nastier elements were referring to Melvin as 'the Personnel Poodle'.

On the return journey, with the eight track stereo giving full bent to a searing Berlioz string line, what none of them knew, including Harold, was that this time Melvin had decided to lead from the rear instead of the front.

After all, was it not Brutus who said: *It is better to see the handle of a dagger than feel its blade.*

6

By the time Melvin had parked his gleaming Mercedes in his customary spot three down from Fred Brannigan's in the executive car park, Jack Matthews had espied him from a top corridor window and had decided to wind him up. His motives were somewhat ambivalent but he was spurred on by a desire to stir things up, to do something, anything that would make someone take notice of what he was saying. He did not wish Melvin any harm because they were buddies, but the depth of his pain caused him to view the emerging world through spectacles whose lenses had been sharpened in the astringent brine of cynicism.

'Had a good meeting, plonker?' said Jack as Melvin trudged down the corridor.

'It's been years since I had a good meeting,' replied Melvin, moving along into his office. He could tell instinctively when Jack was in one of his malevolent wooden spoon moods.

Jack followed him in and slumped his gangling frame on a chair. 'So, have you sorted out your payroll mob?'

'I have taken action.'

'Lying cunt.'

'Partially correct. I know the course of action I'm going to take.'

'That being?'

'A full scale investigation by Mr Rupert Selwyn-Smythe.'

Jack hesitated. Melvin continued.

'Yes, I thought that might give you food for thought, but as it just so happens, on my way round the M25 I came to the conclusion that I have not as yet felt the benefits of Mr Selwyn-Smythe's superior brain power and what better than an in-depth report on your shop steward's allegation of under payments.'

Jack wanted a resolution and now he was going to get one. Nothing like an auditor to ferret out inconsistencies. Needless to say, Melvin was thinking on his feet but the idea had instant appeal. He could send Rupert all over the place, checking up on this and that, it would keep him out of his hair a bit, not to mention Zelda's and the girls. It might also keep Jack at bay for a while; he could do without these constant batterings.

'I trust you will have no objection to the checking of time sheets?'

Jack got up and loped towards the door.

'He can do what he likes as long as it doesn't take six fucking months,' he turned in the doorway, 'and while he's at it, p'raps you'll ask him to scrutinise *your* mileage returns now that you've moved up into the higher echelons of engine capacity and public swanksville.'

Melvin ignored him. Jack threw a parting shot.

'Better sharpen up the porridge gun, dear boy, I hear it's gobbler's paradise with the luscious Lisa next week.'

And with a final leer he was gone. As friendships go, this one was taking some pretty peculiar turns.

The phone buzzed. It was Zelda.

'I've got Outi for you.'

'Oh thanks, I was going to ring her anyway.'

This was the truth.

'Hi,' said Outi flatly, 'were you thinking of coming to see me or what's happening?'

'The training course is definitely on but not until next week. I've got loads to clear up though.'

'So are you coming or not because I want some more paper for my story?'

Outi had a habit of ignoring Melvin's situation in favour of her own which she always considered to be of greater importance. He knew that he would see her anyway and there was no point in delaying things, besides which, he wanted to see Samantha. There were a few things that needed to be sorted out on that front too.

'Yes I'll pop in later tonight, I don't know what time though, my in-tray's about a foot deep,' there was no harm in persevering with the message, 'anyway, I'll bring some paper.'

'Okay, can you make it by eight? Virginia wants to see you about the co-dependants group.'

'I've already said, I'll be in Norfolk.'

He was becoming irritated. Why did so many conversations with Outi always go uphill? She picked up on his temper.

'I know, I know, but I told her you were going away and she wants you to try one out before you go.'

'Oh thanks.'

'Well there's no point delaying things just for the sake of it.'

He counted ten in the space of two. There was simply no point in wasting energy in a fruitless argument. The fact that he might need more time to consider what the hell all this co-dependants therapy stuff actually meant was clearly not an option that was to be afforded to him. The path had been set and that was that. Some day, God knows when, he might just arrive at a state of being where he could actually decide for himself what he did or did not want to do. The trouble was he hadn't got a clue but that didn't mean that he didn't want others to make the choices all the time. 'Others' mostly being Outi.

'Okay, I'll see her.'

'Don't be too late.'

'I'll do my best.'

'And you won't forget the paper?'

'Chrissake, I said I'll bring it.'

'There's no need to snap, it's difficult enough as it is without you losing your temper.'

It was hopeless. An argument was upon them.

'Has it occurred to you that things aren't exactly hunky dory this end either.'

'What's hunky dory?'

'Well, it's not easy, I have a lot of pressures to cope with.'

'You mean like feeding Missoo and getting to work on time?'

'I'm doing two jobs, remember? and strange as it may seem I also worry about you too.'

There was a momentary pause. Perhaps he was beginning to get through? Outi softened her tone a bit.

'I'm just trying to help, you know how you forget things.'

Wrong again. The world as seen by Outi was the one he must address. He decided to throw in the towel.

'Okay, I shall arrive on time and with paper.'

'I'll tell Virginia then.'

'Yup.'

'See you later then.'

'Yup.'

'Bye.'

'Bye.'

He listened to the click and let the line drone on bit before replacing the handset. He looked at his in-try. He could do with a drink. He pulled off a three-page report from the top of the pile. It was entitled 'A Prognosis on the Degradation of the Service Centre Air Conditioning and its Effect on the Energy Conservation Budget (Electrical)'. The author was Austin Dowell his po-faced maintenance supervisor. Austin had loads of impressive electrical sounding qualifications after his name but Melvin couldn't be bothered to read the report as he knew that the entire document would be a minefield of pompous obfuscation. Just the sort of thing to pad out the monthly Energy Conservation Report for Brannigan. 'Time for a bit of administrative action' he muttered to himself 'and I'll bloody well give Rupert Selwyn-Smythe a headache too.'

Momentarily uplifted by such thoughts, he made his way along the corridor and down the spiral staircase into the main service centre.

The parade of feminine beauty in Zelda's typing pool did not fail to touch him. Life was a bag of temptations, was it not? Not that you could refer to it as a typing pool any more. The communications centre was the latest asinine title prescribed by Regional HQ. The onward march of technology had transformed it from a clatter and natter environment to a screen flickering galleria in which the girls would rise like sirens from their designer work stations to press and piddle about amongst the sleek grey slabs of modems and processors whose function Melvin could barely understand, let alone use. Even stereo systems defeated him. He would often chat to the girls about various button pushing dilemmas and when they realised that he couldn't even grasp the principle of double ascending arrows in relation to the playing mode, they sought to pacify him by saying 'oh, don't worry, you're just getting old'. It was all very funny and rather hurtful.

They were a gorgeous bunch, his 'Sabre Dancers' and together they would often put life into perspective with a five-minute chat here and there. According to the grapevine, he was the best agony aunt going. Whatever the case, he felt he provided a little light relief from Zelda's bossiness. She had a heart of gold ensconced in a rubber truncheon.

As he approached the front of the office he warmed to the spectacle of Zelda placing yet another pile of documents on Rupert Selwyn-Smythe's desk.

'There we are Rupert,' said Zelda triumphantly, as she plonked the Fire and Bomb Evacuation Procedures on top of an already enormous pile, 'I think that's about it.'

'Oh, thank you,' said Rupert, mumbling insidiously through his long spotty nose, 'and do you have the master index?'

Most people would have brained the snivelling little shit on the spot but Zelda could eat half a dozen Rupert's for breakfast and was ready with her answer.

'I think you'll find it inside the fly sheet of the Common Services Instructions as per the Secretariat's addendum of 4th July.'

As was typical of all accountants who worked in the Audit department, he didn't acknowledge her response lest he be caught agreeing to something which was subsequently proved to be incorrect. He merely sniffed and fiddled with his greasy grey tie until it hung limply from his neck like a runner bean in a well-boiled stew.

Much to the distaste of Zelda's girls, from the very minute he had sat down at his carefully positioned desk, his slimy demeanour had intruded upon their ambience like a platter of sheep sick at a wedding feast. Although they were aware of the tactics that Zelda and Melvin had adopted, the reality of having to face such an odious visage was not their idea of an inspiring working environment.

'Zelda,' said Melvin, trying hard to conceal his smirk, 'any chance of squeezing Austin's paper into the Energy Conservation Monthly Report?'

'Considering there's nothing else in the report at the moment I'd imagine that would be a definite yes.'

'Oh good, can you bang it out pronto and maybe shove in some graphs or figures from somewhere to make it look good, they needn't be related, just pad it out'

'Same as usual you mean?' They had good guffaw. Rupert was straining his ears to pick up the source of their innocent merriment, 'by the way,' said Zelda, 'I saw Claudia's SNOG message about being out of time so I made a holding reply on your behalf.'

'Great, this morning I told the fat bitch I'd been working on it and she could have it later today.'

'Well it's nearly five o'clock so we better get a move on.'

'May the tablets of Moses be with you, and now, just so's you know what's going on,' Melvin lowered his voice, 'I've got a little project for Rupert the Prick that should give us all a little light relief.'

'Believe me, we could do with it.'

'Yeah, I know, well I'm assigning him to a full blooded payroll investigation because Jack's shop stewards have been stirring it up and if I ask Sid Wyatt to look into it he'll just blow a fuse and rant on about the twenty five percent turnover in payroll staff and how it's the blind leading the blind and it's all my fault, and blah de bloody blah etcetera, so I'll wheel Rupert upstairs now and sock it to him.'

'Good luck,' whispered Zelda, 'I'll see you tomorrow morning.'

'Shalom, sister.'

It was gone half past six by the time Rupert had finally exhausted Melvin with an interminable list of questions.

'I'm not saying that you have to follow them in your car on every job,' said Melvin, struggling to maintain his composure, 'but I am saying that we need to verify the claims they make on their time sheet.'

'Well the only way to verify the time they enter and exit a customer's premises is to take an actual reading on site.'

'I cannot condone spying.'

'Mr Powell, this is not spying, it's standard audit procedure, it is naive to assume otherwise.'

Melvin came close to bludgeoning him with a heavy-duty four-holed stapler. Rupert Selwyn sodding Smythe could give lectures on naivety to somebody else. Obviously he wasn't so perceptive as to realise how close he was to receiving irreparable brain damage.

When they finally parted company Melvin barely had time to dash home, feed Missoo and hurriedly change into something halfway respectable. In the tumult of the last hour he had concluded that the only way to unwind from the frustrations of high office was by way of a massive ejaculation inside Samantha.

By the time he'd pulled himself together, grabbed a quick cup of coffee it was nearing 8 p.m. As he lurched out of the front door, more in hope than conviction, Gladys appeared like a pinafored genie from a plastic teapot.

'Oh, hello,' she said, with contrived spontaneity, 'a late night again?'

He was in no mood to justify his actions and couldn't fail to notice the barbed observation in the word 'again'. Surely, by the time he had been getting home, people of her age should have been sipping their Ovaltine and worrying about drug crazed morons breaking and entering their home and their body? Admittedly, Gladys did have about six mortise locks and chains on her front door but it didn't stop her holding a beer glass to the letterbox like some kind of aural periscope straining to pick up the sounds of the night.

'I expect you're visiting Outi again?'

Needless to say, Gladys had been in on the act right from the beginning. Somehow he had managed to convince her that Outi was suffering from an hereditary kidney problem requiring specialist dialysis treatment.

'Yes,' said Melvin, forcing a smile 'must keep her spirits up,' and then realising that literally speaking that was a highly inappropriate remark.

'How is she then?'

Gladys was a conversational leech. You had to burn her off and decamp to another part of the jungle before she would acknowledge that the communication was at an end.

'Oh, not too bad, she sort of waxes and wanes, you know how it is.'

'Oh yes, I remember when Humphrey's nephew was in Edgware General with suspected malaria, we were practically living there.'

'Well yes, I can imagine and now I really must dash.'

'Oh yes, you hurry along now, mustn't be late.'

'Quite so, one must set an example.'

Nosy old bag, he thought to himself as he escaped down the stairs colliding with a dustbin on his way out.

It was gone 8.30 p.m. when he finally made it to the Friends of Florence Nightingale Hospital. Behind a vulgar sized desk sat Mrs Galapagos the receptionist. A woman in her fifties with lilac eye shadow that matched the carpet and a pair of spectacles that Dame Edna might have worn on her wedding day.

'Good evening, sir,' she said, in a basso rasp that fell somewhere between an inebriated bumble bee and a rehabilitated gin drinker.

'Good evening,' said Melvin, 'I've come to see Mrs Powell.'

'I'll just make a call to the staff nurse.'

'Yes, of course.'

She punched out a number and waited.

'...... I have a Mr Powell to see Mrs Powell......thank you.' She looked up at him with a smile as compassionate as a dried up river bed; she delighted in making Melvin wait whilst she adhered to her formal control procedures, 'Please take the lift to the first floor.'

Out of the lift and face to face with a stocky, balloon-jawed staff nurse who gave him a comforting smile suffused with the smug satisfaction of someone who has just debunked from the NHS in favour of a place in the national caber tossing team. He hadn't seen this particular nurse before.

'Mr Powell?'

'Yes.'

'Would you like to follow me, please?'

He did as he was told and trotted dutifully half a step behind her. She strode purposefully down the carpeted corridor and led him, after a series of left and right turns, to a small but tastefully furnished consulting room.

'Have a seat," she said, 'Virginia won't be a moment.'

Obviously, Outi had made arrangements in advance. He sat down and observed the environment. It was the first time he had been in Virginia's office. Clean, well funded and probably fitted with panic buttons. No doubt utilised by the relatives of patients when receiving their bills. A few minutes passed before the swish of some inner door heralded the arrival of Virginia.

'Hello Melvin. '

'Hello, sorry I'm late,' he stood up, as much as in guilt as in upbringing and found himself politely shaking her warm limp hand, 'I was delayed by an auditor.'

What else could he say? They seated themselves in a pair of low comfy chairs. She gave him a pleasant reassuring smile.

'That's alright, I understand.'

There was something about her that made him believe it was a genuine remark. She was a slim, pale-faced woman in her late thirties, with large, dark attentive eyes. She was tastefully dressed in a modest Camden Town chic sort of way and only her hairstyle gave a hint of her association with souls in torment. It reminded him of the wig Peter Seller's wore as the mad psychiatrist in 'What's Up Pussy Cat?' It was the only oddity in an otherwise normal appearance.

'How are you?' she enquired.

'Okay, I guess,' he could tell that she saw through that in an instant, 'how's Outi?'

'She's rather confused and trying to put on a brave face'

'Is that good or bad?'

'It's early days yet.'

'How long will she be here for?'

'That depends on how she responds to the treatment.'

There was a silence that Melvin did not enjoy.

'Can we talk a bit about you?' she asked.

His immediate reaction was to say 'no you bloody well can't but he knew that at some stage or other he would be obliged to spill the emotional beans. He was part of all this. He was inextricably linked and his deeds and actions, both past, present and future, were as significant to Outi's recovery as her own.

'Well, there's not much to say really, I'm at my wits end and I'm just relieved that somebody else can take the strain.'

Virginia said nothing. She gave him a gentle smile and remained silent. Once again, Melvin felt decidedly uncomfortable. Emotionally speaking, he could handle beans on toast, but bollocks on toast was a definite no no.

'Has Outi said anything to you about the way we like to work?'

'The only thing I can recall is that she wanted me to bring her some paper for something that she's writing for you and I've left that in the car.'

'Are you parked far away?'

'No, just round the corner.'

'Well, you can soon pop out again.'

'Oh yes, no probs.'

'Do you forget things much?'

'Only when it's too late.'

'How do you mean?'

There you are. A nice easy bit of chat and then, zonk, in with the psychoanalysis bit. Well sod it. He wasn't playing ball. There were too many banana skins around at the moment and he was not prepared to go arse over tit in a vortex of cross-examination. He would offer a piece of inept counter play which hopefully she would recognise as such and then leave him alone until next time. There was going to be a next time, of that he was certain.

'Oh, I d'know, just a turn of phrase really,' he crossed his legs and fiddled with his shoes. It was like a soap opera. Surely she would be bound to get the message? It was then that he noticed his odd coupling of socks. Use it, use it, he thought to himself, don't look a gift horse in the mouth - 'there you are, see what I mean, happens all the time.'

She nodded. She had her answer. He was up tight and out of sight.

'How would you feel about joining a co-dependants therapy group?'

'A what?'

'Co-dependants is the name we give to partners of alcoholics or anyone living with somebody with any kind of drug abuse. It helps to share experiences with people who are in similar circumstances to your own.'

Right now, all he wanted to do was shoot off back to the car, pick up the paper and reassure himself that Outi was still in the land of the living.

'Yeah, that's fine by me, I'll give anything a whirl once.'

'It may take a little longer than once.'

'Well, yeah, I wasn't being flippant, but you know what I mean.'

'You can meet some of the others now, if you like. They usually break for coffee in about ten minutes time and most of them congregate in the kitchen.'

'Sure, I could do with a coffee. When can I see Outi?'

'You can go and see her now if you like, we've moved her into a different room, just along the corridor.'

'Righto - perhaps I'll nip out to the car first.'

Virginia gave him another warm smile and gathered up her things.

'I'll show you where the kitchen is, it's in the opposite direction towards the main entrance.'

It was nice of her to bother. Every time Melvin had come to visit he got lost and by now he was something of a standing joke amongst the nursing staff. Off they went.

This time Melvin was conscious of a very lighter footstep in front of him and a motion of the hips that was quite pleasing. As they turned left and right, (or was it right and left, he was completely confused by the geography of the building), Outi appeared in the doorway of the kitchen, clutching a bottle of mineral water. She looked like death warmed up.

'Oh there you are - I'd given you up for lost - did you bring the paper?'

'I've got to nip back to the car for it - I've just been chatting with Virginia.'

'I know. Well, d'you want a coffee or something? - the others will be along soon.'

'I'll see you next Wednesday,' interjected Virginia, 'is that okay?'

'Yeah, I s'pose so.'

And with that, she turned a well-heeled shoe and disappeared down the corridor. Melvin gave Outi a glance, was there going to be another argument? Apparently not, for she returned to the kitchen to put the kettle on.

'May as well talk here, I've been in my room most of the day.'

They seated themselves at a large scrubbed pine table. Very Highgate Village circa 1970. There were packets of biscuits and catering sized coffee tins plus assorted mugs scattered around the working surfaces.

'This is all very casual,' observed Melvin.

'There's nothing casual about the way they stick needles in you.'

'Is that all to do with this de-tox programme thing?'

'Yes, they just pump you full of vitamins. Just as well, because you'd die of starvation waiting for your food in this place, the catering arrangements are a complete shambles, it took me twenty five minutes to get an omelette.'

'I enjoyed the meal we had last weekend.'

'That's just to impress the visitors, the in-mates get treated differently.'

Outi was on her critical bandwagon again. There didn't seem to be anything that she would accept as being satisfactory. He didn't really fancy a coffee either, a large vodka on the rocks would be better, but obviously that wasn't the thing to ask for here.

'How long should I stay for?' he asked, unable to pitch the question in the way he intended.

'You can go now if you like,' said Outi tersely, 'there's not much to hang around for, except me.'

'No, I didn't mean it like that, I just wanted to know the rules.'

'The only rule I'm aware of is that you can't bring alcohol or drugs on to the premises and you have to ask for everything.'

'It *is* a hospital and you *are* a patient.'

'I can always discharge myself if I don't like it.'

'You're here to get better, it's not going to happen any other way.'

Outi gave him a sullen look.

'Want to help yourself to coffee then? there are some tea bags as well.'

It was incredible. They were on the verge of an argument again. It was unfair to expect a glittering repartee from someone who was in the process of drying out, and if he was honest with himself, he'd rather sling his hook and watch Newsnight with Missoo on his lap.

'I'm not sure about this group therapy thing, I've said yes though, what d'you think?'

'It's up to you, wait until you see the others.'

'Where are they now?'

'Just finishing.'

'I thought Virginia was in charge.'

'She alternates with Sue.'

'Who's Sue?'

'The other bloody counsellor, for Chrissake.'

'Okay, okay, sorry I asked.'

This was pointless. Best to grab half a cup and beat it.

There was a chatter of voices along the corridor. He helped himself to a heaped teaspoonful of coffee, brought the kettle to the boil and returned smartly to the table. Somehow, the prospect of meeting a load of strangers who he may be encouraged to share his problems with, was making him feel decidedly edgy.

Suddenly, the room was full of people all milling around grabbing mugs and snatching biscuits. Just your ordinary bunch of everyday co-dependants winding down in post-synergetic bonding syndrome. Quite a few of them looked as knackered as he was. And then, through the door way came a sensual young woman of Malaysian origin, possibly Burmese or Thai. She had the balance and poise of a tiger and her eyes glistened like lacquered coal. Melvin was captivated. He was aware that he was staring unashamedly at her but he could do nothing to avert his gaze. She crossed his line of vision for a mere second, and in that desperately short space of time, they exchanged glances that were volcanic in their desire. Well, that's how he interpreted it.

Melvin flushed and dunked a custard cream in his coffee whilst she turned quickly towards the sink and started to fish out a teaspoon. He was practically on fire. He would have to leave to avoid a heart attack. As he got up to go, quite where he did not know, a tall dishevelled man with bleary eyes and patchy stubble slumped into the chair beside him.

'Hello, Outi,' he said, thumping his mug down and slopping its contents on the table.

'Hi Dillon, have you had a good session then?' said Outi.

'No,' he turned towards the sink, 'hand me a cloth or something, can you?'

The Malaysian tigress tore off a strip of kitchen towel and glided silently towards the table. She bent over and wiped the surface with small, neat swirling actions. Melvin was transfixed. Ensnared. He was convinced her body language said - 'I want to look at you but I daren't', whilst his said, 'I know, that you know, that we know'. What he *didn't* know, but could easily have seen, if only he wasn't in such a state of infatuation, was that she was married to Dillon.

'This is Melvin,' said Outi, to Dillon.

'Hello,' said Dillon rudely. And then said nothing else.

'I'd better get that paper before I forget,' said Melvin.

He hesitated for a second, not knowing which way round the table to go. One direction offered a rugby scrum through the group, the other, a far eastern frisson. He took the other. Would she turn towards him as he passed her? She did not. He was faint with expectation. Fresh air and a slug of vodka was becoming essential.

'Oh, can you get me some cigarettes on the way back?' said Outi, as he reached the threshold.

'Okay,' he said, turning briefly to acknowledge her request. One last glance at you-know-who, and this time it was returned and then quickly averted. Yet again, only a fraction of a second, but their knowingness of the moment transcended mortal definition.

Melvin was not aware of how he returned to his car, for his world was suffused with the delicate aroma of incense, the mystical ringing of tiny bells and a beckoning figure swathed in brilliant red and gold silk, deep in some enchanted forest. It wasn't until he came to rest at some traffic lights that he realised the paper was still on the back seat and Outi was without her cigarettes. He sat staring blindly at the red and yellow of the traffic lights. They turned to green. He admired the change of colour, but did not move. A strident blast from behind him jolted him back to reality. He forgot the car was an automatic and put the lever into 'Park' by mistake. The car behind stood on its horn again. More fumblings. Eventually he got going again and found his way back to the hospital.

Somewhere in the ether, a disembodied voice said 'take it easy now . . . one sock at a time'.

7

In search of some kind of mental equilibrium, Melvin swanned about in mad cow circles until eventually, and purely on impulse, he pulled into a garage. When presenting him with the car, Russell had obligingly given him a full tank of petrol so as yet he had no idea where the filler cap was. After a good deal of mucking about he finally plunged the nozzle in and watched, more in dazed fascination than alarm, as the pump notched up sixty litres before cutting out.

He scribbled erratically across the credit card chit recoiling slightly from the obsequiousness of the attendant's 'thank you'. A couple of tons of Teutonic engineering and already the meaning of service had transcended the usual bored indifference. He pulled away from the pumps and parked a few yards away. He needed to consider his position.

He loved Outi and desperately wanted to see her get better. There was no reason to think that she would not but there was every reason to think that their marriage would not survive the ordeal. The sheer ecstasy of shagging Samantha was more than he could resist but the fact that, in so doing, he had become enmeshed in the sinister desires of Russell was a facet of the relationship that he had definitely not bargained for. Nor had he the slightest notion of how to resolve it. When the heights of sexual passion subsided, his moments with Samantha were a source of peace and contentment the like of which he had never experienced before.

And now he was reeling from the effects of a woman with whom he had not even exchanged a single word! Wasn't infatuation in itself a sign of emotional immaturity? Was he a prisoner of his own desires? Driven by lust he knew he was living on borrowed time. And wasn't this sodding great Mercedes confirmation of that fact? He was as near to resolving his dilemma as a dung beetle dropped in diarrhoea. But hey ho, life had a habit of moving itself forward, so maybe he should shove the gear lever in drive and go see Samantha.

Whilst it was true that he had come into town to see Outi, (although somewhat responding to the pressure to see Virginia), his real motive was a desire to see Samantha. And there was desire creeping in again. Why could he not control it? And was it really such a sin if he did not? When all's said and done, didn't a third of the nation spend its time nipping off to surreptitious liaisons bonkereuse? It was not as if the remaining two-thirds majority appeared to be blossoming on the fruits of fidelity either. As far as he could see, society was a vacuum created by the exit of happiness. Wasn't that why most folks would rather kick you in the teeth than give you the time of day? Unless, of course, you were paying them for it. And in a way, wasn't that the case with Samantha?

Orgasms not withstanding, he could hardly kid himself that he was such a catch that she would jeopardise her entire existence just for him. Of course Russell knew what was going on, it was absurd to think otherwise, and the unpaid for Mercedes was the Venus flytrap. Melvin had already peered into its sickly horn and tasted the beckoning juices of Samantha deep within its throat. And within its bowels he knew that Russell would be waiting. He would deal with that one when he got there.

He switched on the engine. It purred into life. He put the car in drive and headed in the vague direction of Notting Hill Gate. He had no wish to bump into Russell at the Buster

Keaton club, besides which, Monday was always a slack night so Samantha invariably went home early.

Parking was a bit of a problem but at least the walk allowed him to consider what kind of reception he was likely to receive. Surely there was no reason to suppose that she would not be pleased to see him? At least he had the element of surprise up his sleeve. His heartbeat quickened as he pressed the entry buzzer. He had spotted the gleaming Chinese lantern from across the street, so he knew she was in.
'Hello?'
'Samantha?'
'Who's that?'
'Melvin.'
There was a long pause.
'..... You'd better come in.'
He made his way up the stairs as the heavy front door clunk-clicked behind him. Samantha's was ajar but there was no sign of her as he peered across the threshold. She had dimmed the main light until it threw no more than a pale pool of yellow on the carpeted floor. And then he saw her, dressed in her bathrobe and seated on the sofa.
'Oh, there you are.'
'Where did you expect me to be?'
Their eyes jousted momentarily as he moved closer.
'I had to see you,' was all he could say.
She got up slowly and drew him gently into her arms.
'I know,' she whispered.
Their lips brushed tentatively. He could feel her freshly bathed body beneath her robe and her skin was warm and smooth to his touch. He slid his arms around her back but she flinched and he saw the flash of pain across her face.
'Russell?' he said softly.
She averted her eyes. He had the answer. They remained holding each other in silence. There was no need for words. After a few moments she offered her mouth and they began a tender embrace. Another gentle brushing of the lips became a lingering exploration with their tongues, turning and swirling like perfectly matched ballroom dancers gliding across a

polished floor in consummate execution of their art. As their passion mounted she broke off and placed her hands on his chest, gently pushing him away.

'Why don't you get undressed and put some music on while I use the bathroom?' she said.

'I thought you'd just had.'

'I didn't know you were coming, silly.'

They drew apart and he was left to create the atmosphere. He stumbled around in the semi-gloom eventually finding the dimmer switch. He brought up the light a little. Not too much, just enough to discern the CD's and tapes. He had no idea what to put on. He was a classical music buff and hardly recognised any of her choices. Freddie Mercury, lithe and muscular in a tight vest. Rod Stewart looking spiky and wasted and Prince pouting androgynously. All a complete mystery as far as he was concerned. In the end he put on something by Sade. He wasn't sure what to expect but he liked the wide expanse of her forehead and there was definitely something 'after midnight' in the shape of her lips. Silky tones rose sensuously from some hidden speakers. It all seemed very beautiful as he began to undress.

Samantha emerged from the bathroom. He slid underneath the sheets. No point pretending he was Robert Redford, lesser still, Tom Cruise. As yet his body was not quite a lost cause but he had no illusions that for him, muscle tone was something best created away from the gym and fashioned in the dusk with the light behind him.

She moved softly, switching on a subdued table lamp here and there. As she bent over, he drank in the beauty of her calves, the fine chisel of her ankle bones, her long slender back. She moved to the bedside, loosening her bathrobe and letting it drop to the floor.

The next few moments were almost unreal. It was like watching a film in slow motion. He was in it too. It was quite extraordinary. It was as if he and Samantha were destined to become lovers and this was the quintessential moment where every fingertip touch and subtle nuance of the nostril took them ever closer to that glorious realisation. She pulled down the sheet from his chest and slowly straddled his torso. The delicate whiff of her perfumed crotch tantalised his senses. He received the weight of her body as she let his hands wander gently upwards from her hips to her breasts. She stroked his shoulders and chest as his fingers circled her nipples and then dropped lightly to her abdomen and waist. Tenderly they explored each other's contours, lingering here and there to contemplate the substance of the flesh.

He was mindful of her bruising, observing the areas of inflammation, wary of the delicacy of the damaged skin. Every so often, he would pause, placing his hands upon her as if to draw out her pain through the warmth of his inertia. They caressed with their lips. As she lowered her mouth onto to his, they slid their bodies alongside each other. He felt the long softness of her thighs as they brushed against his and then the moistness of her vaginal lips as they slid across his hardened penis. Lightly back and forth they went. The ebb and flow of sex. Moisture became wetness. Hardness turned to heat. And finally they consumed each other.

Their climax was not as frenzied as before, it was a different kind of lovemaking. They reached orgasm in a slow but splendid crescendo, gasping in unison as his semen thundered into her. And then they subsided. Fused together in a deeply satisfying experience.

After a while, when consciousness pervaded in a manner that only consciousness could, the feeling that speech formed part of the communication process slowly emerged in the form of contented sighs and gentle exhalations of breath suffused with a sub strata of meaning that the actual articulation thereof somehow spoiled the very means by which it strode to express itself. Samantha gazed at Melvin and Melvin gazed back. They were aware that on the physical level, the passion and completeness of their union had signified an understanding of needs and utterances which words themselves could not describe. And yet, as the after effects of their orgasm subsided, a faint but tangible shroud of reticence began to form between them. As if sensing the dissolution of something incredibly fragile and precious, they began to caress each other once again. It was not a re-run of foreplay since the factor of anticipation was no longer present, but it was as if they were aware that some kind of sensory stimulation was needed before they could move into the disturbing world of speech. Eventually Samantha spoke in whispered tones.

'Will you leave Outi?'

Her directness caught him unawares.

'We're not really together now.'

She searched behind his eyes for the real answer.

'What are you going to do when she comes out of hospital?'

It was impossible to answer because he simply did not know. He did not know what he was going to do about anything. Never before had he felt so utterly out of control in terms of what he was going to do next. He ran his fingertips lightly across her jaw and gently up into her hair. She eased her head upon his chest and he enveloped her in his arms.

'I expect that Outi will do what she will want to do and no doubt I'll find a way of fitting in with whatever all that is.'

It was the nearest he had come to openly admitting what he perceived was an inherent weakness in his character. It wasn't that he was patient or docile or accommodating, he was usually the opposite with most people. But with Outi it was different. In the face of her iron determination and the sheer force of her will power he chose to acquiesce and appease. On every occasion he was troubled by the likely outcome, particularly in terms of his own needs and feelings, and yet he always chose to back down. The line of least resistance always seemed to present respite from the inevitable argument and tension and although he knew that it could only ever be a short-term solution, that was the path he took.

The one thing he could not voice however was the sense of freedom he was experiencing since Outi had been hospitalised. It had given him space and time and in spite of the fact that he didn't seem capable of managing either facet particularly well, it was undoubtedly a new and pleasurable experience. In fact it was not far short of a bloody revelation. Should he feel guilty? Did he feel guilty? And why did he still not know what to do next? When in God's name was there ever going to be a break through or at least some indication that his prevailing life condition was taking a turn for the better instead of the worse? He was convinced his face was a picture of confusion and yet Samantha offered no response. Nevertheless, he felt a wave of unspoken questions flickering between them.

'And what about you and Russell?' he said.

It was her turn to examine her conscience and it was no more comfortable for her than it had been for him.

'Eventually he'll leave me.'

She spoke in a tone of flat resignation.

'Why do you say that?'

She raised her head slowly and eased herself onto her elbows. There was anguish written all over her face.

'Because he really prefers men.'

The implication of her remark was not lost on either of them. He wanted to ask her why, if that were so, Russell chose to beat her up, but he already knew the answer. Russell was evil and sick and they were both of them powerless to do anything about that.

She slid down beside him. They pulled the sheets over their shoulders and engaged in a soft lingering kiss. When their lips parted, she said

'You won't leave me, will you?'

'. . . No,' he whispered hoarsely.

A simple reply that ushered in the awesome spectacle of total deep shit.

8

At around ten o'clock the following morning, three people observed Rupert Selwyn-Smythe drive his red Mazda through the main gates of the North London Regional Service Centre of British Energy Services Limited. One of them was Claudia, who immediately consulted Fred Brannigan's executive movement sheet to see whether Melvin had included Rupert's movements as she had suggested to Brannigan he ought to. Typically he had not. She huffed and puffed. As the General Manager, Mr Brannigan's instructions should be obeyed, (she had even sent him a copy of her SNOG message to Melvin). It was disgraceful that people like Melvin Powell should put two fingers up to a new procedural rule. She would speak to Mr Brannigan about it.

The second person to observe Rupert's exit was Jack Matthews, who turned to Zelda and said:

'I bet that spotty little creep is off to spy on my Shop Stewards.'

'Well, you have rather brought it upon yourself, don't you think?' replied Zelda.

She was in no mood to see Melvin criticised for his actions, even indirectly. Jack gave Zelda a non-committal stare. He didn't like it when Zelda took him on because somehow he could never quite get the upper hand. Being Jewish, she always had the last word. And being Zelda, she was prepared for the one after that as well.

Jack considered his response. Ever since the SNOG email system had been installed, it seemed that ninety-nine percent of all managers had disappeared underground. There was very little one-to-one talking, which was Jack's favourite method for routing out Achilles' Heels or building new alliances. It was becoming increasingly obvious that most people preferred to sit in front of their computer and tap out innocuous little messages that harboured a smouldering time bomb with the reams of pages that were merrily pinned on the end as 'an attachment'. Impatient by nature, Jack would usually trash the entire contents and to hell with it. When his own line managers started to develop their own little 'attachment culture' he immediately rang them up and called them arseholes. Quite apart from the fact that his big clumsy hands were not inclined to dance the light fantastic across a keyboard, he considered that managers should manage and leave their typing to Zelda. And since he had no wish to jeopardise that service, he batted a middle of the road reply.

'Maybe, maybe, but I don't feel at ease when vipers like that are let loose.'

'Us neither,' replied Zelda cheerfully, 'which is why we're taking snake charming lessons. You gotta know the right tunes to play.'

Jack accepted that there was no mileage in further criticism so he left matters at that. He needed Zelda more than she needed him. And that was bad enough in itself. Somehow he was losing his touch.

Rupert parked his car in the multi storey edifice that abutted the regional headquarters building. He was relieved to find a vacant bay that wasn't situated beneath one of the many faulty seams that dripped a limey substance onto the cars beneath them. He had complained to Property Services about it but they had issued an incomprehensible reply that seemed to imply that the original aggregate had been defective although this fact was not technically proven at the time of its construction. In any event, they were constrained by the lowest priced tender which, as a member of the Audit Department, he would naturally appreciate they were bound to abide by. These days, the 'up yours' factor was spreading like bind weed in a well-fertilised bog. Well, he would let it go for the time being, he had greater issues to report on. There was nothing so juicy as the discovery that the Director of Personnel was misappropriating funds and diverting costs down illegitimate channels. The Director of Finance would love it and he would be the golden boy with yet another golden star.

'Well, I think we need to start gathering the evidence, don't you?' said Gerald MacNab, practically dribbling at the thought of humiliating Nigel Denmark in the bloodiest crucifixion the company would ever witness.

'I think that would be a wise course of action,' sniggered Rupert, fingering his filthy tie in anticipation of the task ahead.

'I need hardly say that for the time being this must remain between the two of us.'

'Oh yes of course, Mr MacNab.'

'Now, what about Melvin Powell?'

Rupert was not quite sure what to say. He had not expected Melvin to give him a payroll investigation nor with such a wide ranging brief. It was a pleasurable dilemma that he strove to explain with a note of caution. They both knew about Melvin's forthcoming week in Norfolk, (in fact it was the forward payment to a certain Management Consultant called Julian Weekes that had put Rupert onto his final stage of discovery) and any notion that someone other than Zelda could actually take over control of administrative matters was naive to say the least.

'Well, if I were you, I'd concentrate on payroll matters and let Zelda Solomons run the show,' said Gerald, matter of factly, 'if Fred Brannigan gets stroppy about anything I'll remind him of the thirty-two percent adverse variance on his salaries and superannuation account for the third quarter running.'

Rupert glowed inwardly. Money was power and he was in cahoots with the Director of Finance. What better position to be in at the start of a major reorganisation?

'Is there anything else then?' enquired Gerald.

'I don't think so,' said Rupert, wondering whether he was supposed to offer an addendum to the dynamic already provided, 'Mr Brannigan tends to leave me alone but Claudia his secretary is a very nosy person and I get the impression that she thinks she's somebody very important who has to know everything.'

'Never underestimate the power of a personal secretary,' said Gerald, with a wry smile, 'most of them know more than anybody else anyway. Just let her think she's in control and she'll become a passport to all sorts of useful information.'

Rupert looked non-plussed. Developing human relationships was not something he had found particularly relevant to either his life or his work. Gerald persevered.

'I suggest you try building some bridges with Melvin Powell too.'

'How will that help us? He breaks every rule in the book, so I can't imagine that he'd be a reliable witness, whatever the outcome.'

At this point, a moment of doubt flashed across Gerald's mind. Was he really placing too much trust in Rupert? Was it really possible for someone to gain a double first at Cambridge without picking up on at least some understanding of the basic elements of human nature?

The moment passed. It was brushed aside by the intoxication of revenge. To destroy Nigel Denmark utterly and completely. To wipe him, if not off the face of the earth, at least from the company. Two years ago the bastard had somehow managed to block his plans for expansion, but now at last he had the upper hand and he was not going to let it slip through his fingers.

'The point is Rupert,' he said, trying hard to speak as evenly as possible, lest any hint of emotion should cloud his pearl of wisdom, 'Melvin is in charge of the project, so he will know what's going on and why and where,' (Rupert's face was as a potato absorbing gravy, a slow realisation that a certain state of being was about to be influenced by another but with little appreciation as to whether this was good or bad), 'he's that kind of manager, and what's more, he's friendly with Harold

Hogger and Harold will be taking his instructions from Nigel Denmark, therefore . . .' Gerald tailed off.

'I appreciate the connection,' said Rupert.

Gerald smiled in no small relief. The sauce bottle had at last met the stew.

On his way back to the service centre, Rupert wondered how he might go about ingratiating himself to Melvin. Perhaps he could prepare a preliminary payroll report or something?

Rupert had been back at his desk a good half hour by the time Melvin swung the Merc imperiously through the main gates and came to rest in his parking bay. Events at Samantha's had rather overtaken him. Their first awakening had been around seven o'clock and in the drowsy aftermath of love and confession it had seemed like a good idea to snuggle up in each other's arms and slumber blissfully on. It was nine o'clock by the coffee and toast stage, by which time Melvin had come to the conclusion that his managerial responsibilities paled into insignificance alongside the earth-shattering realisation that he had actually fallen in love.

Eventually they had parted and the priority of the day was to return home and feed Missoo. She was not amused by his total disregard for her well-being and made that perfectly clear by sinking her claws, lightly but firmly into his thigh as he wrestled with the can opener. Not surprisingly, Gladys just happened to bump into him on his way out again and that was another ten-minute diversion as he tried to extricate himself from the banalities of neighbourly discourse.

'Well I'm so glad she's feeling better and do give her my love.'

'Yes, of course, byee.'

'And do tell me if you want to stay late at the hospital or whatever, I know how these things are and I can always feed Missoo if you want me to.'

'Yes, thank you, we'll have to organise a key.'

As Melvin got out of the car, George Potless the overnight security guard was knocking off duty.

'Is this your new regular vehicle Mr Powell?'

'Yes.'

'Oh, righto then, only nobody's told me officially and not even Zelda would confirm it.'

'Oh, sorry about that George, my fault, stick it on the register.'

'I've already logged it on the security sheet because as you know I have to keep track of all alien vehicles that come on site.'

'Absolutely. Well this one's a friend. I'll sign whatever later if that's okay with you, only I've got a meeting I really must get to.'

'That's okay Mr Powell, I'll walk over to reception with you, I'm knocking off now as you probably know.'

'Oh really - I mean yes of course.'

Jesus Christ, how quickly some people can spoil your day. The sodding man was a limpet. Perhaps he should introduce him to Gladys? The two of them would get along fine. They might even marry each other.

'What colour should I call it, Mr Powell?'

'Pardon me?'

'The car - it's rather an unusual colour.'

'Wet Sahara.'

'I'm glad you told me, it looks more like camel dung to me.'

Belinda on reception cocked a sympathetic eyebrow as Melvin finally extricated himself and fled upstairs to his office. He had not been inside long when Jack stuck his head in.

'Where the hell've you been wanker? There was an ops meeting in Brannigan's office at 10.30 a.m. to which you were noticeable by your absence.'

'Well, I did nominate Rupert in my place.'

'Don't piss me about wank head. Rupert bloody Selwyn-Smythe was driving out of the main gates half an hour earlier.'

Melvin was about to respond when Zelda appeared with half a ton of post.

'I don't know what you said to Rupert last time you were briefing him but I think he's undergone some kind of personality change. He actually said good morning.'

'Oh really, what did you say in return?'

'Piss off you prick, I hope,' interjected Jack rudely.

'Well, as a matter of fact,' started Zelda, 'I asked him he'd like a cup of coffee.'

Jack was about to launch in with another obscenity when Brannigan and Claudia appeared in the doorway. Fred Brannigan's massive six and a half foot frame with its bovine head and thyroid eyes, dominated the doorframe like a bull in a chicken shed.

'Have you got those service contract figures yet?' he said directly to Jack, ignoring Melvin completely.

'Oh, I didn't know you wanted them this soon.'

'Our meeting finished an hour ago, what've you been doing since then?' Brannigan's voice was deep and growly.

'I'll get them to you' said Jack tersely. He knew it was unwise to put up a defence. Brannigan turned to Melvin. The hairs on Claudia's big peachy cheeks were raised in anticipation.

'Alright, lad?' said Brannigan.

'Yup,' replied Melvin.

'I hear you're going to Norfolk next week, for some training?'

'Motivational psychology, as I understand it.'

'Well, as long as everyone in the admin. department remains motivated whilst you're gone, I shall be a happy man.'

Coming from such a morose pig as Brannigan, Melvin felt that it was a comment best left unremarked upon.

'Well as long as we've got Rupert's sheet I think we could all be bit more cheerful,' said Claudia, giving everyone a duplicitously benign smile. The stupid fat cow actually thought that she had convinced everyone that she was being witty.

'It will be on your desk, have no fear of that,' said Zelda in a tone of such resolution that it was practically a parody of mockery itself.

Melvin's phone rang. He snatched up the receiver.

'Hello,' said Outi.

'Oh,' stammered Melvin, 'I didn't realise they'd put the call straight through.'

'Does that make a difference then?'

'Well, I'm just in the middle of a meeting so can you hang on a sec?'

Brannigan's bulk was already receding and carrying all before it. He wasn't interested in other people's phone calls as long as they jumped when he rang them. Claudia brought up the rear like a tug in a docking operation and as Jack made a beeline along the corridor, Zelda took up a chatty position along side her. The flotilla set off.

'If you've got a template set up on SNOG,' said Zelda loudly 'p'raps I can take a copy and I'll put Rupert's movements in as soon as I open up.'

She pulled the door behind them leaving Melvin in relative peace.

'Okay then,' said Melvin, sensing that bad vibes were afoot, 'what's the score then?'

'I don't know about any score,' replied Outi truculently, 'but I shan't be staying here much longer after what's happened today.'

Needless to say Melvin was obliged to ask what and before the words were hardly out of his mouth, Outi launched into an angry saga that oscillated wildly between the inept administration of the hospital and some impending crisis with all the counsellors. Melvin could hardly keep up with the convolutions of the story but it sounded like everything was in turmoil and professional principals were being savaged.

'So, Virginia is bringing the therapy group forward to tonight and she's holding it off site as part of her private practice, so can you make it?'

Melvin was flummoxed. He was planning on seeing Samantha tonight and this had cropped up.

'Er, well, I er, well, yes I s'pose I could, but where is it? I mean I have to allow time to get there, don't I?'

'It's on your way if you were coming here,' said Outi directly, gearing up to give directions, 'it's in one of those very big houses along the Finchley Road, Virginia says about half way between Swiss Cottage and Golders Green, I'll fax you a map with the number on it, only don't attempt to go in the front entrance because it's all double yellow lines and main road traffic and you have to go round the back and park so's you can walk first across and then down the side and into the back entrance when you come in from the garden, it's all on the map, so you'll be able to find it.'

'I can't wait.'

'Well, you do want to go, don't you?' said Outi half accusingly.

'Yeah, yeah, it's just that I want to get my head in gear.' Melvin's psychological positioning was not something she felt she could contribute to, besides which, her own course of treatment was now in jeopardy and if things didn't get any better she would have to consider suing somebody.

'Well, I'll send you the fax and you can make it, okay?'

He could but say yes and that was an end to it. They rang off.

Almost immediately he punched nine for an outside line and rang Samantha's home number. There was no reply apart from the answer phone. He hesitated. What if Russell got to hear it? Sod it, he knew what was going on anyway, didn't he? Melvin left a cryptic message just in case. He wanted to be tender, to give her some signal that he would never leave her as he had promised but somehow he just couldn't make it sound that way. He rang off in a strange mixture of confusion and angst. He needed this fucking therapy class like a hole in the head.

The rest of the day was one long frustration. He wanted to leap frog everything until it was nearing midnight, that being the time when he would probably arrive at Samantha's.

Zelda told him emphatically to go and he took her advice. 'There's no point in staying when you can't think straight, go and see your wife, she needs you.'

He hadn't quite managed to say that he wasn't going to the hospital but rather on some half-baked journey or self-discovery or some bloody nonsense.

He crashed Missoo's dish in the sink and flung down a helping of dried biscuits. He was dying for a quick cold lager and took the decision to nip across to Ajit's before setting off.

'Hello Mr Melvin,' boomed Ajit, taking a four-pack of Pils from the fridge, 'd'you want to settle up now or later?'

'I'll stick it all on my card if you like. I'm a bit short of cash though, any chance of doing a cheque?'

'Sure, sure, no problem, how much you want? I can do thirty.'

'Yeah, that's fine, that'll do great.'

Ajit raided the till with a flourish and gave Melvin a big beam as he handed over the cash and zapped his credit card transaction. Back in the car, which was parked in the gloom of a side road, Melvin unplugged the can and savoured the full rasping liquid. 'Nectar or death, I know not which' he muttered to himself as he headed toward Friern Barnet and Finchley.

Virginia and her colleague Sue ran an independent counselling service that just happened to pick up a lot of work from the Friends of Florence Nightingale Hospital. Their sessions were held in one of several vast old houses that served as colleges on the sprawling campus of London University somewhere along the Finchley Road between Golders Green and Swiss Cottage.

By the time Melvin had found a parking space and remembered that he was supposed to enter the building from the rear garden and not the main road, he was already ten minutes late and seriously in panic. He also recalled that Virginia had said they would start with some relaxation exercises and these would be run by an Australian movement teacher called Marylin. Oh really, how nice. Rock on cobber. He needed to loosen up.

He stepped through the doorway into a large student type kitchen (these days he seemed to be making all his entrances like a tradesman) and was greeted by Virginia with her kind, gentle smile. Everyone else, all seven women of them, had already got their tea and biscuits.

'Hello Melvin, we haven't started yet, help yourself to a cup of tea or coffee if you want one.'

Deliberately avoiding everyone else's eyes he focused on a large urn on top of a huge metal trolley only to find that standing beside it was that beautiful Malaysian girl who had so captivated him last night. She, who had induced a temporary memory loss, seemed more bewitching than ever. He had never seen such incredible poise and stillness. There was no turning back now. He began to fumble with the cups when she looked at him and said:

'What you want then, tea or coffee?'

She spoke in that funny, truncated style of English so peculiar to the oriental races and yet there was a hint of the Mile End Road in her accent. He was fascinated by the contradiction.

'Tea, please.'

'Okay, I put this bag in, you take milk and sugar?'

'Yes.'

'How much?'

'Just a dribble and one level spoon.'

She moved with speed and dexterity, her small lean hands forming delicate shapes and positions above the crockery. When it was ready she handed him the mug with a disarming smile.

'Okay, I'm Shaida, what your name then?'

'Thanks, I'm Melvin.'

'Okay, we going in now.'

And indeed they were. So much for not starting yet. Everyone was downing their mugs and filing along the corridor. He took a few gulps, burnt his tongue and followed suit.

Marylin was an Australian of Amazonian proportions. Well over six and a half foot with strong muscular thighs and massive wide shoulders that supported a high falling cleavage that Fellini would have paid homage to. She had broad cheekbones and enormous blue eyes that seemed to dilate and twinkle like the hypnotic snake in Walt Disney's Jungle Book. She wore her hair in a ridiculously long plaited ponytail that flopped indecently across her rump like a flaccid egg cholla. Standing dishevelled and tired in his crumpled suit, Melvin looked up at her in an aura of total inadequacy.

'Okay everyone,' said Marylin, in a soft throaty voice, 'just copy me and let's relax and enjoy our bodies.'

As an introduction to group therapy it was second to none. After a series of straightforward exercises, he imagined that Marylin would tell them to lie on the floor as she played a soundtrack of waves washing gently to and fro on some sun kissed shore whilst angels and fauns caressed their vocal chords from afar. He knew something about these things. It was all in those alternative magazines. But he was horrified when she said:

'That's really very good, now choose a partner and we'll build some trust through touching.'

He tried to fade into the wall paper. There was no way he was making any such statements before being properly introduced. They really ought to just float a bit and then go elsewhere for the chin wag. Perhaps he could go to the loo instead? The lizard was twitching.

As tentative alliances were formed he found himself staring at Shaida. She met his gaze and moved towards him. Never before had he seen such exquisite and fragile beauty. Her classically contoured face broke into a broad friendly grin. Only when she spoke was the vision in dilemma. She was a beguiling mixture of East and West. Exotic yet honky.

'Yo Melvin, you wanna see if I got tits?'
There was an explosion of laughter. Definitely girls on top.
He wished the floor would swallow him up.

It didn't.

9

The cast iron radiators of the Flint Shingles Country Club Hotel were caked with heavy cream paint like an old whore's make-up. The central boiler took its function rather literally and since temperature control did not appear to be a feature of the ancient system, the pulsating ironware had branded many an unsuspecting guest with scarlet buttocks. It was a topic of discussion that took flight in the bedrooms but was contained, albeit rather painfully, in the dining room. Somewhat surprisingly, considering the distance from any recognisable centre of sophistication, the staff were extremely pleasant even though their sense of service would not win them any medals.

In a funny way, in spite of his serious misgivings about the whole venture, Melvin's arrival at the hotel was a source of blessed relief. The closing stages of the previous week had subjected him to a series of emotional conundrums the like of which had caused his psyche, were it ever to become tangible, to resemble a pin cushion that some disgruntled seamstress had vent her fury upon. Things were closing in on him. Outi had rung him at work the day after his first therapy session (an experience that had left him feeling like a two dimensional cartoon character that had just been flattened by a steamroller) to declare that she was discharging herself from hospital in support of Virginia and all the other counsellors who had been blamed following the discovery of drink and drugs in certain patients' bedrooms. By the time the fracas had subsided, he had spent three consecutive evenings at the hospital trying to hold a rational conversation with Outi who was hell bent on suing the administration and had demanded chapter and verse on the small print of their medical insurance. He couldn't even make head nor tail of the main conditions let alone anything else and in desperation had enlisted the help of Zelda. She went through the policy like a dose of salts and said it all hinged on whether they could get the hospital's resident psychiatrist to side with the counsellors in order to prove professional negligence, or something.

'You've got to get a professional opinion on your side otherwise they'll close ranks and freeze you out, believe me, you can forget the hypocritical oath, Americans play dirty'

There was little doubt in his mind that Zelda was right but the most disconcerting aspect of the entire fracas was not knowing whether Outi was coming home or staying in. To make matters worse, Christina had appeared on the scene, apparently at the behest of Outi, and her air of moral superiority and pious inclination tested his self-restraint to breaking point. There was always the thought at the back of his mind that the gang from Ahus Ericsson might just take it into their heads to get rat-arsed during a long haul at the Buster Keaton club, and as he was convinced that the chemistry of his affair with Samantha was practically palpable.

He had this recurring nightmare that one night she might just appear out of the blue smoked gloom like a pristine incubus, to point her perfectly manicured finger in gesture of triumphal cognisance - 'ah Melvin, I thought as much, well I'm not surprised and I don't expect Outi will be either' and then she would dismiss him with something like - 'I don't think I can drink my Dubonnet any longer' as if his behaviour alone was responsible for soiling the very air she breathed through her precious nostrils.

Although such a spectacle never happened, it was not far removed from the reality of being cross-examined by Christina in the coffee bar of the Friends of Florence Nightingale. To compound his discomfort, Shaida was there too. It transpired that Dillon and Outi had forged some kind of in-mates liaison - 'he's very intelligent and sensitive' insisted Outi, and needless to say, Dillon was at the centre of the brouhaha.

In spite of his embarrassment at the therapy class, Melvin still felt impossibly drawn towards Shaida. When the session had ended, she had said:

'You wan cup of tea in the student refectory?'

'Umm'

'Yuh, come on, I show you, my throat is like a drain.'

And there they had sat, for nearly an hour, supping student tea and discussing their spouses. She did not so much as flirt with him as allow him to enter her personal space. Towards the end he was conscious that they had moved physically closer and were talking in hushed tones and with incredible eye contact.

'I want Dillon to get well but I don't think he's capable of it.' They brushed knuckles across the table. There was no sexual frisson, just a shared moment of mutual understanding and support. And maybe something deeper? Something to do with their destiny?

'What you think about Outi?' she said.

He looked into her deep black eyes.

'The same.'

And now there was Christina, trying to tell him how to run his life and what he should be thinking.

'Of course, Outi can always stay with me if you cannot look after her, and naturally she is aware of my offer too.'

'Oh yes, and no doubt you are of what her innermost wishes are.'

'Melvin, there is no need to be sarcastic just because you do not know what to do.'

'How long you been a co-dependant?' Shaida cut in.

Fierce black eyes locked onto indignant blue ones.

'I really don't see what that has got to do with it.'

'Yuh? well that's why you gotta stay out of it, you not family so you don't know.'

'I am very close to Outi, we are both Scandinavian.'

But Christina knew she had met a greater force. A higher intelligence.

'The only people who can make this decision are Outi and Dillon themselves - we not interfere - only remind them we are here.'

'That is what I've been trying to say all along,' replied Christina affecting agreement, 'they need our support.'

'When did they not have it?' said Melvin, more in statement than in question.

'Yuh,' said Shaida, just in case Christina had any doubts that it was not two against one.

'Well, that's settled then,' said Christina, 'we must leave them to make up their own minds.'

By midnight it was all wrapped up. Everyone stayed put. Virginia had agreed with the Administration that she would hold her co-dependent's therapy classes off site. It was an astute gesture that carried the implication that it was others beside the nursing staff who had been lax in their security arrangements. There was an uneasy alliance. A Balkan peace tick tocking away.

Christina disappeared haughtily into a cab and Shaida asked Melvin if he fancied a Big Mac.

'Not really, but I'd murder for a cool crème caramel.'

'They don't do that at MacDonalds, I buy you an ice cream.'

'Okay.'

It was too late to pay a call to Samantha and in some respects he was glad that the hour of the night had made the decision for him. He was emotionally exhausted. A deep and lurid sleep rendered him even more exhausted the following day.

When Rupert made one of his typically stupid suggestions concerning some minor point in the depths of an already incomprehensible payroll system, Melvin finally snapped.

'Tell Jack Matthews that I'll slap the whole bloody lot of them on flat time if they don't sign their time sheets in Sanskrit capitals,' he yelled.

'How will that solve the problem?' enquired Rupert, with the perspicacity of a budgerigar. Melvin was about to swing his chair at him when Zelda walked in for the umpteenth time.

'Shouldn't you be going or is there something I don't know about?'

And eventually he had thrown the towel in and gone. He had tried to ring Samantha and then thought better of it and then changed his mind twice and finally rung. He put the phone down in panic and confusion when Russell answered.

And now here he was in this creaking hotel, supposedly to discover the meaning of human behaviour and demonstrate the qualities of leadership. In the absence of anyone to lean on, he made a beeline for the bar. And that was where he saw the pair of them. Julian Weekes the Consultant and Lisa Joplin his Project Team Leader.

He knew who they were because he just did. Lisa was the give-away. He remembered seeing her at one of the company's ghastly, inept, so-called sales launches. She'd been in Sales then and had been voted Wonder Woman of the Month, or some crappy accolade so favoured by Sales, and had made an impromptu speech that was remarkable for its wit and candour, not the least from somebody who had barely turned twenty one, (he found that bit out later) and just about every male in the audience, pissed or sober, had got a hard-on.

And here she was again, seconded to a high profile project by some inadequate sales manager who felt threatened by her dynamism and achievement. Such was life.

He took in the scene, which meant he took in her utterly dong riveting body and startling good looks. Somehow he managed to feign respectable eye contact as he neared the bar.

'Hello Melvin.'

Why did so many people in the organisation seem to know him? Anyway, thank God she hadn't called him Mr Powell, but why did she have to be so attractive? Things were complicated enough as it was without further temptation. An efficient hag was what he really needed. Or perhaps a bloke that he could say fuck off to ten times a day.

'Hello,' he beamed.

'I don't believe you've met Julian Weekes have you?' she said, indicating a rotund man with the girth of Friar Tuck and then more some. She had obviously got herself up to speed pretty quickly.

'No.'

'Good morning Mr Powell.' said Julian Weekes oozingly.

'How d'you do?' replied Melvin correctly. He'd taken an instant dislike to the fat toad and was buggered if he was going to say 'do call me Melvin'. He didn't like fat people, and he disliked grossly fat people even more, and he positively loathed grossly fat people with transparent personalities culled from the pages of a Consultancy Skills Handbook.

He ordered a double vodka on the rocks and after a bit of fart arseing about, managed to get a glass of iced water to accompany it. No point being sober now that he didn't have to drive anywhere and clearly Julian treacle-oozing-platitude-smarmy fat fucking Weekes wasn't giving up as easily as that.

'Shall we sit down with our drinks?' said Julian, with a velvet toned smile.

'No,' said Melvin, 'I've been sat in my car for the last three hours.'

'Okay, fine, I understand that.'

So the three of them remained standing. He knew it was a stupid, petulant remark but at least it signalled that he wasn't to be taken for granted. Just because he hadn't been able to select his own team didn't mean to say that he wasn't capable of leading it (albeit from the rear, he hadn't changed his mind about that one).

Lisa watched the way the wind was blowing and concluded that her new boss might just be as mercurial as Harold Hogger had suggested. It was one of several conversations she'd had with Harold when he'd first approached her about the job and although she'd had to look 'mercurial' up in the dictionary, she had come to the conclusion that what with the grapevine reports that Melvin wasn't somebody who ever ducked a decision and enjoyed pissing about a lot, nine months away from a shabby service centre in Luton was not a bad idea. Besides which, she needed a bit of space to sort her head out about Troy.

Things weren't going too well between them but the trouble was he didn't seem to notice. The first six months had been great, especially the sex, and let's face it, she loved sex and Troy had terrific stamina. It sort of went with the job, building labourer and trainee JCB driver and all that. Not too high on the imagination stakes but then you can hardly expect everything from one man. The last six months had been a disappointment and quite frankly these days Troy seemed to be more interested in rugby, Chinese take-aways and pumping iron than developing a relationship. She had tried to explain what her new job entailed.

'I shall have to stay away nights.'
'So?'
'You won't resent that?'
'We've got the weekends 'aven't we?'
Terrific. A rock solid relationship. And these days a quick bang was all he could manage. So, a little bit of distance didn't seem a bad idea.

She trusted Harold Hogger too. It wasn't anything to do with the fact that he was the Regional Training & Development Manager, he just seemed a straight sort of man. He had an old world courtesy and wisdom about him that appealed to her. Melvin was clearly different. Obviously he didn't like Julian Weekes and hopefully he wouldn't knock back too many vodkas before things got out of hand.

Harold had told her that Melvin was an instinctive, intuitive kind of manager and if they got off to a good start (which he was sure would be the case) the project would be extremely beneficial to her both from a personal as well as a career development point of view. Clearly, she needed to tune into Melvin and since she had already been bored rigid for the last twenty minutes by Julian's facile conversation, she decided to take action.

'Julian, I hope you don't think I'm being too rude but I need to update Melvin on a couple of things and we've both been so busy of late that we haven't had a chance to get together before now.'

'No, no, of course not,' said Julian, with the affability of an apple pie, 'you carry on whilst I make myself known to the others - mustn't hog the managers.'

And with that he turned on his axis like Mr Blobby and waddled towards a cluster of people who somehow or other he had discerned were part of the team.

Melvin and Lisa moved to the corner end of the bar. Melvin was intrigued by Lisa's intervention and also relieved. He knew he had behaved with abominable rudeness.

'Some opening, eh?' he said.

'Are you always like that?' said Lisa.

'Only with fat prats who've weaselled their way into a corporate account they don't deserve.'

She chose not to ask why Julian didn't deserve it because she had already arrived at her own conclusion that he was a bull shitter. She was more interested in getting to know Melvin. There was something about his slightly dishevelled appearance that was rather appealing. It wasn't the superficial untidiness (she quite liked long hair) it was more to do with his air of indifference. So many of the company's senior managers were either boring old farts or arrogant know-it-alls that it was kind of refreshing to find somebody who, as far as she could tell, was a tad unhinged.

'So, what's going on?' said Melvin. It seemed a good idea to throw her the line since she had taken control anyway.

'Nothing much. The rest of the team are all booked in. There's the usual moans about a company of our size giving the workers a crummy hotel and the rest of the stuff's all about how long they think they'll be in a job, and what the hell are they doing on a project like this, and why are they here, and what are you like, and how come you didn't interview them and generally being rather negative.'

'Thanks, so what did you tell them?'

'I said I was going to keep an open mind about things, including you.'

She grinned at the last bit.

'So, how am I doing so far?'

'I think you need taking in hand.'

She grinned again.

'Too bloody right Lisa. I shall dazzle everyone with my managerial expertise at some later stage, meanwhile I suggest we agree some kind of game-plan to cope with this . . .' he hesitated, indicating Julian who was now holding court with the others -

'Wanker?' said Lisa.

'Precisely.'

He could see they were going to get along like a house on fire. She was young enough not to be flawed by the corrosive influence of cynicism yet mature enough to suss the situation. What's more, she wasn't giving him all the I'll-just-do-whatever-you-want-me-to-because-I'm-your-project-team-leader crap, and that pleased him immensely. Dear Harold had made an inspired coupling (if that was the appropriate word) and what with her HND business studies Distinction she clearly had brains as well as beauty. Forget the efficient hag bit, she was gorgeous and zappy. And why shouldn't he accept the fact that for him, a positive motivating factor was a stunning young woman. And who cared if he was old enough to be her father? Bollocks to the feminists. There was nothing wrong with lust, it was what you did with it that mattered.

And two nights later the pair of them did something with it. What was so great was the fact that neither of them pretended not to be interested in each other. They were careful not to make things too obvious and that generated an excitement all of its own.

In the evening, by the time everyone was well and truly pissed off with Julian's fatuous pontifications and heaving belly, and the lounge bar was the only sensible place to be, they would circulate amongst the team and yet somehow just happen to keep on meeting at the bar simultaneously. It was a kind of subtle foreplay and there was no doubting the syncopation of their rhythm At midnight, as the chimes of the hotel's grandfather clock clanged into action, Lisa said -

'Okay, so's mine a bacardi and coke, and I promise not to turn into a pumpkin.'

'Oh, and what will you turn into then?'

'I'll still be me - in the flesh - okay?'

'Absolutely.'

And the sex was terrific. Lisa was sublimely uninhibited and deliciously dirty and to his intense delight (and hers as well) he had no trouble in joining in. He hadn't had such fun since - Jesus Christ - was he really only sixteen at the time?

He remembered a curly haired Irish girl who had pressed against him in the arena of the Royal Albert Hall during a Prom performance of Bruckner's Seventh Symphony. As the blazing chords rose to their final climax he was convinced that before day break their physical union would be moulded in equally golden proportions. And it had. Chinese noodles in South Kensington afterwards, somebody or other's party and then alone together in a bedroom off the Earls Court Road. She was much older than he was with the experience to match. 'May as well get on with it' she had giggled, like the good Catholic girl she was. And in the early hours of the morning, he had bent down to kiss the moss on the Blarney Stone. Ever since then, he'd always had a soft spot for Bruckner.

As yet, he and Lisa had not discussed the merits of large scale architectural symphonies but he was in no doubt that they were capable of fornicating their way through quite a few of them. The following night they were at it again.

'Lisa,' he gasped, his head above her thrusting pudenda, 'you do realise this is no more than unbridled lust?'

'Yes, oh yes,' she groaned, 'but arise Sir Muff Diver, you have done your duty.'

It was undeniably fantastic.

At eight o'clock the following morning, back in his own bed, the telephone rang. It was Samantha. Morning had broken.

'I just wanted to warn you that Russell's coming.'

'Jesus Christ! what here?'

'Yes.'

'But how?'

'He forced me.'
There was a cold awful silence.
'Are you alright?'
Another silence and then a small voice saying -.
'Do you still want me?'
'...Yes.'
'Take care.'
And then the line went dead.

It really wasn't funny how one minute you could be enjoying yourself, really, really enjoying yourself, and then bang, the next minute deep shit happened. Really, really deep shit.

He put the receiver down and went to the bathroom. He cleaned his teeth, gargled and then threw up. He cleaned his teeth again, then gargled, and then made a cup of tea. There was something about the soft podginess of the tea bag that reminded him of the vulnerability of human flesh vis-à-vis your average Stanley knife. He threw up in the bathroom once more and decided to give breakfast a miss. He didn't want people to get the wrong idea about his shaking hands. The day's session was due to start at nine o'clock but he didn't appear until gone eleven thirty.

When they broke for lunch, Julian approached him with mock concern oozing from every pore.

'Is everything alright, Melvin?'

'Yeah, yeah.'

'Okay fine, only it's just that you've always been so prompt and I thought you looked a little pale this morning.'

'I'm fine, I'm fine.'

'Okay, well if you need to leave for whatever reason you know that's alright by me.'

'I don't need yours or anybody else's permission to leave or stay in this poxy bloody hotel.'

People began to look around at the sound of his raised voice.

'No of course not,' continued Julian, dropping his voice to an ultra soft level that served only to aggravate Melvin further. Julian knew that everyone was ear wigging like hell and he enjoyed showing them that he was in control of himself even if Melvin was not, 'I'm not suggesting you should, but I do know that you're carrying an enormous responsibility, more so than ever I could, let's be frank about that, but I just wanted you to know that if there was anything you wanted to share with me I'd be more than happy to listen.'

Melvin came to the boil. He had to hit out at *something*. The fear of forthcoming events had nowhere else to go and, with hindsight, watching Burt Reynolds suffering in Deliverance on the bedroom video had not been a good idea.

'Now you understand this, you fat fucking toad, you are the last person on this Godforsaken fucking earth that I would want to share anything with.'

Everyone fell silent. It was difficult to ignore what was going on.

'Okay, fine, I understand that, you're obviously angry about something and I respect your right to privacy, in any case I don't think the synergy of the group will be affected now that we've all bonded so well.'

That was too much. Melvin exploded.

'Listen to me you fat cunt,' he yelled, (just as Russell pushed through the main doors of reception like a bouncer on duty) 'the only thing that's going to bond around here is your fucking bollocks to that chandelier.'

And with that, he stormed towards the lounge bar straight into Russell. The receptionist had already summoned the manager and was wondering what to do next when Russell took over.

'Melv, my ol' ray of sunshine, now what 'ave you been doin' to get yerself into such a fine ol' laver?'

He had a grip on both Melvin's shoulders. Most of the guests remained frozen to the spot. They were convinced there was going to be a fight. The assistant manager appeared and then rather wished he hadn't.

'It's alright squire,' said Russell, 'this gentleman's my patient.'

And without more ado, guided Melvin through the main doors and across the gravelled courtyard to his Jaguar XJ6.

Fortunately, it was the last day of the course and there was only the plenary summing up session to go before everyone could pack their bags and get the hell out of it.

But Julian Weekes had already decided that it would be the start of something else.

10

'Christ Almighty, Melv,' said Russell, as he ushered Melvin into the waiting Jag, 'I couldn't fink what I'd walked into, you really 'ad me worried for a minute.'

'Oh, well as long as it was only for a minute,' said Melvin feebly, as he sank into the front seat shaking like a rabbit. Without explaining why or how he was there, Russell drove the car sedately across the crunching stone courtyard and down the long driveway.

'I mean, I says to Sam, I know, I'll just pop in and see me ol' mate Melvin, I could do wiv' a little break, and bugger me, when I comes through the door, what do I see but you going all ballistic wiv' that fat geezer, I mean what a bloody spectacle!'

'He annoyed me,' said Melvin, aware that his voice had risen by about three octaves.

'No fucking kidding, I mean bloody 'ell Melv, I never seen you so mad before, cor dear oh dear, I shall 'ave to watch me p's and q's in future, I can see that.'

It was a form of torture and he was enjoying it. The car picked up speed along the country lane. He continued.

'I mean, it's not nice to lose yer rag like that, is it? I try to avoid it as much as possible, mind you, don't fink I'm being critical like, I mean there comes a point when enough's enough and you 'ave to do summink abart it.'

'Yes.'

'I gotta say though Melv, I kind of admire you really, 'cos if that'd been me and I was as uptight as you obviously was, I wouldn't 'ave give 'im no verbal, I'd 'ave just kicked his fucking teeth in. But that's where you and I are different innit? I mean, I sort of lack your self restraint, y'know what I mean?'

'Yes.'

'I know you're not posh or anything like that, but as I said to Outi once, you're a sort of gentleman, you got manners, and that's why I like 'aving you in the club.'

'Thank you.'

'I fink a stiff brandy might be a good idea, don't you?'

'Yes.'

'Yeah, we'll 'ave a nice little chat and calm down a bit.'

After a few miles of silence they pulled into a pub. Russell read out the name like a tour guide.

'Case is Altered - well bugger me, they do 'ave some funny names around 'ere.'

'I think I've seen that name somewhere in Warwickshire,' said Melvin, trying to get a grip on things. Was there really the remotest hope that he might see the end of the day in one piece?

'Now that's summink else I like about you Melv,' said Russell, giving him a friendly pat on the thigh and leaving his hand there, 'you've got an inquiring mind, you sort of remember fings, take fings in, like. Come on, let's go and 'ave a drink.'

They entered the lounge bar which was crowded with lunch time drinkers. The predominantly middle class county clientele peered suspiciously at Russell in his Armani suit as he commandeered centre position and waved a twenty-pound note.

'When you're ready luv.'

The bar maid, who was clearly the proprietor's wife and did not like being addressed as 'luv' finished serving a Norfolk hacking jacket and a twin set and pearls and engaged Russell with a cautious but disapproving stare.

'Yes sir?'

'One large Remy and a Beirut Twister please.'

'I'm sorry, I'm not familiar with the last one.'

'It's Bocha liqueur and lime juice.'

'I'm afraid we don't serve that one here, sir.'

'Oh dear, what a shame, well I'll 'ave a double schnapps with grenadine and tonic in a long glass and lots of ice.'

She served the drinks as if there was a bad smell under her nose.

'Got any pork scratchings, luv?'

'I'm afraid not, sir, we have a selection of crisps and peanuts.'

'Right, I'll 'ave one barbecue beef, a packet of dry roasted and what d'you fancy Melv?'

'I'll just stick to the brandy thanks.'

'Righto.'

As he took his change, Russell pushed a fiver back across the bar.

'Give us another dry roasted while you're at it luv.'

The woman completed the transaction in icy contempt and Russell made a point of ignoring her completely as they turned to take their seats.

'Fucking snooty cow, wouldn't last five bleedin' minutes at the club, eh Melv?'

'I guess not.'

'No bloody way, not like our Sam, eh?'

Melvin knocked back his brandy. Surely Russell wasn't going to create a scene, here of all places? He wouldn't put it past him though. He'd been an observer of his tactics for a long while and there was definitely a working class chip on the shoulder at work somewhere in the midst of all the psychosis. Nothing gave him so much pleasure as to push the frontiers of decency to their limit, knowing that violence, his ultimate weapon, his ultimate joy, was something that most folks recoiled from. His engagement at the bar was deliberately orchestrated to give maximum offence. It was his sport.

They settled themselves back in their seats, which meant that Melvin continued to perch himself on the edge whilst gripping the table with his free hand. Russell sprawled backwards, propping one foot across his knee in a blatantly balls akimbo gesture.

'Now the fing is,' he continued, raising his voice so that everyone could hear without straining impolitely, 'wiv' Sam what you get is a smile 'ere, and a smile there and a lovely pair of tits, like on a platter, but definitely not for touching. A class act.'

Melvin chose to say nothing. Samantha's physical attributes was not a topic he wanted to be drawn into but he knew only too well why Russell was leading him there. The atmosphere in the bar tightened as Russell's crudity permeated the normal cosy affluence. Melvin remained glued to the spot, knowing that he was powerless to affect the ensuing events, whatever they may transpire to be. Russell was in control. He had him in the jaws of a trap and he had only to release the spring and he would be crushed and mutilated beyond recognition.

'Could I possibly have another brandy?'

'Melv, I'm so bloody sorry, of course you can. Dear oh dear, there's me rabbiting on about Sam and completely forgetting what a nasty upper and downer you've just 'ad.'

Russell returned to the bar. Everyone pretended not to watch him but all eyes were skinned.

'Another Remy, luv, make it a large one,' the woman served him and handed him his change as if he were a leper, 'ta luv, 'ave you got a menu?'

'Are you eating in the restaurant or the bar, sir?'

'Well, as long as you've got summink beyond prawn cocktail and Black Forest Gateaux I wish to dine wiv' me colleague in the restaurant.'

She handed him a large menu and barely managed the thinnest of smiles.

'I'm sure you will find something to your taste, sir.'

'Most grateful, I'm sure.'

Russell returned to his seat with obvious enjoyment. Melvin downed his second brandy and prayed for the alcohol to take effect. When in God's name was all this going to come to an end?

'Being a bit presumptuous, as you know I can, I thought a bit of high class nosh would not come amiss, after all, you and I 'aven't exactly 'ad time to put the world to rights of late, 'ave we?'

'No.'

'That's what I thought. Wodja fancy then? I'm 'aving steak Diane wiv' them little Julian carrots, I love me veg all shredded.'

Melvin wondered for how long he must endure this charade? He felt like a mouse that was partially traumatised and every so often the cat would pretend to ignore it and let it run for cover before sticking its claws in again and tossing the poor demented creature into another series of hellish convolutions.

The answer came when they had completed their main course. Russell had devoured a second crêpe suzette and Melvin had given up the struggle with his third crème caramel. Surprisingly, he had found that the act of stuffing his face with food was a way of relieving some of the tension.

'Mmm, fucking lovely,' said Russell, 'I absolutely adore these fings. D'you want another one of those squaw's tits?'

Melvin shook his head. By now the brandies, together with a bottle of wine had taken effect and Melvin was beginning to think that there might be something noble in presenting himself as a sacrificial lamb for the slaughter. But, as usual, Russell had another trick up his sleeve.

He began by revealing to Melvin the fact that Samantha had indeed confessed all about their affair. How she came to do this he did not say and Melvin was not about to enquire either, all his effort was concentrated on following the minutiae of Russell's behaviour. Would he suddenly explode or would there be a continuance of his ordeal? What was Russell's final move? What did he actually want?

'Now, the fing is Melv,' he began quietly, 'we both know you 'ave been a bit of a bastard, no doubt about that, no doubt whatsoever,' Melvin lowered his head and gazed forlornly into the remains of his third crème caramel, 'you 'ave transgressed the boundaries of normal friendship, that's to say, you an' me being mates, an' all that.'

Melvin considered his position and came to the conclusion that he was indeed morally deficient and there was no point in denying it.

'Yes,' he mumbled, 'I know, I'm sorry.'

'You're sorry Melvin, you're sorry are you?' Russell cracked his knuckles and heaved a sigh of abject mortification, 'not half so sorry as I am. I mean, fink about it Melv. Here's me and Sam, an item, subject to life's slings an' arrows an' all that fucking shit, but trying nonetheless to 'ave a loving relationship, man and woman struggling along together like.'

Melvin was not so drunk as to choke on the sheer biblical hypocrisy of the man. It was a calculated insult to his intelligence, but what could he do? Samantha had warned him to take care, as if he didn't need reminding, but what should he do, what *could* he do? The truth, unadorned, bereft of false embellishment was being spelt out to him, and the fact that he had absolutely no respect for the human being that was dishing it out, did not detract from the fact that he knew he was morally guilty. Russell pressed on relentlessly.

'And then, out of the blue, along comes you, already married to a smashing bird like Outi, wanting for nothing as far as I can seen, and what 'appens? And what fucking 'appens Melv?' - any diners who had lingered for whatever reason were now long gone, 'you stick your fucking little prick - maybe it's a big one Melv, maybe that's the fucking attraction, 'ow should I know? but you stick your fucking prick right up inside my Sam's fanny and you dump your fucking essence right inside her like I don't matter. Now if that ain't a fucking insult, I don't know what is, truly, I don't know what fucking is.'

Melvin toyed with his crème caramel, which had long since lost its erotic attraction.

'However,' Russell moved himself closer to the table and leant across it, signalling to Melvin to do likewise. When their heads were no more than a foot apart he fixed Melvin with his steely grey eyes.

'I wouldn't want a friendship like ours to come a cropper just because of a woman,' Melvin felt Russell's hand on his knee and remained frozen as it moved slowly but inexorably up his thigh until it came to rest clutching his balls in a firm but definitive gesture, 'there are some blokes that I waste no time in wasting, as you may know Melv, but wiv' you I fink we still 'ave a chance to sort this problem out like mature adults, wouldn't you agree?'

Melvin was incapable of speech. If he believed in Jesus, now would be the time to offer a prayer for mercy, but unfortunately he did not and he had yet to discover a viable alternative. Russell squeezed gently and the first dart of pain raced through his nervous system. Russell's eyes gleamed as he pressed home his advantage.

'Eh, Melv?'

His testicles were throbbing and he could feel the blood pounding through his temples.

'I suppose so,' he croaked.

Russell released the pressure and his mouth broke into a triumphant grin.

'Well there we go Melv, see what I mean? fings are taking a turn for the better already.'

His grip changed and he began to fondle Melvin gently with the tips of his fingers.

'Like I said, it don't 'ave to be a load of aggro, we're mature adults you and me . . . two fully grown men.'

The effects of the alcohol had vanished completely and Melvin's mind was racing blindly ahead trying to work out what Russell would do next. Would he take him back to the hotel and bugger him? The man was an animal, capable of anything.

Melvin glanced at the restaurant clock, it was gone three o'clock and at least that meant that by now Julian Weekes would have wrapped up the final session and everyone would be well on their way home. Home to their loved ones and a normal decent life. Having achieved his aim, Russell snapped into a different gear and they were out of the pub in no time.

Driving back along the country lanes Russell addressed Melvin with a kind of conversational casualness.

"Ow's the Merc then, enjoying it?'

'Yes, it's lovely.'

'I knew it would be. Are you alright to drive, by the way, I mean you do look kind of shagged out?'

'I'll be okay.'

They exchanged no more words until Russell brought the car to a rest right outside the hotel entrance.

'Now listen, my ol' ray of sunshine, now that we've 'ad our little natter, I don't think there's any need for me to say anything to Outi.'

Melvin's head was already working overtime on the permutations of his position.

'Thank you.'

'And I know I was a bit harsh about Sam but then I 'ad to get it off my chest.'

'I understand.'

'Naturally she is disappointed about the turn of events and depending on 'ow fings work out in the long run, I may be in a position to consider some kind of accommodation, if you see what I mean?'

The sick bastard had thought of all the angles.

By the time Melvin was back in his room, having been handed a message slip by an extremely wary receptionist, he had broken into a cold sweat and was trembling uncontrollably. He dived for the bathroom and threw up in the toilet. His hands were still shaking as he sipped a cup of instant coffee and opened the note from Lisa.

I'm on your side and so are most of the others. Ring me at home if you want to. Troy knows you're my new boss so there's no need to worry if he answers.

It was the understatement of the millennium.

11

By the time he had joined the North Circular, Melvin had rejected the idea of becoming a mature recruit in the French Foreign Legion. The last thing he wanted was to be surrounded by a load of sex starved men with fixed bayonets. As he skirted the RAF base at Mildenhall, he had also kicked into touch the thought of becoming a Roman Catholic Priest. As for becoming a Tibetan monk was concerned, well, that notion evaporated at Newmarket when the isolation of the A11 was more than he could cope with.

Never before had he so welcomed the seething mass of outer metropolitan humanity as he did today. If nothing else, there were more places to hide, assuming that you didn't get killed trying to change lanes at Edmonton. Rush hour traffic was a revelation of character. Perhaps, if he didn't waste his time trying to be so courteous to other drivers and instead just cut the bastards up like everyone else, life in general would pan out a whole load better. Becoming more aggressive was all very well although he was beginning to realise that his temper had got him into more trouble than it had got him out of it.

A Ford Transit express courier van came along side menacingly and then cut in front of him and tailgated the driver in front until swerving dangerously again to overtake on the inside and then back out again. Mass road rage was building up nicely but Melvin was reminded of the lecture he had attended where the Police officer had said 'never antagonise an already reckless driver'. The trouble was that a Peace Brother sticker on the rear window no longer had the same effect as in the days when most drivers had only eyes for Lucy in the Sky with Diamonds and traffic lights on red became a pause for divine rapture.

Any further thoughts on reasonable behaviour were abandoned when Gladys took twenty minutes to hand over the door keys. Even Missoo showed signs of irritation by knocking over her potted geraniums when she continued her saga outside on the concrete veranda.

'Ooh, you cheeky little puss, she's having one of her little tantrums just because you're home, aren't you, yes, cheeky miss tantrum, that's what you are.'

Missoo gave a sour hiss and went back inside, a clear indication to Melvin that she would discuss the restoration of a less patronising programme of care and attention when he had got rid of the silly old boot and changed her litter instead of recycling it.

No sooner had he unpacked his suitcase and cracked open a can of Pils from the fridge than the telephone rang.

'Ah, Melvin, I'm so glad I've reached you.'

It was Christina. His spirits sank. Did he really deserve her after a day like he'd just had?

'Hello, how are you?'

He was trying, he was trying.

'I am okay, thank you, but I think Outi would appreciate some attention and she is a little upset that you appear to have ignored her all week.'

The pious bitch, why couldn't she just fuck off and join Mother Teresa?

'Well, as a matter of fact, I telephoned Outi on three separate occasions during the week and each time I was told that she was either in therapy or was sleeping.'

'That is as maybe Melvin, but you know in these hospitalisation programmes one has to be, how shall I say, a little circumspect when it comes to matters of communication with the patients.'

Circumspection in mid-shag with Lisa was the last thing he was capable of, not that he actually chose to ring Outi right then, but all the same, he had tried to ring her three times.

'Obviously, but when one is entrenched in the middle of a highly intensive and extremely demanding training programme, with the welfare of team members to attend to, to say nothing of according the appropriate courtesies when an external consultant is present, one is not always in a position to be as circumspect as one would like.'

(and stuff that up your Swedish tundra).

'Melvin, I understand that you have certain responsibilities to discharge.'

'Oh good.'

'Melvin please don't interrupt me when I am trying to explain the situation.'

'I am already aware of the situation but you do not appear to be cognisant of mine.'

There was a pause. Nothing like a rich vocabulary to silence the cow for a few moments.

'I'm just saying that Outi would appreciate another call as soon as possible.'

'Oh good, I thought for a minute you were saying something else. Goodbye.'

He slammed the receiver down and went for a piss. He took the opportunity to inspect his penis. It was still there and he passed his water comfortably. No dreaded lurgy as yet. Jolly good.

As he enjoyed a passing moment of gratitude he wondered idly what sex with Christina must be like. She lived with a Hungarian art dealer called Karel whom he had only met once, that being the last Ahus Ericsson christmas party when they had demolished a litre bottle of blue Finnish Korskenkorva vodka and Karel had confessed that Christina insisted he wash his entire genitalia in a fifty percent solution of Dettol before he could penetrate her. And that was before he put the condom on. Apparently, until he had discovered the merits of Nivea hand cream, it had given him the most awful dried skin flakiness which had precipitated a fearful row during which she had accused him of consorting with prostitutes.

Melvin flushed the loo and counted his blessings. After he had showered and shaved, (the latter he knew not why because he certainly wasn't going anywhere) he decided to put in a call to Outi. She was, after all, his wife, and the nearest he could get to a known constant in life, however inconstant that may be.

Outi was not in her room so the call was put through to the recreational lounge where someone had said they thought they had seen her. Moments passed whilst yet another tinny version of Vivaldi's The Four Seasons began to wind him up until Shaida came on line.

It surprised him and then again it did not. She spent nearly every evening visiting Dillon and it made him feel guilty, but there was more to it than that. There was something about her that he felt drawn towards and although he found her waif like figure and oriental beauty undeniably alluring, he was aware of the beginnings of something that was almost spiritual in its depth and mysteriousness. He was aware too that he did not choose to question it but merely to experience it. He had encountered no other woman in his entire life within whose presence he felt such a comforting aura of calmness. It even transcended his moments of tranquillity with Samantha.

'Hi Melvin, how's it going?'
Her chirpiness was the best thing he'd heard all day.
'Oh, so-so, you know how it is.'
'Yuh, I guess so. Why you not here?'
'I've only just got back from Norfolk and I'm totally knackered.'
'You had hard time?'
'You could say that.'
'Okay. I wanna talk with you but not on the telephone, when you coming up?'
'I don't know, probably tomorrow, how's Outi, is she there?'

'She was until ten minutes ago, now she gone walking with Dillon.'

'What do you mean, gone walking?'

'They can go out for limited periods and so that's what they've done.'

This was a new development that he was not aware of.

'So what about you? What are you doing?'

'Outi say I can go with them if I want to but Dillon say I am just in the way.'

He paused, trying to separate the past week's events from his own. All sorts of imaginings crossed his mind. Had Outi and Dillon bonded? Christ, he was sick of the sound of the word. Presumably it was not more than one could expect, given that like-minded souls were incarcerated together and required to examine their consciousnesses. What advice had Virginia to offer to mere co-dependents like himself and Shaida?

'Is Virginia there?'

'No.'

'How long are they gone for?'

'I don't know but they have to be back by nine o'clock.'

'Do you think they've gone on a bender?'

'No, they both serious about things.'

He wasn't quite sure what things they were both serious about unless it was the business of remaining sober.

'Perhaps I should come up?'

'What you want to do, Melvin?'

It was at this point that he realised he needed to talk to her too. About everything.

'I'd better come up.'

'Okay, but I'm not sticking around here any longer.'

'Where shall we meet then?'

'You know the Mermaid and Cutlass in Chalk Farm?'

'Who doesn't?'

'Okay, I'm going there.'

'Give me forty minutes.'

'No need to rush.'

'Okay.'

They rang off. It was incredible. He had automatically complied with her agenda in the absence of any well-defined one of his own. He had genuinely thought about Outi during the week and had been annoyed, then worried, and eventually confused by her apparent non-availability when he had tried to reach her. And now he wanted to sit and talk with Shaida. He wanted to talk to Lisa too, but not just yet. He also wanted to see Samantha but likewise not just yet. One thing he was definitely certain of. He did not want to talk to himself.

The Mermaid and Cutlass was a large decaying Victorian oddity in the middle of somewhere that you could never direct a stranger to and was frequented by a loose mixture of artisans, labourers and layabouts. An enormous heavy oak bar extended like an elongated horseshoe under one vaulting roof and every strata of customer drifted towards their chosen drinking clan quite happily. Unaccompanied women were not an unusual sight although they were invariably joined by a gang of friends at some later stage. Student graffiti in the bog was of a particularly high standard and there was one very talented cartoonist who plugged the Republican cause with great wit; you could literally piss on your shoes laughing.

When he entered the crowded bar, Melvin spotted Shaida perched on a high bar stool with her drink positioned on a narrow ledge. She was bathed in a warm glow thrown from a beautifully ornate wall mounted brass light fitted with two tasselled lampshades perched at cock-eyed angles. She was a most reassuring sight.

'Hi,' She gave him a lovely grin.

'Hi, how long have you been here?'

'About twelve and a half minutes.'

They laughed.

'I haven't laughed all week.' (with Lisa, he'd only gasped and groaned)

'Me neither, at least not with Dillon - have a beer,' she pushed a Budweiser towards him, 'I got this in just in case there was a crush, you know what it's like sometimes.'

'Yeah. Cheers.'

He grabbed another high stool and tucked himself in. As they drank at close quarters he caught a whiff of her perfume. It reminded him of Marylin's movement class when she had lain on the floor and publicly teased him. And then the long chat afterwards. And now this. Nothing sexual, although she was definitely sexy, but something very comforting. That was it. He felt comforted by her presence.

'So, I wanna talk about Dillon,' she said directly. He nodded and said nothing. She continued. 'I don't think he loves me any more.' She held him with a steady gaze.

'What makes you think that?'

'I found condoms in his suitcase after his last trip and he don't wanna talk about it.'

Again he said nothing. He knew it was important to listen. Dillon was a foreign correspondent with one of the big dailies and it meant he was away from home for long periods of time. Perhaps it was a straightforward case of too much separation but then again perhaps it was not.

He listened intently as Shaida discussed her relationship and marriage. Some of the things she said about Dillon tied up with remarks that Outi had made about him; Outi and Dillon had clearly found a common wavelength beyond the one of booze. On those occasions when Melvin had sat with her in her bedroom and she had just talked, he had suspected that theirs was not the only marriage that had taken a battering.

During the first co-dependents therapy session, Virginia had encouraged everyone to open out and put their trust in one another, but for Melvin, that was too much too soon and with too many women. But now, as he listened to Shaida, he was deeply affected by the trust she was placing in him. There was no doubt in his mind that she took her marriage vows very seriously and was deeply wounded by Dillon's apparent unfaithfulness. He wondered how Outi might react to his? There was nothing apparent about that. He had managed a double whammy plus forthcoming options and a sickening aberration.

'So, I'm not saying that Dillon and Outi are having an affair, I don't think that's physically possible under the current circumstances but I know that he doesn't want me around any more,' she took a long gulp on her drink, 'what you think?'

Was it his turn now? How could he possibly sum up his marriage, explain his infidelity, let alone comment on the actions of others? He drank his beer and tried to find a starting point. He wanted to say something that would be helpful and meaningful to her but his life was so full of garbage and guilt that he doubted its usefulness to anyone.

'You shocked by what I say?' she said.

He stared into his drink and shrugged.

'Not really.'

Right now he felt she was his only lifeline to sanity but he did not know how or where to begin.

Raucous laughter burst from across the bar. It had become noisy and crowded. It was Friday night in a London pub and people were revving up for a fun weekend. How had all this normality evaded him? He shifted uneasily on his stool.

'You having an affair, Melvin?'

He could not look at her.

'You needn't be ashamed, I not sit in moral judgement.'

The cat was out of the bag, the beans were spilled, whatever way you cared to describe it, Shaida knew. This time he looked directly at her.

'I am in the most God awful mess.'

His guts were turning as he fought hard to retain his composure. She squeezed his hand gently.

'Yuh, I thought as much.'

'Christ, is it that obvious?'

'Melvin, you might just as well've put up a gigantic big advertising poster in the street 'cos it was written all over your face. Y'know, I take only one look when I first see you and I say to myself, this guy's in deep shit.'

Amazingly, her remark actually gave him some relief. Nothing had been resolved, nothing had even been discussed and yet he felt that the first tentative signs of some kind of breakthrough had suddenly emerged.

'You wanna talk about it?' she said.

'Yeah, let's have another drink.'

'Okay, you save our places, I get the drinks, they know me here, it's quicker that way.'
And off she went.

By closing time he had told her everything. Absolutely everything. Afterwards, she had offered him coffee at her flat and he had accepted. She showed him her wedding photographs and he remarked how handsome Dillon was. They gazed at his clean-cut image and clear blue eyes, so different from the dishevelled wreck of today, and then she shed a tear.

'I know,' he said softly, 'I have a favourite photo of Outi too. She has beautiful skin and a smile as big as a sunflower but I think they are lost forever.'

At the doorstep, they kissed each other lightly on both cheeks and he departed. He drove home in silence save for the echoing of her final remark.

'Don't lose your self respect Melvin.'

Presumably, that meant he still had some?

12

As the Stanley Knife severed his penis he awoke with a jerk. Russell was nowhere to be seen. He was drenched in sweat and shaking all over. As nightmares go, Hieronymus Bosch on LSD could not have done better.

He drank his third cup of coffee in a steaming bath and decided that he wasn't capable of shaving. A fine start to the day. In the lounge, he flicked on the radio in search of some music. Classic FM was being rumbustiously jolly with a march by a lesser Strauss, and on Radio 3, a brass band conductor from Lancashire was explaining to school children why they shouldn't use spearmint lip seal when developing an embouchure. He silenced them both.

He opened the curtains and contemplated the visage before him. There was Ajit across the road in his off licence, laughing and gesticulating in a cobalt blue turban of such radiance that it practically outshone the fluorescent lights. He was not sure whether he could cope with the man's genial bonhomie at the start of the day so he lit up a small cigar and settled down to an old 70's recording of Nitai Dasgupta singing a morning raga. Normally, by the time it reached the open throated wobbly bits at the end, he would have arrived on some transcendental plane but, unfortunately, the residue of his nightmare had transmogrified the experience to the point where it had become a nation wide broadcast of his infidelities. Outi was ceremoniously throttling him to death to the cheers of an all female audience. In the mental stability stakes, the outlook did not look promising.

He decided to ring Shaida.

'Speak to Outi,' she said, 'you don't have to tell her everything just yet but I think you need to make contact, just say hello again.'

So he rang Outi and said hello again.

'Oh, so you're back from the dead are you?'

It seemed the day had gained a certain imprint that was going to be very difficult to shake off. Did he really have put up with this? Just because she was struggling with demons didn't mean to say that he wasn't either. There were reasons for his infidelity and wasn't he entitled to a bit of support and understanding too? What happened to all the 'and in sickness and in death' bit or did that become a one-way process when one partner had actually made it into hospital? He was not disputing that it took two to tango (well three if you knew the steps) and he wasn't denying his relish to get on the dance floor but all the same, as Virginia had said 'you cannot take responsibility for other people's actions'. (it was quite an asset being able to quote one's counsellor). So he felt it was not unreasonable to state his case.

'As it just so happens I've had a very demanding week and what was I supposed to do when you were unavailable every time I rang?'

'You could have left a message.'

'I did.' (this was true, he had).

'Well I never got any.'

'So whose fault is that? Did you try ringing me? I notice I didn't get any messages either.'

'Well you know what the administration is like in this place, I can't be responsible for everything, anyway when are you coming up? I've got forty pages of my life story written and we're supposed to be analysing them this week and there's not much point if nobody can read my handwriting and you promised me you'd type them because otherwise how am I supposed to get them done, I can hardly hire a secretarial service can I or maybe that's what you think I should do.'

'Yeah, yeah, alright, alright, I hadn't forgotten, but what about all the other things *I've* had to do this week, you've obviously dismissed those as unimportant.'

'I'm the one who's bloody ill, not you!'

'Well thanks for the vote of confidence,' by now he was yelling too, 'I'll arrive when I bloody well feel like it and if you're still unavailable then perhaps you'd better leave your manuscript with the sodding room service or something!'

He slammed down the receiver. Well, bollocks to it all. He had his own life to run hadn't he? He would pick the bloody stuff up alright but in his own time and in accordance with his needs and his agenda.

He rang Samantha. There was no reply. Impetuously, he rang the club, bugger it all, he wasn't going to be intimidated by Russell.

'Hello, Buster Keaton.'

Her voice was music to his ears.

'Hello again.'

'Oh God, I've been so worried about you, are you all right?'

'Well sort of, how about you?'

'The same - look I can't talk now - can you come to the flat at about midnight?'

'Yes - what about Russell?'

'He's going over to Islington to look at some jewellery.'

'Okay.'

'Bye then.'

'I love you.'

'Bye.'

Her voice was a whisper. She must've felt the same, surely? He glanced at his watch. He wasn't wearing one. He flicked on the telly. A load of Grand Prix smoke and roaring and no time check. He switched off and picked up his wallet from the coffee table. There was the note from Lisa. He rang her. Another impulse.

117

A coarse male voice answered
'Yeah?'
'May I speak to Lisa Joplin please?'
'She ain't in.'
'Oh righto, I'll try again later if I may, will she be long?'
'No idea mate, who's calling?'
'Mr Powell.'
'Oh yeah, I'll tell her you rang.'
The line went dead before he could say thank you. Not that it really mattered because Troy was obviously socially dysfunctional.

How on earth did such a vivacious and intelligent girl as Lisa end up with a moron like him? Okay, she had admitted that she was turned on by his muscles and apparently his dick was as magnificent as the Beachy Head lighthouse, but surely it wasn't only the sex? She had a mind as well as a body. He had plundered her body right enough, or to be more exact, she had offered it to him and they had thrown themselves into a frenzy of such orgiastic pleasure that he knew he could not resist were it ever to become available again.

And was that his real motivation for ringing her now? In spite of all the risks? In spite of all his troubles? In spite of knowing that it could not lead to anything except more disaster? After such intimacy, was it really possible that their relationship could become platonic and they could derive pleasure from intellectual stimulus only? Or at the very least, succeed in doing something together, manage the project for example, so that they could look back on their achievement with pride and satisfaction? He very much doubted it. They would continue to screw each other's arses off until their bodily fluids hit the fan. Was this really the stuff of life? Somewhere, somehow, there had to be something more ennobling than that. But how to find it? Aye, there's the rub, my cockies. In the absence of any answers, he cleaned Missoo's litter tray and went for a walk.

Gladys watched him amble along the road from her lounge window and thought he looked very tired and woe begone. Poor man, he couldn't look after himself properly, the sooner Outi returned the better. An hour later she was still peering out of the window when she saw him return with a newspaper and enter Ajit's off licence.

He emerged with a large cardboard box that took both his hands to carry. By the time he had made it round the side of the building and up the stairway she was out the front door polishing her letter box.

'Good morning, and how are you today?' her pink lips broke into a rubbery smile as garish as her marigolds.

'Not too bad.'

'Been shopping already I see.'

'Yes, just stocking up.'

There was the familiar clink of bottles as he put down the box to open the front door.

'How's Outi, will she be coming home soon?'

'I hope so, I'm going to see her tonight.'

'Oh that'll be nice for you, I expect you've missed her all week.'

'Yes.'

The front door swung open and Missoo criss crossed in front of his legs as he tried to enter.

'I bet Missoo's pleased to have you back.'

'Oh, no doubt about that.'

'I expect she misses Outi too.'

'Well actually, she told me that she could go another week provided I gave her Whiskas selected meat cuts in gravy.'

Gladys looked slightly perplexed.

'Well, I mustn't keep you any longer, I expect you've got a lot of cleaning to do.'

'Yes, 'fraid so.'

He pushed through the door into a safe haven. Nosy old bag, she'd obviously been scouting round the flat all week and hadn't failed to notice the piles of dust and fluff that he'd allowed to build up. Well yah boo sucks.

As it just so happened, the fresh air had done him some good and he'd already decided to pull himself together by concentrating on the mundane necessities of life. Two hours later a major clean of cathartic proportions had been achieved and he was beating the rugs outside just in case she hadn't got the message. He slung them over the brick wall to air and afterwards Missoo sat on top of them to watch her master take an afternoon can of Pils in the autumn sunshine. He didn't even bother with a glass. Later on he went inside and fell into a deep sleep on the sofa.

He felt much better on awakening and put the Merc through a car wash and did some late night shopping at Sainsburys. He fed Missoo and cooked himself a risotto with fresh peppers and onions. Bearing in mind his assignation with Samantha, he showered and put a change of clothes and some toiletries into a small overnight bag. Before leaving, he checked his appearance in the mirror. Not bad, all things considering. A knot of uncertainty was still knawing away in his system but that was only to be expected.

As he entered the Friends of Florence Nightingale Hospital, he was even taking a philosophical view of the overall situation. He was no longer angry with Outi and apologised for his temper. She accepted it without comment and they settled down to a relatively mild conversation. She gave him her manuscript in a plastic folder and he promised to type it as soon as possible. He'd already decided to hand it to Zelda as she could be trusted with anything and would turn it round ten times faster than he could.

'Has Dillon written as much as you?' he enquired tentatively, hoping that this might open up another avenue of discussion.

'I don't know but he's been banging away on his laptop for days.'

She didn't volunteer any further information. He pushed a bit more.

'Did you enjoy your walk last night?'

'Sort of. Did you speak to Shaida then?'

'Yes, you were both out when I rang.'

'Did you ring later then?'

'No, I was too tired, I went to bed, I've had a very demanding week.'

There was an uneasy silence.

'Maybe everything is too demanding,' she said.

'What d'you mean?'

'I don't know exactly but this is the first time in years that I've been able to think things through clearly and maybe some things have to change when I come out.'

'When are you coming out?'

'I don't know but we don't think we need this place any longer.'

'Who's we?'

She lit up a cigarette before replying.

'Dillon and me.'

He felt a small knot of tension in his chest and he was sure his pulse had quickened.

'And what sort of changes had you in mind?'

Outi drew several quick snatches on her cigarette. It was a habit she lapsed into either when she was very drunk or when she was about to get angry about something. It was a sure sign of trouble.

'Depends,' she replied enigmatically.

He felt his throat tighten.

'Depends on what?'

'I don't know . . . but you don't love me that's for sure.'

He felt a leaden weight descend upon him. This was an old familiar conversation and he could hardly believe that they were back to square one again. The only difference this time round was that she was stone cold sober. Usually he would reply by insisting that he did love her and this would lead to a spiralling argument in which she would pile issue after issue on top of him until he was bludgeoned into a raging silence. There had to be another way. He knew that he did love her but somehow he could not offer it in the way that she needed it. It had nothing to do with their lack of physical passion, that was merely a symptom of deeper causes running deep. The fact of the matter was that they had grown apart and had become two very different people to the exuberant couple they were at the start of their marriage fifteen years ago. Was this what was meant by irreconcilable differences?

Outi was pushing ash round the ashtray. She inhaled deeply and then spoke with a steady voice.

'So, you're not denying it this time?'

He wondered if this was the beginning of the end of his marriage or had that occurred when he'd first made love to Samantha? He responded calmly although his insides were pretty churned up.

'I don't think it's a question of me denying it, but I do think that we've both had an opportunity to look at ourselves in a way that we haven't had before.'

'And what's that supposed to mean?'

'Well, perhaps we could discuss these changes that you're on about.'

'Maybe I'm not ready to yet but I think we should separate for a while when I come out.'

This did not quite come as the bombshell he had imagined, nevertheless, he felt his heart miss a bit. Discretion being the better part of valour, he chose not to ask whether Dillon came into the equation. He was pretty certain he did but it was best to take one step at a time. For all he knew, Shaida might be having the self same conversation with Dillon at that very moment.

'So, you agree then?' said Outi with typical directness.

'What have we got to lose?' he replied steadily, 'certainly not our happiness.'

That was the turning point of their conversation. They had finally reached agreement on something in a rational manner. Outi was never one for small talk and he sensed that she needed her personal space to consider what came next, as indeed he did. Ten minutes later when he stood up to leave he felt a tremendous sense of relief although already his mind was working overtime with the permutations of exactly where he stood now. He was not without a paddle but the creek was definitely still shitty.

On the way out he checked with the ward nurse to see if Shaida had called. She had and there was a note for him. *I'll be in the Nag's Head until closing time - Shaida.* What an operator she was.

The Nag's Head was a plastic grot hole two blocks away but the beer was reasonable and the bar staff were friendly.

Shaida would be okay there. He set off immediately in a strange mixture of elation and apprehension. He realised that he needed to talk to Shaida urgently to find out the latest news about Dillon but he was puzzled by his emotions concerning her well-being.

On the one hand he didn't want to see her marriage affected by any complications with Outi, Dillon meant so much to her and yet, if something unforeseen had developed between Outi and Dillon, she would need his support and he had this strong urge to give it so that it would draw them closer together. He didn't want to see her hurt and yet he wanted something to happen that would allow him to show her that he wanted to care for her. Be near her.

There was half an hour to closing time as he entered the smoke filled pub and found her on a bar stool in front of the pumps. He gave her a peck on the cheek, it seemed a natural thing to do. There was no room to move anywhere else so he remained standing and ordered a round of drinks. Her eyes were red and puffy and told the whole story.

'Dillon wants to go abroad with Outi,' she said.

'Christ, that's more than she told me.'

'What she say then?'

'She wants a separation, I agreed to it, but the only bit about Dillon was that they both think they've had enough of the hospital.'

They both took a slug on their drinks.

'You know,' said Shaida, 'Virginia told us that it was normal for close relationships to develop between patients and that we shouldn't be worried if we felt excluded.'

'I think that depends on who the patients are, once Outi makes her mind up, there's seldom any going back.'

'Yuh, I guess as much - same for Dillon, he bloody stubborn.'

They returned to their drinks. There was no need to state the obvious.

'I'm not seeing Outi until Tuesday,' he said after a while, 'I promised her I'd have her life story typed up by then.'

'Dillon don't want to see me all week, he say he want his personal space.'

She looked as if she was going to cry, so he put a comforting arm around her. She felt small and very precious and spoke softly.

'You coming to Virginia's group on Wednesday night?'

He hadn't thought about that. So much had happened since then and he wasn't sure that he was up to baring his soul to seven women all of whom were total strangers bar one.

'I don't know. I've had enough of bonding to last me a lifetime and as long as I can talk to you I think I should be alright.'

There was a surge of activity as the bell for last orders went. Normal conversation was becoming difficult and they agreed that neither of them wanted another drink and would prefer to break free from the jostling.

Shaida had tucked her little blue Fiat up a side street which they reached first. She unlocked the door and turned to him.

'You see Samantha now?' It was incredible how women knew these things. He shrugged sheepishly. 'Take care, Melvin,' she kissed him lightly on the cheek, 'maybe you come on Wednesday for me.'

She gave him a funny sad smile, started the engine and was gone.

Forty-five minutes later he was in bed with Samantha. Her ordeal with Russell had been as expected and once more he caressed her naked body with the utmost care and attention. She moved her hand between his legs but he needed no stimulation.

'I don't want him to have any part of you,' she whispered feverishly.

Her words did wonders for his imagination.

13

As orgasms go, Lisa's came and went, which was to say, she never got there at all. As for Troy, well, he thrashed about in Ramboesque convulsions and then collapsed on top of her like a redundant bag of cement. In terms of a shared experience it never got further than zilch. Troy eventually rolled over and not being a poet of the post coital school of expressionism went straight to the bathroom for a short sharp shower. Lisa was left to ponder on the meaning of satisfaction.

It did not take her long to arrive at the conclusion that physically speaking their relationship had reached its nadir. In fact the rest of it wasn't that far off either, and yet they remained together. She had an uneasy feeling that she was just beginning to realise why. The devil in your bed was the one that you knew.

Troy had no such complications. After his shower, he towelled himself down vigorously whilst whistling a meaningless ditty. The heights of his musical appreciation were usually scaled during television commercials and cup final singalongs. Life for him was pretty good. A fantastic looking bird, a set of trendy wheels and enough dosh for piss ups and iron pumping sessions at least three or four times a week.

For Lisa, it was somewhat different. She reflected that in the early days Troy had definitely been a major event. When she had first met him he'd been wearing a really smart Italian suit which she now knew had set him back at least three hundred and sixty five pounds. Quite promising for someone whose arse hung out on a building site. There had been the usual crush of bodies at the Tally Ho Saturday night meat parade and somehow he had just been there in front of her. 'Okay, what yer 'aving then?' he had said. And she had ended up having him.

Nowadays he lumbered about in a lime and apricot coloured shell suit and when she had queried his choice of colour he had merely said 'Well, *you* know I'm not a fucking pooftah, so what's the problem?' Subtlety had never been his forte but of late she had begun to find his coarseness irritating. She wasn't sure what to do about it although last week had demonstrated that in reality she did. It was all a bit of a revelation really. Talk about managing change.

A familiar crashing and banging signalled the availability of the bathroom and Troy gave her a hearty thump on the bum as she rose from the bed.

'Ouch, that hurt.'

'It was meant to,' he guffawed.

She ignored him and made her way into the bathroom.

The shower was hot and inviting and her fingers found herself lightly. Ahh yes, Melvin. If unbridled lust could produce orgasms like last week then she was happy to be Helen of Troy knickerless astride the Trojan Horse.

Eventually she towelled herself down and put on her bathrobe. Back in the bedroom, she slipped on a pair of clean knickers and decided that she wasn't in the mood to dry her hair and get dressed. Events of the past week had been rather hectic and she felt that she had earned a lazy day, it was Sunday after all.

As she went downstairs, Troy was stuffing his rugby gear in a holdall.

'You didn't tell me you were playing today.'

'You didn't ask.'

It was going to be one of those mornings.

'Anyway, I ain't playing, I'm training.'

'Well what difference does it make? It still means you're going out.'

'Yeah, well I'll still be coming back an' all, so what's the problem?'

'There's no problem, I just think I'm entitled to know.'

He zipped up the holdall, snapped on his sportsman's watch (the one with the white plastic wrist band) and picked up the car keys.

'I'll be back at lunch time.'

'What lunch?' she retorted.

He turned in the doorway.

'Now what's the bloody matter?'

There were times when she could hit him and this was one of them. The trouble was he was just as likely to slap her back. He could be bloody awkward at times and when he was like that there was little point in trying to reason with him. All the same, she didn't like being ignored and it was her weekend as much as his, what was left of it anyway.

'Well, in case you hadn't noticed, I've been away on a training course all week and it was bloody hard work, plus the fact that you wouldn't help me do the shopping yesterday, nor did it even occur to you to ask me if I wanted to go out, but in spite of all that I'm expected to cook the Sunday lunch as per usual.'

Troy dumped the holdall on the floor and slung the car keys on top of it, he could be quite melodramatic at times.

'Look, I know you've been away all week, at some bloody hotel 'aving posh dinners every night served up by some poncey waiter in a bow tie, so don't come the 'ard done by story - anyway, who's this Mr Powell bloke?'

The remark stopped her dead in her tracks. She tried not to show her agitation.

'Who?'

'Mr Powell, the geezer with a posh voice who rang yesterday.'

'You never told me he rang?'

'Oh, so you do know 'im them?'

'Yes, he's my new boss, I told you last week.'

'Oh yeah, well I forgot. Was he at this hotel an' all?'

Lisa hesitated for a second. If only she knew what Troy and Melvin had spoken about but Troy wasn't letting that much out of the bag. He could be pretty thick at times but he wasn't stupid. She went for honesty.

'Yes, as a matter of fact he was.'

'Well, if he's been with you all bleedin' week, 'ow comes he's got to speak to you before Monday?'

She managed to convince herself that now was not the time to get in a flat spin. If she chose her words carefully and didn't antagonise him any further, with any luck he'd leave and right now that was probably the best thing.

'I don't know, he had to leave before the end of the course to attend a meeting, he probably just wanted to firm up the go-live arrangements for Monday.'

Troy scowled at her. He didn't like it when she used that arty farty business language.

'Well, as long as he's not firming up you that's all bloody right then, innit?'

He picked up his things and went out. She was on the point of asking whether Melvin had left a number but then thought better of it. Hopefully, there weren't too many Powells in the telephone book.

She waited until their purple Suzuki Vitara had pulled away from the kerb in a screech of burning rubber and went in search of the telephone directory.

Samantha woke first as the morning sunshine filtered across the duvet and crept lazily upwards to create pleasing fan shapes on the walls and ceiling. Melvin was still fast asleep, his body completely inert as if moulded into the contours of the bed. She observed his sleeping form and wondered, with no small discomfort, whether the time would ever come when they could be together as true lovers, free of the fear and anxiety that permeated their relationship at present.

She did not know why she loved him or indeed could recall the point at which she realised that she did. For so long he had been a withdrawn and reticent figure, slumped in some corner of the Buster Keaton Club whilst Outi and her office mates drank and smoked the night away. He had never seemed to be part of their reveries and yet he abided by their ebb and flow.

At first she had thought he was a rather lonely and pathetic figure, always on the periphery of things, never invited to join in but always there because of Outi. It was only when he moved from the tableside to the bar that she had begun to engage him in conversation and found him strangely appealing. There was nothing crass or sexist in his manner, just a mixture of vulnerability and confusion that somehow suggested, were it not for his sense of humour, that he was on the verge of collapse. It was ages before he would take the initiative on conversations and then always falling silent when others were within earshot. Especially Russell.

She had watched the two of them closely, never obviously, but always keenly. She noticed how Melvin cowed in Russell's presence and even recoiled as Russell had pushed his physicality rudely between them. She knew that Russell wanted him and was powerless to stop him as he slowly manoeuvred himself to the point where she knew that he would start calling the shots. She had seen it so many times before. He was cold and calculating and took a sadistic delight in turning the screw. She had come to the conclusion that he was incapable of love.

Their relationship had started in bloody origins when Russell had beaten up her ex-husband who had foolishly come to the club to cause trouble. From then on, Russell had become her protector, a sort of employer bodyguard. It was months later that she found herself in his bed and that was only out of loneliness. She had been aware of Russell's bisexuality, his violent temper, and had witnessed them both. However, following a vicious and bitter divorce, such had been her feelings of low self-esteem that she had chosen to ignore them.

Russell had provided her with a paid job, a reason to pull herself together in the mornings, an escape route from depression and aimlessness and from there she had simply taken life one day at a time. In the beginning she had felt gratitude towards him and had enjoyed his energy and brash posturing, and even admired the craftiness of his double dealing, criminal though it was.

But as time went by she realised that there was no relationship at all. Russell existed to please himself. A self-contained, emotionless man with a twisted soul. He lacked humanity and it was that which she feared the most. When it finally dawned on her that she was no more than a piece of window dressing for the club, an object of lust for drunken males to slobber over, she had begun to consider the quality of her life, to look beyond the needs of daily survival, to contemplate the future.

It was then that she had noticed Melvin. Their conversations at the bar gradually drew them together and then there was the night he came in without Outi because she was in hospital. From their first passionate satiation they had gradually found deeper expression until, with mounting intensity, they realised they were in love. That much she had denied to Russell when he confronted her about Melvin.

'So, I'm not bloody good enough for yer, am I?' he punched her in the shoulder and sent her crashing against the wall, 'so what's he gonna give yer, a better bloody job, eh?' another blow thundered in, this time to her rib cage causing her to buckle and fall, 'and a bit of dick on the side,' a clenched fist smashed between her shoulder blades, 'don't take the fucking piss darlin'' a vicious kick to her legs, 'don't take the fucking piss.' And then he left her in a heap. But she never uttered a word.

And now, several days later, she felt the warmth and tenderness of Melvin's arms, the reassurance of his body close to hers, and finally his passion, deep inside her, reuniting them and drawing their destinies together. Was it too much to hope that one day they would be free of Russell?

Melvin stirred and moved his arm sleepily towards her. She took his hand and held it to her breast as they lay there side by side in the morning sun.

Lisa tried Melvin's number a third time, she was sure it was the right one, but there was no reply and he clearly didn't believe in answer phones. She was in a bit of a quandary, she didn't know what to do next, which was untypical of her. She wanted to know what it was that had caused Melvin to explode and who that sinister looking guy was that he had suddenly disappeared with. And what was all that about him being 'a patient'.

She wanted to tell him that the project team were pig sick of Julian Weekes and were privately dancing with delight at the incident although they had pretended to be shocked and appalled when the slimy Julian had tried to elicit their support afterwards. She wanted to know how he was, and sod it all, she wanted to see him, feel him and touch him and for Christ's sake she was getting horny just at the thought of him. And then she remembered she had Harold Hogger's home telephone number. 'Please ring me any time no matter how daft it may seem, I understand the nature of these things'. Dear Mr Hogger, do you really mean that? You're not just saying that to make me take the job? Is there something about Melvin Powell I should know? He's a whiz in bed and I'm sick of Troy so please don't spoil it for me.

Lisa pondered on how she might justify a telephone call to the Regional Training and Development Manager on a Sunday. Given that the last time the project team had observed their project manager he had apparently suffered some kind of apoplectic fit and was hell bent on adorning the hotel's lighting system with male genitalia. When all's said and done, there were some serious operational problems afoot. She rang Harold. His polite, avuncular manner was most reassuring.

'Well, he's always had a bit of a short fuse and I do know that he was unhappy about certain elements concerning the project initiation.'

'To be perfectly honest Mr Hogger, none of us feel particularly confident just at the moment and as I've already said, we're none too impressed with Mr Weekes and I just wanted to let Melvin know that he has our support and understanding.'

'I'm sure he'll be delighted to hear it, look, why don't you leave things with me for a while and I'll get back to you later?'

There wasn't much else to say except 'yes' although, as she rang off, she realised that the conversation had resolved nothing and she was still in a peculiar state of unrest. With any luck Melvin might ring again before Troy came home.

She poured herself a dry Martini and plastered the chicken thighs with Mexican salsa. If Troy really had suspected her of something, there was no way he would have mentioned Melvin just in passing. There would have been a big scene on Saturday night ending with him storming off to the pub and threatening to rearrange Melvin's back teeth if she had been lying. Where human relationships were concerned, Troy could be awesomely Neanderthal at times.

She poured herself another Martini. She was still fretting. Surely, there was no way that Melvin would have dropped them in it? She had warned him that Troy was jealous and possessive and he had simply said 'show me the male who isn't'. On their second night together, when they had finally disengaged their bodies to collapse in post coital sleep, Melvin had stirred fitfully in the night and shouted - 'a retractable blade, you must be joking'. She had chosen not to mention the incident fearing that it might be something deeply significant and maybe embarrassing. Thinking back on things, she had found his threat of physical violence against Julian Weekes rather exciting. And who knows what might happen if it really did come to a Troy versus Melvin punch up?

But of course, these were matters that girls took no part in.

14

'Believe me, Nigel, it was only because it was such a public insult that I'm bothering to mention it at all,' said Julian Weekes, milking the moral high ground for all it was worth, 'otherwise it would have been in one ear and out of the other.'

'But Julian, this is absolutely appalling,' said Nigel Denmark, cursing under his breath, 'we can't possibly condone behaviour like that, I really am so very sorry, I cannot apologise enough.'

At the other end of the telephone line, Julian was practically basting himself in the oils of moral rectitude. The situation, as he had described it, gave Nigel no other option other than to throw himself on the ground in a paroxysm of apology and there was nothing that Julian enjoyed more than to wallow in somebody else's discomfort, and he did so, like a hippopotamus in a mud bath.

'I understand entirely, please don't feel embarrassed, as you can appreciate, my main concern is for the welfare of the project team who have bonded together so admirably during the last week.'

'Oh quite so, quite so.'

The last thing Nigel was concerned about was the bloody project team; they could bond to a fly paper as far as he was concerned. What was happening to the launch of his project? Was Julian Weekes signalling disaster or what? The trouble with having a vision about a company of this size was that you couldn't finger all the buggers that were working to their own agenda.

'Naturally, I was able to deal with the immediate issues during the final plenary session, which unfortunately Melvin was no longer able to attend,' said Julian, pressing home the point that he alone was the saviour of the occasion, 'nevertheless, I wouldn't be at all surprised if, during the weekend, some, if not all of them, will have reflected on the incident and may very well have some concerns about the integrity of the leadership they will be receiving in the future.'

Julian thought that slipped the knife in very neatly and eagerly awaited the response.

'Oh indeed yes, we must support them in whatever way we can.'

Well, there it was, thought Julian, Nigel Denmark knew sod all about anything. The potential for a nice, juicy, lucrative extension to his contract was beginning to materialise.

'Of course, I'm sure you will do what's best. Well, I'll leave things with you. I do hope you have no objections to my ringing you first thing Monday morning?'

'Good Lord no, I'm only too pleased you did Julian.'

Gotcha. He had the blind, pompous twat on the run. This was the very stuff of bread liberally buttered on both sides.

'And if there's anything you would wish me to do to address their concerns, please don't hesitate to ask.'

'Of course Julian, and once again, I'm so sorry.'

'That's quite all right. I do hope Melvin recovers and I wouldn't want to think I've initiated a knee-jerk reaction to something that clearly has its seeds in something very deep in his life.'

'Oh clearly, very deep.'

Well, that was it. The man was a total idiot. He had swallowed the biggest load of bollocks that a Monday morning could dish up. He was ripe for picking.

'And I would just mention that when I finally checked out, the hotel manager was none too pleased about the adverse comments made by a number of other guests, apparently some of them quite vociferous. I wouldn't be too surprised if you received a letter of complaint in the not too distant future.'

'I see, well thank you for putting me in the picture Julian, I expect I'll be talking to you again soon.'

'Okay Nigel, well I won't keep you any longer, um, perhaps I should delay sending my invoice until you've had an opportunity to review the overall situation?'

'Indeed yes, possibly so.'

They both said goodbye together.

'Get me Harold Hogger,' snarled Nigel into the intercom, crushing a handful of chocolate chip cookies in a glistening rage, 'and tell him it's urgent.'

The last thing Nigel wanted was bad publicity. He had spent his entire career perfecting the art of blame deflection and credit piracy and now, just as the project was about to enter the public arena, Melvin Powell had put his foot in it. Well, Harold would have to lock into the grapevine instantly and report back; no doubt the project team would be flapping their yaps all over the place. It was difficult enough getting forced volunteers in the first place never mind giving them ammunition on day one. Powell would have to be carpeted before he ran amok throughout the entire company. No doubt he was a member of the Senior Managers Union, most of the bolshie ones in Marketing were. Bloody hell, what was keeping Harold so long? Nigel stumped about the office and then called Heather for some more coffee.

'And bring me some Jaffa Cakes will you and get hold of Clive and tell him I want to speak to him urgently.'

'Clive is in London and won't be back until this afternoon.'

'What the hell is he doing there?'

'I believe he's representing you on the National Psychometric and Strategic Goal Profiling Cross-Pollination

135

Steering Committee,' replied Heather politely, 'but he's due back at four p.m.'

Nigel cursed and rang off. He had promised his daughter that he would take her to her piano lesson in Watford that afternoon and now Clive wasn't around when all this had blown up.

Clive Pettifer was his Employee Relations Manager and he needed him to set about organising Melvin's disciplinary. Forget the other side of the picture, what Julian Weekes had told him was bad enough, and as far as he was concerned, whatever this deeply seeded thing in Melvin Powell's life was all about, he wanted his bollocks on a plate and Clive was the man to do it.

Lisa's first sight of Melvin was in Zelda's typing pool which now had a posh acrylic sign hanging from the ceiling declaring that it was a Communications Resource Centre. She had spent most of Sunday trying to ring him, even putting in a call when Troy was in the toilet, which was quite frequent given that he had returned from the rugby club fairly plastered and with a twenty-four flat pack of Newcastle Brown in tow which they had both made considerable inroads into during several hours of bickering and bitching. Not to mention a burnt offering of spiced chicken which she had periodically douched with irritable splatterings of Tabasco sauce before finally snatching it from a roaring oven.

By ten p.m. Troy had collapsed in a dishevelled, snoring heap and she had got through to Melvin. He had sounded strange and remote and wouldn't take her into his confidence. Despairing of making any real connection she had opted for salacious memory recall.

'You've got a tongue as long as a chameleon and sixty-nine's my favourite number.'
There was a long pause and eventually he said:
'My porridge gun is ever at your service.'
There was something in the tone of his reply that didn't quite relate to the uninhibited passion they had shared such a short while ago but nevertheless she sought to pursue the only available opening.

'Will you take me like that again?'
Another strange pause before he replied:
'As night follows day.'
Troy stirred.
'I have to go now,' she whispered, 'take care.'
'I'm trying to,' he replied.
She put down the phone as Troy farted for the umpteenth time.

And now she observed Melvin gesticulating to Rupert and passing papers back and forth to Zelda. He looked rather flustered, and since Harold had not come back to her to say what he had found out, if anything, she was batting in the dark. She needed to get him alone and relaxed. There didn't seem to be much chance of that at the moment so she ran off a couple of implementation schedules on the photocopier hoping that he might catch sight of her. Eventually he did.

'Morning,' he said, in a tone of such normality that she guessed he must holding something back.

'Are you alright?' she said.

'Depends what you mean by alright,' he replied.

They moved out of general earshot.

'I rang you several times on Sunday but there was no reply,' she said, searching his eyes for clues.

'No, I was out all day, with friends,' he added the qualification with what almost seemed like a tinge of guilt, 'after a week of the fat man's clap trap I needed to switch off a bit.'

'Did you enjoy yourself?'

It wasn't the question she really wanted to ask but there were too many people milling around to get into deep conversation. As far as she could see, he was still the same Melvin and she felt her desires stirring again, but he had a kind of edginess, a sort of preoccupation about him that told a different story.

'Not so bad, how about you?'

She shrugged, 'Troy went off to play rugby and came home drunk and belligerent.'

'Was he driving?'

She knew something wasn't right, polite conversation was definitely not how she envisaged their relationship developing. As she had travelled into work that morning a few things had fallen into place, the main one being that Troy was now on borrowed time whilst she explored alternative options, Melvin being one of them. Well, numero uno, to be exact.

'Look, is there somewhere else we can talk?' she gave him her best gaze, hoping he would pick up on the vibrations of understanding and desire.

'Yeah, sure, umm - is the team alright?'

'Yes, no problems, they're troupers but I think you should have a chat with them sooner rather than later about the Friday scene,' she chose her words carefully, hopefully transmitting more messages of support, 'especially as the Fat Friar was making such a meal of it afterwards.'

'One is surprised,' he replied, his cynical tone giving the impression that he was getting back into the swing of a normality, 'let's meet in the social club in about an hour, apparently, according to Rupert Selwyn-Smythe, I have to countersign for the weekend bar takings or some stupid procedure like that, I've never done it before but the little runt has inspected just about every piece of paper he can put his hand on and I don't trust him an inch.'

'Okay, I'll see you there.'

Further discussion was interrupted by Zelda.

'Hello Lisa, nice to see you're part of the Melvin support club - Melvin just a quickie, Harold Hogger's on the phone, he said it's rather urgent, where d'you want to take it?'

'In my office.'

They split up and Melvin raced to his office passing Claudia in the corridor who gave him her usual artificial fat faced smile.

'Good morning, Melvin, did you enjoy your week of psychology?'

'Yeah, fantastic - I now know how to analyse a couch potato on a couch - can't stop, got a call waiting.'

Harold was his usual reassuring self.

'Greetings, Enlightened One,' he chortled.

'Not so I'm afraid, I remain mystified as to how this organisation can devise a procedure that requires a million signatures for a weekend's bar takings but doesn't bat an eyelid when it comes to coughing up a small fortune to have Friar Fuck bore an entire project team rigid with his promulgation of the Beano theory of transactional analysis.'

'Do I detect a tiny note of displeasure?'

'You most certainly do, but I trust we have now seen the back of him?'

'Well, that's what I want to talk to you about. I gather there was a passing moment of unpleasantness in the closing stages of an otherwise momentous week which, needless to say, have reached the impartial ears of the Director of Personnel who has been good enough to share his feelings with me.'

Melvin could imagine their conversation.

'And presumably he did not like his office repainted in Burnt Sienna?'

'Something of that nature. The thing is, I have been instructed to discuss matters with that epitome of non-judgmental thinking, the Employee Relations Manager.'

'Jesus Christ.'

'No, but He will probably be chairman of the appeal panel.'

'So Julian Weekes has squealed, one is surprised.'

'Listen dear chap,' continued Harold in a kindly but more serious tone, 'Nigel has just confirmed his instruction via SNOG with a copy to Clive, so he's clearly on the war path and Heather has tipped me off that at the moment Clive knows nothing about it because he's in London and I've got to see him at HQ at the end of the day, so we need to talk before then.'

'Okay.'

'Room 502b is free at five p.m.'

'I know it well and shall look forward to sitting amongst the detritus and congealed coffee cups of other people's meetings.'

They rang off.

Melvin was not surprised at the turn of events. Nor was he particularly bothered. British Energy Services, like most corporate organisations, took particular delight in salving its moral conscience and justifying its inefficiencies through the imposition of disciplinary procedures. The occasions when some poor wretch actually deserved the punishment far outnumbered the cases where cover-ups and double standards were enacted. Hypocrisy had always run rampant but now, as people covered their backs and tried to stab others in theirs, it was like an enema in full flood.

As far as he was concerned, he would listen to Harold, take his counsel wisely and then, if it came to a formal disciplinary, enjoy revealing to the panel what an utterly incompetent pseud Julian Weekes was and how totally unprofessional the Director of Personnel had been by allowing his judgement to be influenced by the volume of liquor the Fat Friar had poured down his gullet. But of course, it would not make the slightest difference to the outcome. Revealing the truth was the last thing the company was interested in. As long as the ruling elite could keep the proles in order and maintain the status quo that was all that mattered. And was it not the way of the world? Nobody wanted a revolution these days, it ruined the economy. Provided there were clean hand towels in the executive toilets then creeping mediocrity was somebody else's problem.

If only Melvin had known when Russell was about to enter the hotel he could have arranged to send Julian ahead of him to share his concerns with Russell and negotiate a peace settlement. Now that would have been a piece of transactional analysis worth watching.

'Hello wanker,' said Jack Matthews strolling into his office, 'what d'you know then?'

'What do I know about what?'

'Anything, aren't you s'posed to be Doctor Psychic or something?'

'Doctor Sick is more like it after the garbage I've been exposed to for the last week.'

'Yes, so I've heard.'

It had not taken Jack long to plug into the grapevine or for certain members of the project team to spill the beans. There was no point in denying anything so Melvin told Jack enough to satisfy his curiosity being careful to ensure that it did not reveal the turmoil of his personal life.

It was good to be able to take Jack partially into his confidence again and rather satisfying to string him along a bit. They chatted away like schoolboys discussing the relative merits of each other's conker collection, pausing only to elaborate on points of contention but finally wrapping up the state of the nation to their mutual satisfaction.

Zelda had put through several calls but now, as they were beginning to flood in for Jack, he stood up to go.

'Well, yours won't be the only disciplinary if Rupert Selwyn-Smythe's preliminary payroll findings are anything to go by, I doubt if I'll even be left with a viable workforce.'

'Too late to complain now - you wanted action and action is what you got.'

'Yeah, and don't I bloody know it - the little turd nose has been lethally efficient and what's more I can't bollock him because he's actually done a good job in an exemplary manner, Christ knows how you briefed the pus faced bastard.'

'I just threatened him with a chair.'

Melvin's reply elicited no response as Jack loped through the doorway. It was time to meet Lisa. God knows what that would lead to. This morning she had looked absolutely ravishing.

He made his way to the social club which was situated across the staff car park from the main building. As he disappeared through the main doors, Claudia checked that Fred Brannigan did not require her services and mentioned casually that she was just going on her milk round. He took that to mean that she was dropping off important papers on various people's desks and generally noting who was being industrious and who was not. On this particular occasion however, she had only one destination in mind, and that was the social club.

With a glutton's heightened awareness for sources of food, she had noticed that whenever there was a late night function on Sunday, the catering staff were more anxious to go home than check every nook and cranny for forgotten food stuffs. It was a feast waiting to be had and she was practically slobbering at the very thought of the rich pickings of crisps and crunchy bars, or maybe even the remains of a cold steak sandwich which she could wop in the microwave. She had the operation down to a fine art and, gathering some papers as a kind of administrative smoke screen, she waddled off on her mission of gastronomic gratification.

By now, Melvin had entered the social club bar from the kitchen and there was Lisa, propped up on a stool and doodling on a notepad.

'Hi, sorry to keep you, you know how it is.'

'That's okay.'

As she turned to acknowledge him he caught a fleeting glimpse of a long golden thigh through the slit in her skirt, and as her cotton blouse tightened across her breasts, two magnificent nipples rose like ripened raspberries atop an iced Pavlova. He was incapable of pure thought. In heart beating silence they drank each other in. By now their earlier discourse had dissolved into insignificance as memories of their white hot passion flooded back to them. Now they were together again and nothing else seemed to matter.

'We could go in the stock room,' he whispered.

'Won't it be locked?'

'Authorised key holder,' he grinned, dangling the keys in his hand.

They moved across the bar to a heavy door in the far corner. Melvin inserted the key and they entered the windowless room racked high with shelves and boxes. There was no need for further conversation as their minds were as one. Who cared a toss about the consequences when temptation blinded all reason in a blistering firmament of longing? They moved closer to touch and smell each other's craving. Hardness and wetness flooded their senses. They wanted each other. They had to do it. They had passed the point of no return. Their mouths interlocked, their tongues danced and played as they fumbled frantically with each other's clothing. Desire threw caution to the wind. They sank to the floor bringing down cardboard boxes and cartons around them. Rolling, grasping and groaning, flesh seized upon flesh as they locked in sublime and feverish coupling.

And as they thrust and pounded with mounting intensity, the door swung slowly ajar and there, concealed in the shadow of a corner was Claudia, chocolate dribbling from her wide open mouth, staring with Mars Bar'd incredulity at the unfettered animality of their fornication.

15

At about the same time as Melvin was ejaculating into Lisa, Clive Pettifer was accessing his SNOG messages from a remote terminal at national headquarters in London. His face furrowed in distaste as he absorbed the content of Nigel's angry message. Well, he wasn't going to say 'I told you so' but there was no mistaking the fact that his reservations about Melvin had now been proved right.

Personally speaking, he had always thought that Melvin Powell was a most unsuitable candidate and he couldn't understand why Nigel had been so insistent about him. In fact he was most concerned that he had not been privy to the project appointments much earlier, before political considerations had come into it. Just because the Change Management Programme was a national initiative did not obscure the fact that no extra funds were being provided for it. As it was, the manpower forecast was proving to be an absolute nightmare and yet again Gerald MacNab was being particularly unhelpful about the phasing of the projected salary costs. And why had Nigel been in such an unholy rush? If only people would just sit down for a few months and plan things properly. He rang Harold and they agreed to meet in Clive's office. It was gone 6.30 p.m. by the time their discussion had ended and he was not impressed with Harold's defence.

'Look Clive, I know there are aspects of Melvin's behaviour that were utterly reprehensible.'

'Aspects! good God Harold, the entire incident was a disgrace and a very public one at that, heaven knows what we do if some local reporter gets wind of it, as it is we may yet receive a formal letter of complaint from the hotel.'

'I understand all that and I'm not trying to make light of it but we've both known the chap for a number of years and it's the first time he's behaved like this outside company premises.'

'I don't exactly find his behaviour *inside* the company a role model of managerial good conduct.'

Harold knew he was not making much headway. Perhaps there was one last tack that might persuade Clive to listen with a grain of common sense.

'Well, I appreciate that you have to recommend some kind of action in line with company policy and right now Nigel is hopping mad. However, we do have to consider that Management's response will be viewed by others in the cold light of day and must therefore be appropriate to the misdemeanour as opposed to just an angry reaction.'

'Well of course I'm aware that the Director may calm down in due course,' (Clive would always refer to Nigel as the Director when he felt that his judgement was being questioned, it reminded people that he was, after all, number two in the Personnel pecking order) 'and I am constantly striving to demonstrate the need for balanced and considered judgement in disciplinary matters.'

Clive was puffing himself up with self-importance and Harold reckoned there was a fifty-fifty chance that he might just swallow the next ploy.

'Quite so, Clive, and therefore I think we should position the matter in the context of the company's declared adherence to the principles of Total Quality.'

Clive's forehead puckered up. He had read just about every book, dissertation, and thesis on the subject but, like most senior managers in Personnel, steered clear of actually doing it.

'Oh yes, but of course,' (what on earth was Harold driving at?).

'So perhaps I should just take Melvin to one side and remind him of the need to lead by example.'

Clive began to twitch. This was not how things were done in the past. And since when did the implementation of a Total Quality culture mean that you could throw away the rule book? Tut tut, Harold was clearly getting a bit long in the tooth.

'Naturally, I shall be very stern,' added Harold quickly, seeing disapproval spread across Clive's face like a dog fart at dinner time, 'and I shall make it quite clear that such behaviour will not be tolerated in future.'

Clive was mortified.

'The point is Harold, the company will not tolerate it *now* and I am here to ensure that the code of conduct is seen to apply to everyone all the time.'

Harold had made his exit shortly afterwards leaving Clive to thumb through Melvin's personal file again. It was like a bad smell under his nose. For heaven's sake, the man hadn't even got a degree. If the project really *was* as important as Nigel had said, then why hadn't they appointed an operational line manager with appropriate gravitas and qualifications? A Chartered Engineer for example? A proper professional, not some vulgar Marketeer with an 'O' level in woodwork. There were no standards anymore. He sniffed and looked at his watch.

Like the majority of senior managers in the Personnel Headquarters Directorate, he rarely went home before seven p.m. That was the culture on the tenth floor. By staying late, it gave everyone a feeling of importance. It fed their egos and convinced them that they were doing something incredibly significant. Some of them even came in during the weekends. Clive Pettifer was one of those too. He inhabited a world of policies and procedures. They were the be all and end all of everything. The reason for existing. After all, wasn't that why Nigel Denmark had given him the job? As custodian of the Company Oracle it was his honour and duty to uphold and promulgate its tenets. He could not understand why the company actually needed a change management programme in the first place, let alone an implementation manager to front it. As far as he was concerned, the only reason why management had failed to get to grips with things was because they had not adhered to the principles of Effective Rationalisation and Output Identification Criterion as set out in his third Strategic Planning and Development Paper.

Clive Pettifer was so immersed in his theories, and so mindful of his position as a Human Resources professional that he seldom came out of his office to see what was actually going on. In short, he was a pompous, insufferable snob. And yet, Nigel Denmark, who seldom had an original thought in his head, trusted his judgement implicitly. Obviously, it was entirely appropriate that the Director had delegated responsibility for a satisfactory resolution to him but nevertheless, it concerned him that managers as mature and experienced as Harold could be influenced by an organisational philosophy that had, let's face it, originated in the United States of America for God's sake. He was going to make an example of Melvin Powell to deter other managers who might be mistaken into thinking that vulgar emotional outbursts in public was the British way of responding to the economic threat from the Pacific rim. In fact, he felt a strategic policy discussion document was upon him.

He turned to his VDU and launched into yet another interminable litany which he considered would be a model of communication. Like all the others before it, it would be received with universal derision and loathing. To most people, the Employee Relations Manager was a condom on the prick of progress.

As Clive's computer screen flickered, so too did the dashboard lights of Rupert Selwyn-Smythe's Mazda as he switched on the ignition and pulled away from Regional Headquarters. A short while ago he had presented his latest findings on Nigel Denmark to Gerald MacNab and was excited at the way things were hotting up. Why did people think that being in Audit was so dull? At times like this it was riveting.

Here before his very eyes was evidence that the Director of Personnel had not only been diverting funds from accounts that were the personal responsibility of the Chairman but had actually contrived to raise a bogus supplier invoice to pay for goods that he, Rupert Selwyn-Smythe, Assistant Controls and Investigation Officer (Finance HQ) nay Assistant Administration Manager, Outer Metropolitan Area (Seconded) had successfully linked to the Director's personal charge account at a local John Lewis department store. And it had been going on for at least eighteen months. Everything from lingerie (had he got a mistress?) to a three-piece suite (would there be a dawn raid by police?). Gerald MacNab had practically knighted him on the spot. He could hardly contain his pleasure.

'Well done Rupert, well done.'

'Thank you.'

'Can the transactions be refuted in any way?'

'No, absolutely not, the IT Systems Information Manager has a monthly master disc of chronological listings for all financial transactions at NAC levels one to six since system implementation in June 1995.'

'How does he hold them?'

'As high security bar coded computer files in the central computer suite which the Director of IT will only release on written authorisation of the Chairman,' Rupert glowed with pride, 'but I have microfiche copies of NAC level accounts transactions for the last two financial years as per national finance directive number thirty-four stroke five-A.'

Gerald MacNab's eyeballs had difficulty remaining in their sockets. Sweet revenge was on nigh.

'I think a meeting with the Chairman would not be amiss,' he replied, playing with his balls through his trouser pockets, 'and how goes the Change Management Project?'

'Well the rumour is that Melvin Powell went berserk in an hotel foyer and Julian Weekes the consultant has made an official complaint.'

Gerald nodded casually and made a mental note to ring Harold Hogger the following day. It seemed like a nice head of pandemonium was building up. Things were moving along exactly as he had planned.

He dismissed Rupert and sat alone in his office fantasising on the day when he would control the entire organisation. With delusions of grandeur running through his mind like tokens spinning in a fruit machine he watched Rupert climb into his car as an autumnal dusk lowered its shroud of dampness on all the surroundings.

It was completely dark by the time Rupert remembered that he had left his other brief case at work and since this contained his draft final report on the payroll investigation, he thought it prudent to retrieve it. Using his electronic security swipe card, he entered the main building through the back entrance.

As he skirted the management suite he spotted the large and familiar figure of Claudia rummaging through papers in Melvin's office. It was unusual for her to be working as late as this. He drew himself behind a coffee vending machine to observe her actions. She was peering intently at a red folder and appeared to be writing something down. He remained in the shadows until she was gone, her body language, vast though it was, displaying all the signs of a cat who had just got the cream.

He sneaked round the corridor, entered Melvin's office and located the file she had been looking at. It was once of several that Melvin had placed on a table adjacent to his desk. He was very neat and methodical in his way and it was easy, for a trained auditor, to spot the break in the symmetrical placings. Within the folder, his eagle eye further observed a tell tale sign and he extracted the sheet of paper that was not quite properly aligned with the rest. It did not seem to be of any great significance. Just a project file with details of the project members, a short career profile with qualifications and experience etc. and the usual personal details. Against the last entry he spotted a tiny indentation. The tell tale sign of someone who had inadvertently allowed their biro to touch the paper at the spot which had so held their interest. But Rupert was still non-plussed.

What was so important about Lisa Joplin's home telephone number?

16

'There you are,' said Zelda, plonking a nicely bound sheath of papers on Melvin's desk, 'one life history all done and dusted.'

'Utterly amazing, once again your delegation has been faultless.'

'Big-end Brenda, need you ask?'

He did not and what's more, he knew that total confidentially was assured. If there was one advantage of being a bewildered male in the post-feminist world it was that you could happily accept that no man was ever likely to achieve a typing speed of one hundred and eighty four words a minute with a hundred percent accuracy whilst simultaneously confronting the threefold challenges of varicose veins, cellulite and a bum as big as Brenda's. The glistening, pristine pages were graphical testament to the superiority of women to conquer a balls-aching task.

'Bloody marvellous,' he replied, admiring the beautifully laid out text on posh paper with front and back covers, 'Outi will be delighted.'

But that was wishful thinking. Within the walls of the Friends of Florence Nightingale Hospital a different set of values prevailed.

'I'm surprised you haven't raised an invoice,' said Outi, throwing it on the bed like it was last week's junk mail that the cat had pissed on. It was a bit of a bummer he could well do without, nevertheless, during the years of disintegration (a poignant description of their marriage that he felt had a certain noble attraction) he had long given up on sarcasm as an effective method of verbal retaliation. But tonight was different.

'I just wanted to upstage Dillon,' he retorted, noting that he had scored a definite point. Outi scowled and then, after a pause that seemed more awkward than it was tense, said:

'So, what do you do with yourself nights?'

It caught him off guard, or rather reminded him that he needed to be on it. His immediate thought was that either Outi was just trying out a diversionary tactic or that Christina, that wretched female pestilence, had spotted him in or around the Buster Keaton club and had been dropping her usual polite and helpful innuendoes. Either way he was becoming fed up with the number of people to whom he seemed always to have to answer or account to. He wasn't taking any bait however and plumped for a casual reply.

'Not much, you know me.'

'I sure do.'

So, this was how it was going to be was it? Although she looked physically better there was no sweetness or light in her manner. Apart from some kind of matrimonial obligation, which he immediately rejected as fruitless, he could see no reason why he should tolerate her sourness. Of course she was still struggling and of course it was no small battle but bugger it all, in between whiles she had charted out some kind of life plan which did not happen to include him and he had been made aware of that in a very off hand manner. No wonder the divorce rate had gone through the roof. I mean, what was the point of it all? One partner's aspirations were another one's disillusionment. To be subsumed or not to be subsumed, was that the question? Since Outi's declaration of a new direction he felt that he had become as valued as a used railway ticket. And it was getting him nowhere.

'Okay, so what's the problem?' he said eventually.

'Mine or yours?'

'Well, I'm coping alright, maybe that's of interest to you?'

'Coping with what?'

'Life in general, Missoo, Gladys, the unrelenting stimulus of daily work.'

Outi lit up a cigarette and blew a length of smoke across the room.

'Have you been to the Buster Keaton recently?'

This was a potentially dangerous situation. He decided to procrastinate.

'Depends what you mean by recently.'

She blew another line of smoke out.

'There's no need to side step the issue, I already have the answer.'

He shrugged. The cow-bitch Christina was obviously hell bent on achieving the snitch of the year award. He was debating the wisdom of asking why she had asked him if she already knew the answer when there was a tap on the door.

'Who is it?' said Outi.

'The Virgin Mary,' replied an Irish male voice.

Outi opened the door to Dillon.

'Come in, Melvin and I were just trying to have a conversation but I don't think we're getting very far.'

Dillon nodded a greeting before slumping on the bed, 'Oh well that's a pity, but I know the feeling, maybe I can add another dimension?'

'You don't have to be polite on my account,' said Melvin, resenting the intrusion at the same time as welcoming it, 'and anyway I was about to call it a day and leave.'

'Melvin's very good at leaving,' said Outi tartly, 'it saves him having to confront the truth.'

'Oh, and what truth is that?' enquired Dillon with his Irish lilt.

Melvin felt like telling him to mind his own business but then he had second thoughts. This was Shaida's husband after all and if he and Outi had something going then staying was a way to find out.

'The truth is that I'm just not appreciated today,' he said.

'There's always tomorrow,' quipped Dillon, 'in this place they like you to take it one day at a time.'

'I don't doubt it but then I'm not the one who's in this place.'

'So it's not your problem is that it?' interjected Outi.

'I just like to be appreciated once in a while, that's not too much to ask is it?'

Things weren't going quite as expected but since it was two against one he may as well get his oar in first.

'Now I wonder where I've heard that one before?' said Dillon, with more than a hint of sarcasm.

'Oh take no notice of him,' said Outi, 'unless he gets his daily intake of gratitude it's a cause to sulk for the rest of the day.'

Outi offered Dillon a cigarette and the two of them sat side by side on the bed blowing clouds of smoke in Melvin's direction. Dillon propped his long frame against the bedside wall.

'Would this have anything to do with the gratitude factor?' he said, picking up Outi's neatly bound life story.

'Well first you have to understand that as far as Melvin's concerned, every request for assistance carries some kind of credit and debit entry, everything has to balance out otherwise nothing's fair.'

'I don't see why I should be taken for granted that's all.'

'Nobody likes being taken for granted, Melvin,' said Dillon, almost mockingly, 'but it happens, it's a fact of life.'

The man was definitely getting up his nose, who did he think he was? They hardly knew each other. And was Outi seriously thinking that this lolling Gaelic hack-wit was a better option than he? Clearly she must've poisoned his mind because how else would he have cause to be so patronising? It buggered belief. And what on earth did Shaida see in him?

As he sat uncomfortably in the chair trying to recall what items of tenderness Shaida had attributed her husband with, he became aware that he was being consumed by a powerful loathing for the man. This man who presumed to engage him on matters philosophical, who was attempting to steal his wife and had already cheated on his own. This man who was now sprawled across Outi's bed in a position of calculated insouciance and was rolling up Big-end Brenda's immaculately presented typescript as if he were about to swat a fly.

'If you don't mind,' said Melvin, making a grab for the papers, 'a lot of work has gone into that.'

'Oh, so it belongs to you, does it?' taunted Dillon, holding firmly on to the other end of it. They glared at each other like two kids struggling over a Christmas cracker, each hoping the other would fall over backwards empty handed when the cardboard strip went snap.

'Let's just say I have more of a stake in it than you do,' hissed Melvin, giving a sharp tug to no effect.

'Let's just say you might be making some assumptions you've no right to.' And then a counter tug that coincided with a tap on the door.

'You may as well come in,' said Outi, 'there's a bit of a floor show going on.'

Shaida entered as the two men began to wrestle with the typescript like it was a super-glued baton in the relay of life.

'What going on?' she exclaimed.

'I'm warning you, you'd better let go,' yelled Melvin.

'Oh yeah, and what if I don't?'

'Just don't bloody mess with me.'

'Oh dear, will you issue a formal disciplinary letter or something?'

'I'm warning you, don't take the piss.'

'Oh Mr Macho Manager, now I'm seriously worried.'

Melvin suddenly let go of his end of the paper giving Dillon a violent shove as he did so.

'You fucking failed hack, at least I don't stuff my suitcase with cheapo condoms!'

Dillon crashed back onto the bed and then suddenly sprung back up again, eyes ablaze with anger. Without stopping to break his momentum he followed through with a right hook that slammed into Melvin's jaw with a resounding smack.

Shaida screamed, 'Dillon! stop it!'

Melvin staggered backward and smashed into the hand basin mirror sending Outi's toiletries flying in all directions amidst the shards of glass.

'For God's sake!' yelled Outi.

'Come on let's get out of here,' yelled Dillon, grabbing Outi's arm, 'I've had enough of this place.'

Outi put up no resistance as the two of them made a beeline down the corridor. Shaida hesitated.

'Melvin?'

'Oh bollocks,' he gestured to her to go away.

There was an anguished moment before she turned and ran down the corridor shouting after Dillon.

Melvin slowly eased himself up to pick his way gingerly out of the perfumed detritus. 'Fucking bastard,' he muttered as he stumbled across the screwed up typescript, 'fucking life story,' and threw the crumpled scroll angrily into the metal waste bin. He headed towards the door and then, seeing Outi's cigarette lighter on the bed, grabbed it impulsively and set light to the contents of the waste bin. 'Fucking life,' he muttered, and watched transfixed as the flames took hold on the edges of the paper. Suddenly there was a muted bang like a damp firework and the waste bin shuddered and spewed its burning contents all over the carpet.

'Jesus Christ!' gasped Melvin, as a snake of fire raced across the floor and sped upwards into the curtains. He raced to the sink intending to throw some water about but slipped on the broken bottles instead.

'Jesus fuck!'

The bed was alight, the carpet was on fire and acrid smoke was billowing everywhere. Things were out of control.

He panicked and ran coughing and spluttering out of the door and down the corridor. Reaching the top of the stair well he spotted a fire alarm and smashed the glass frantically with the little metal hammer. All hell let loose. Bells erupted everywhere as he catapulted down the stairs at breakneck speed with only one thing on his mind. Escape, no matter what.

By the time he reached the ground floor there was a fair build up of confused and frightened people spilling out into the streets. He glanced briefly up and down the main road but neither Shaida, Dillon nor Outi were to be seen. His jaw was aching and he felt in need of a stiff drink. As the sound of fire engine sirens drew closer he resolved to make a quick dash to the Buster Keaton.

There was a definite nip in the air as he climbed out of his car five minutes later and entered the club. The prospect of a welcome drink overshadowed his apprehension at meeting Russell again. Some things had to be challenged though, and if there were to be more Sundays with Samantha as beautiful as the last one, then he had to get a grip on his life, become more proactive and cease to duck the issues.

Brian, the bent CID copper was one of a small band of blokes seated around a table near the bar, all of them consumed in a blue circle of cigarette smoke. There was nobody behind the bar but there was a God-awful noise going on somewhere behind it. Somebody was having their head bashed in. There was a heavy thudding like a sack of potatoes hitting the wall and then a flatter thump followed by stifled agonised groan like a stopped note on a French horn. The kind of sound when some poor bastard is having their stomach kicked in and can't scream on account of their attacker's hand being clamped across their face. After that there was comparative silence, save for the scraping and banging of a fire door somewhere out back.

'Customer liaison,' said Brian with a sneer, and his cronies yukkered in cynical laughter. More dragging of fags and the circle of smoke moving sinuously around them like Ali Baba's cave at planning time.

'Ex fucking customer, more like it,' growled another.

There was more low life guffawing as Russell entered a few moments later, his face glowing with menace and satisfaction. These were challenging moments indeed.

"ello Melv,' said Russell, grabbing both his shoulders in a vice like embrace, 'join the party.'

What else could he say but 'cheers'?

The party turned out to be a mixture of criminal plotting, lewd shaggy dog stories and a general slagging off of law-abiding citizens. As the meeting began to break up, Russell said:

'Gotta a little bit of paperwork for you to sign Melv, sorry it's taken so long.'

He was of course referring to the bogus HP agreement for the Mercedes Benz. The fake proforma had been sufficient to convince Harold that it was a genuine transaction and bingo he had authorised Melvin's company loan. Nigel Denmark was definitely miffed when he realised that Melvin's opulent stagecoach, albeit a much earlier model, far outshone his manual 190E which did not have air conditioning. But he could not really complain since his instruction to Harold had been perfectly clear - 'you deal with the admin and just consult me on policy'.

Russell produced the document and laid it on the table.

'The usual legal clap trap but nothing to phase a man of your intellect Melv,' he said mockingly, putting his arm round Melvin's shoulders as Melvin tried to concentrate on reading the small print, 'just sign on the dotted line, as they say.'

In the background Brian was glowering and looking at the two of them through yet more clouds of incessant cigarette smoke. Melvin signed.

'I'm afraid I haven't got my cheque book with me.'

Brian broke out into laughter. Russell continued to hold Melvin.

'This is cash all the way, Melv,' he said grinning, 'but don't worry if you're a bit strapped right now, 'cos I know you only dropped in on the off chance of seeing Sam who incidentally isn't 'ere tonight on account of doing a little errand for me.' Brian apparently found that amusing too. 'p'raps you'd care to fuck off for a few moments Brian,' said Russell sharply, 'while I 'ave a little up close and personal with Melv.'

Brian grunted and shambled off into the gloom. Melvin could smell the whiskey on Russell's breath as he pulled him closer, still with his arm around his shoulders.

'Might not be a bad idea to pop over to Notting Hill Gate though, just to reassure her about our accommodation which I fink she is still coming to terms wiv.'

'She's not the only one,' blurted Melvin involuntarily.
And then Russell's hand snaked under the table to grab his testicles.

'Jesus!' exclaimed Melvin.

'He won't 'elp you, sunshine,' snapped Russell, pulling him roughly into a full bloodied embrace. Melvin nearly gagged as a coarse whisky laden tongue thrust down his throat. He could feel the stubble at the edge of Russell's lips. It was a strange, awful sensation. Russell suddenly unlocked him and pushed him back into the chair.

'Cash every month, Melv, now piss off.'
Melvin did not need any encouragement to go. He fled shaking.

And indeed, fled straight into the arms of Samantha into whose flat in Notting Hill Gate he burst a short while later in a fit of shock and anxiety. The shock for him, the anxiety for her.

'He's like this,' said Samantha, pouring him a mug of coffee, 'don't let him get to you.'

'But for Christ sake, the man grabbed my balls and French kissed me!'
She added a tot of brandy to the steaming mug.

'Drink this, it will make you feel better.'
He followed her bidding. After a while, when the hot smooth liquid began to steady his nerves, he became aware of Samantha's stillness, that strange aura that seemed to arise from an acceptance of things as they were, the precise opposite to him.

'He also said that you were taking things badly but it certainly doesn't look like it to me.'
She lit up a cigarette.

'I know how his mind works, there's no point in panicking.'

'Oh, thanks very much, I'll remember that when it comes to bending over to think of England.'

She looked at him but did not answer. He fumbled in his pocket and found a small cigar. His hands were still shaking as she gave him a light.

'Anyway, I seem to recall you saying that you didn't want him to have any part of me.'

She drew deeply then exhaled at length.

'I don't.'

An honest enough statement in itself but he was hoping for something a bit more reassuring. The fact was that they were up against a force of evil whose power was more than the two of them could cope with. Russell controlled them. There was no going back and there was no going forward. They were in a box made in hell.

'Well, I don't want to appear selfish but have you any bright ideas how we might be able to stop him?'

Samantha gave him another one of her long steady looks and then moved closer to kiss him lovingly.

'Do you really love me?' she said

His heart was beginning to palpitate. He didn't know whether it was her or the brandy.

'Yes, you know that.'

'Then how far are you prepared to go, for both of us?'

Her eyes were burning with a strange intensity.

'What do you mean?' he replied nervously.

'Melvin,' she said quietly, drawing him into her arms, 'I know this man, it can only end in bloodshed.'

'Yours or mine?' he replied inquisitively.

'No - his,' she whispered fiercely.

He was transfixed by her gaze. Was this the face of Lady Macbeth? There was no getting away from it. Honour, duty or integrity?

Yet again, his life was full of options.

17

'Don't be ridiculous,' said Shaida, as they sat in the student refectory supping tea, 'that's the quickest way to end up in jail.'

She was absolutely right, of course, but then her wisdom was something that he was becoming increasingly aware of. This odd, spunky, sparrow of a girl was never far off talking some pretty straight sense.

'Anyway, you get buggered inside as well, so it not too clever all way round,' he was rather surprised at how angry she had become, 'you gotta see things as they really are, Melvin, that's what the group were saying tonight but you don't wanna hear them do you, 'cos you live in fantasy.'

She was laying it on rather heavily and he was beginning to think it was a bit too much, given that Virginia's co-dependent's therapy session had more nearly resembled his moral court martial. Not that he had blurted anything out about his latest twist of fate, but when seven women (mercifully excluding Shaida) had all pronounced him a moral failure and a two-timing sonofabitch, it was enough of a bummer for one evening, thank you very much.

As yet he had not been linked to the fire in the hospital, (which struck him as a minor miracle), and it seemed that Shaida had been too concerned with the state of her marriage to question him closely about what had occurred after she had chased after Dillon and Outi.

'Well, what the hell do I do?' he exclaimed.

'You pay off Russell, you stop mucking around with other women and you show Outi you love her.'

'It's not quite as simple as that, besides, I thought Virginia said we had choices about our lives.'

'You think the mess you're in you got choices? You only got decisions Melvin.'

There are occasions when some kind of remarks come zinging out of the deep blue yonder to zap you in the solar plexus like an Exocet amidships. This was one of them. No doubt to her it did look as straightforward as she had said, but the difference was, she wasn't *experiencing* it. And isn't that always the trouble? No matter how much they're trumped up to be, foresight and hindsight might just as well be as blind as bats when the actuality of the moment renders them totally *out* of sight. And how do you know what the right moves are at the time of taking them? It isn't as simple as that.

As far as the consequences of his actions were concerned, Melvin knew, if not exactly, then certainly on the dartboard, what the general outcome would be. Admittedly, there were occasions (and of late there had been far too many) when the results had been completely unexpected. There could be no argument there. How many of us, he reasoned, have been around when the fickle finger of fate, without so much as a by-your-leave or it's-for-you-hoo, came snaking out of the sea of carnality to smack one round the chops with the cold kipper of reality and a spiteful 'gotcha!'. Deny it if you must but how do you stop it?

Even if, at the moment of conception, one's DNA is suffused with love instead of lust, there's no guarantee that out of a gerzillion spermatozoa there isn't one little wayward wriggler who can't wait to play nooky in the next available life. That being yours. And if it doesn't get you in the balls, it gets you in the brain. And there's even a back up system in the soul. Nature. The Mother of all Motherfuckers.

Shaida was almost right. But not quite. He wanted rid of Russell and he definitely wanted Samantha. And he was going off Outi in a major way. So, if he were to pursue that line of thinking, was he being selfish? And if so, then all this stuff about choices that Virginia and the group kept wittering on about was just so much hogwash.

What he needed now was a large vodka and a liberal dose of fully enlightened now-sight. And a bloody good shag with Samantha. Or Lisa. That was the bit that Shaida hadn't got a handle on. Sexual gratification was the only release from the stresses and strains of modern life (excluding listening to Bruckner symphonies) that left him simultaneously pleasantly knackered and wonderfully invigorated. Well, most of the time. It wasn't that easy to predict the knock-on effects of knocking off the wrong woman. By wrong he didn't mean a bad knock, he meant a bad decision, which is to say one based on lust as opposed to the loftier levels of the human condition. Wasn't that something that the majority of the male of the species had yet to successfully crack? Not that such things were entirely one sided. Admittedly, with Samantha it had been a reciprocal need and whilst there was no denying the sexual aspect of their relationship, it had grown into one that embraced tenderness and feelings (although recent developments had begun to cast a sinister shadow of doubt).

With Lisa it was different. She had been gasping for it and indeed had made all the running. So why was he in such a mess? Damn it all, even Roman Catholic priests had shattered the purity of driven snow, so what chance had he, a mere mortal, to scale the noble paths to enlightenment? Did the answer really lie in Shaida's prognosis?

After years of wounding rows, for which he was fully prepared to accept his proportion of the blame, Outi had discarded him. The terms of their loving were no longer acceptable to her and she had made her decision. Finish. Out. But with another woman's husband. And that was the woman who was now seated opposite him, urging him to follow the path of common sense and righteousness. Granted she was wiser than him, in a sassy sort of way, but not that wise.

'So what do I do if Outi decides to take off with Dillon and more to the point, what do you do?'

'We gotta reconnect with our spouses.'

It was extraordinary. Shaida was sounding like a cross between a marriage guidance counsellor and a Victorian landlady.

'Why, what's the point? When I gave Outi her manuscript last night she never even said thank you. I've been frozen out, Shaida, I know my wife. I'm ex-rated.'

'Melvin, you're so defeatist, you gotta fight for what you want. Don't you want a happy marriage?'

'I'd rather fight for you,' he suddenly said, not knowing where the impulse came from.

Shaida fell silent.

'What you mean?' she said quietly.

He felt himself sweating. The truth was he knew exactly what he meant but he had only ever kept it in the deepest recesses of his mind, tightly locked up under twenty-four hour control. And now it had suddenly sprung free. He had not even sensed its coming, nor felt the preparation of its leap into the here and now. She was the one that he wanted a normal happy relationship with! Wasn't that why he had tried to behave properly towards her? Wasn't that why he actually sodding well had? He knew it wasn't simply because she was married whereas Samantha and Lisa were not. It went deeper than that. But he wasn't ready to disclose his feelings and was there really any point? She wanted to save her marriage and that was that.

'I don't know, I just sort of blurted, I guess you touched a raw nerve or something. I'm sorry.'

She knew he was covering something up but hadn't the heart to press home for it. If Dillon was going to run off with Outi, or vice versa, (did it really matter?), they would cross that bridge when they came to it. She was aware that she wanted Melvin to cross it with her but was not prepared to say so. He had enough on his plate without her.

'I think we should go home now,' she said, in as level a tone as possible, 'we both got jobs tomorrow.'
He nodded agreement and they left the brightly lit room to emerge into the evening rain.

Melvin opened the passenger's door of his big Mercedes Benz like a dutiful chauffeur and they drove home in silence. It was not an uncomfortable silence. It was how they chose to communicate.

'Thanks for picking me up,' she said at her doorway, as the rain splattered heavily on a big black umbrella that he had surprised them both with, 'you drive carefully now.'

'Sure, I'll be fine.'

'And thanks for coming tonight.'
He smiled and nodded. And then they kissed each other lightly on the cheek, and then paused . . . and then parted.

When her front door was shut, he closed the umbrella and enjoyed the sensation of rain as he walked back to the car.

18

The news of Nigel Denmark's suspension from duties pending further investigation spread like wild fire. Clive Pettifer took over as Acting Director of Personnel and parked his car in the Director's bay the following day. The Chairman, being mindful of the damage to the reputation of Personnel, decided to put Harold Hogger in overall charge of the Change Management Project. The next biggest news however, was that Harold would report directly to Gerald MacNab and not Clive Pettifer. As a consequence, Gerald's sphere of influence increased ten fold and Clive's remained exactly where it had always been, except that now it was publicly acknowledged as such.

The effect on the organisation was dynamic. Which is to say, negatively dynamic. Most senior managers thought Nigel Denmark was a lazy incompetent turd and were delighted that some kind of major come-uppance appeared to be in the offing. Details of his misdemeanour were the subject of wild speculation, particularly as many folks remembered his previous fanny flaffing incident with a cleaning contractor's supervisor and subsequent promotion to national headquarters.

However, a repeat of the 'Feather Duster Affair' as it was popularly referred to, was soon kicked into touch when no lesser personage than the Chief Auditor himself appeared at the portals of the I.T. department's high security central data bank suite, with Rupert Selwyn-Smythe lapping at his heels, to remove a large number of computer tapes. Rupert was so beside himself that he bashed his little document trolley going through the sliding doors and spilt the tape boxes all over the floor. Immediately, half a dozen data processing technicians materialised as if by magic (normally you'd be lucky to get a SNOG reply in three weeks) to helpfully gather up the tapes as if they were the crown jewels.

But it was the implication of the steely hand of Finance that sent the strongest tremors through the organisation. In contrast to Nigel Denmark, Gerald MacNab's reputation was one of ruthless stealth. The take-over by Gerald of the change management project was a clear signal to those who were in touch with reality that they should continue to fear for their jobs. The last round of manpower budgets had been notable for its bloody squabbles and few Directors could forget that most of their desperate arguments to maintain at least some of their numbers had been crushed by Gerald with a viciousness that denied the very existence of reason or mercy.

His deep hatred of Nigel Denmark was well known, and now that he had him ensnared, his fangs were raised for all to see and woe betide anyone who dared to cross him. Already, people were speculating about what position he would be given in the re-organisation, some even saying that he would oust the Chairman. Allegiances were springing up and disintegrating daily as one rumour contradicted another. From the very top to the very bottom, nobody was prepared to make a decision without looking over their shoulder several times, and in most cases, the majority chose not to make one at all. To Gerald's delight, a culture of fear was firmly embedded and this was exactly what he wanted. People who were usually competent would be making mistakes all over the place and he could pick them off one by one. To add lustre to the machinations of his mind, Rupert had somehow managed to sniff out the details of

Melvin's disciplinary and, as a consequence, Gerald had now got his game plan neatly in place.

'Well Clive, there it is,' said Gerald affecting a tone of world-weariness, 'it's a shocking business and one can only hope it won't affect the share price.'

'I'm sure we can pull things together,' said Clive, who was in a state of shock. Gerald had just promised him a directorship in the new company. The Director of Personnel no less! That had always been his goal, his dream. He could hardly believe it but Gerald had not minced his words and they remained like a golden cassette tape in his brain.

'Off the record Clive,' he had said, 'I admit that I had difficulties in working with Nigel and this was generally known, but I always tried to maintain a professional relationship for the good of the company. It was evident too, not just to me, but to the whole Board, including the Chairman I hasten to add, that the formulation of the company's HR policy and its attendant strategic direction was really being shaped by you. So the Chairman and I think the time has now come for you to take the credit for that fine work and help us to give the company the progressive and dynamic culture it so badly needs.'

As Gerald's peroration reached its climax, Clive was practically wetting himself in self-congratulatory smugness. In his excitement, what he had failed to see was the malevolent glint in Gerald's eye. The look of a hawk that has just spotted its supper. The promise did not come without strings attached and the question of not being a favourable witness in Nigel's disciplinary and taking no further action against Melvin Powell had yet to sit comfortably with him.

On the other hand, what had Nigel ever done for him, except delegate his entire workload and get the wrong end of the stick at Board meetings? It took a situation like this for the truth to dawn on him that Nigel had never given him any recognition or praise, in fact, now that Gerald had mentioned it, Nigel had actually suppressed his career by selfishly taking all the credit for his hard work. And now all this brouhaha with the accounts.

The stature and credibility of the entire Personnel directorate had been put in jeopardy, and if he was not careful, his own reputation would be at stake, and that was simply intolerable. To be perfectly frank, he was viewing Nigel in an entirely new light. And Gerald too. Gerald was not allowing personal enmity to cloud his judgement, he was putting forward his argument in a rational manner. The sign of a true professional. And if there was one thing that Clive thrived on, it was professionalism. A company could only be successful if the status quo was maintained for reasons of professionalism. One had to guard against the hoi polloi being given a voice in matters that were clearly above their station. Gerald was behaving correctly and being very honest. In fact those were his very words.

'To be perfectly honest Clive,' said Gerald, 'I admit that my field of expertise rarely strays beyond the world of finance and it may very well be that Nigel has some personal problem that could in some way mitigate against his actions but I don't think the Chairman would look too kindly on a situation that has yet to impact on the stock market.'

'No of course not,' said Clive. He felt that the stock market was not the domain of an HR professional such as him but naturally he must consider his position vis-à-vis the Chairman's.

'And once this wretched business breaks,' continued Gerald, 'well, I need hardly say that the shareholders will not take such a sympathetic view of such fraudulent behaviour.'

Clive's brain was swimming. The Chairman, the stock market, his directorship, the possibility of introducing his strategic rationalisation programme and all the seminar engagements arising therefrom.

'So what I'm saying Clive is that you need to consider the position of the company and your contribution to its business performance in the global market place.'

'Gerald, I have no problem whatsoever in identifying my priorities.'

'I'm so glad we see eye to eye,' said Gerald smiling thinly, which Clive interpreted as acknowledgement of their growing intellectual compatibility, 'however, there is the problem of Melvin Powell isn't there?'

Clive could not for the life of him see why they shouldn't convene an immediate disciplinary and dismiss Melvin for gross misconduct on the spot, especially as the general manager of the Flint Shingles Country Club Hotel had now written a formal letter of complaint.

'The Chairman is naturally concerned that we support the painful process of re-organisation with a positive, supportive culture and that means giving more than just lip service to our programme of Total Quality.'

Clive wasn't aware of any such programme but perhaps that was something else that Nigel had failed to be forthcoming about.

'I couldn't agree more,' he said.

'So, making an example of the very person to whom we have just entrusted such a programme could lead to some confusing signals.'

Clive was completely confused. How many programmes were there and what signals was Gerald alluding to?

'Yes I understand entirely,' he said.

'In fact it could have the opposite effect to the one we wish to achieve . . .'

Clive gaped like a goldfish.

'. . .namely, to engender a culture of trust and to establish a system of shared values and beliefs.'

Clive had absolutely no idea what Gerald was talking about but he understood the word system and clearly Gerald had the ear of the Chairman.

'So I suggest you have a word with Harold Hogger and then we can all get on with the job can't we?'

'Absolutely Gerald.'

Gerald gave another one of his thin smiles which Clive was convinced came from the cradle of mutual respect and understanding.

'I think that just about wraps things up don't you?' said Gerald.

'Indeed I do,' said Clive.

'Notwithstanding what I've said about maintaining a positive culture, I'm sure you appreciate that Harold must continue to report directly to me in order that management do not lose site of the business focus that is the bottom line of all our activities.'

'Oh absolutely, that's so necessary.'

'Nevertheless Clive, I need hardly say that I shall always welcome your advice and no doubt, if all goes well, I shall be returning control of the project to you.'

As Clive got up to go, he realised he had pooped in his pants.

19

A can of Newcastle Brown narrowly missed Lisa's ear and landed on the toaster.

'So did he bloody screw you or didn't he?' yelled Troy.

'For God's sake, he's never even touched me!'

'That's not what that woman said.'

'What woman?'

'The one on the bloody telephone, I've told you already, now don't piss me about.'

'Jesus Christ Troy, just where are you coming from?'

Lisa was desperately trying to buy time, even a few seconds would do. Troy was in a Neanderthal rage and she could hardly believe his accusation. It was of course true, but who on earth would have had any reason to go near the social club during working hours and more to the point, what kind of bitch would go to the trouble of shopping her and why? Jesus, some people were real shits.

'I don't know what's going on, somebody's just stirring the shit.'

'Yeah, well it's some bloody shit aint it?'

'For God's sake Troy, calm down, there's got to be an explanation somehow or other.'

'That's what I'm bloody waiting for innnit?'

Lisa knew that she had little chance of reasoning with Troy when he was in a rage. Somehow she had to bring him off the boil. There was no point bursting into tears, that would only make him smash the kitchen furniture up and she had spent enough time queuing up to get out of Ikea as it was. Perhaps a stab at being devastated might do the trick.

'Have you thought what this wild accusation is doing to me, what it's doing to us?'

'What I wanna know is why this woman should go to the bother of ringing me in the first place, there's no smoke without fire, that's what I'm thinking about.'

Obviously that was the wrong tack and the skin of the cat was nowhere in sight. Perhaps a red herring would do?

'There are some very sick people about, take Melvin's wife for example, she's in hospital for alcohol abuse.'

'The woman what rung me was stone cold sober.'

'I'm not saying whoever it was that rung you was drunk, but I am saying that there's a lot people around who've got all sorts of problems and they just do things like that because they can't handle it, they get jealous and resentful for no particular reason.'

Troy cracked open another can of Newcastle Brown and glowered angrily at her. She reckoned he was about half a degree down from half a minute ago and that meant progress, so she pressed on.

'It could've been anyone from the Luton office, there's quite few there who resent my getting on and they're more likely to know our telephone number.'

'Luton ain't Barnet and this woman said your boss was banging you in the Barnet social club on top of a load of cardboard boxes like there was no bloody tomorrow.'

He was getting angry again.

'Troy, offices are the same as building sites, people are just as nasty to each other, they just go about it differently, but they still stir the shit because of their own inadequacies,' (Troy wasn't quite sure what she meant but he understood the bit about people being shits) 'and on cardboard boxes for God's sake, you know me better than that, I've got standards when it comes to what I lie on. Why d'you think I change the sheets every week?'

She had a point he had to admit. It drove him mad the way she fussed about the cleanliness of everything, always puffing up the pillows and turning down the bed sheet. He couldn't imagine her getting horny on a load of cardboard boxes. All the same there was something fishy about it. He saw the way other blokes looked at her. She was beautiful and sexy. A real catch. *His* bloody catch. If Melvin Powell's old lady was in hospital then of course he'd be looking around for a bit on the side, it went without saying didn't it? And when was she in hospital then? No doubt when him and Lisa were at that hotel in Norfolk. He wasn't bloody stupid.

'Yeah, well if there is summink going on, your bloody boss is gonna find his back teeth rearranged.'

Inwardly, Lisa sighed with relief. Troy had moved away from accusation to macho threats, which at least she could deal with.

'Troy, listen to me,' she said, adopting a softer tone and drawing up a chair to sit opposite him. As she drew closer she felt his towering anger. He was like a wounded beast. One false move and he would lash out. God help Melvin if he really did find out.

'What I'm trying to say is that there's just you and me but there's some sicko out there who's got a grudge about something.'

Troy swigged on his beer. He wanted to believe her and maybe he did. She had never mucked around before. Not that there wasn't a first time for everything. He swigged a good third of the can in one big guzzle. Lisa sensed she might just make it to shore.

'There's a lot at stake in this job and it's not all for me.'

'Wodja mean?' said Troy.

'Well, if I can make a success of things then it could lead to better opportunities even if it means leaving British Energy Services which is more than probable.'

'Wodja mean?' said Troy again, still truculent and uncomprehending. Lisa began to wonder how long it would be before Troy's horizon of understanding would raise itself above the level of a building site

'Everything's changing, there's going to be hundreds of job losses, nothing's guaranteed including my future, so if I can deliver the goods then it's going to look good on my CV and maybe I'll get a better job elsewhere, more money.'

'So what's that go to do wiv us?'
Christ it was hard work but there was no stopping now.

'Troy, I don't blame you for being angry, I'd be the same if I'd taken a call like that, but the thing is you were angry before then, and it's all to do with your frustration at work.'
Troy remained as sullen as an ape who had just been told that Darwin got it wrong and therefore his species no longer featured in the grander scheme of things.

'Maybe, if I could get promotion, or another job with more money, you could take a day release course and study surveying or something like that, you've always said you wanted to.'

Even as the words departed her lips, she could not fail to register the sheer outrageousness of her suggestion, nevertheless, the look on Troy's face said she had scored a bull's-eye.

Yeah, Lisa had a point. He'd been shovelling shit for nearly two years now and the only sign of advancement was half a day a week on the JCB. He could do better. What he really wanted was to have a job where you got issued with the best donkey jackets and spent the day walking around with those little telescope on tripod things and stuck your arm out like a traffic cop so that some other geezer had to shovel the shit higher or take it away. Marking out or surveying, either would do.

He cracked open another Newcastle Brown. Eventually, when the clouds of infidelity had finally departed, they settled down on the settee to watch telly. When the late night film titles began to role Troy said:

'Coming up then?'
'And why not?' said Lisa lovingly.

When they were both in bed, Troy pulled Lisa towards him with all the finesse of a JCB on its last scoop of the day. But she was already prepared for this and obligingly opened her legs to facilitate his mechanical pulverisation of her pelvic region.

'Oh Troy!' she gasped, as she sensed he was near to some kind of hydraulic burstation, 'it's only like this with you, only you!'

To hell with the neighbours, she knew that if Troy got his end away good and proper then as far as he was concerned, *everything* was back to normal and right now that was the perception she wanted him to have. So, go, go, go, Geronimo! Sod the bruising, this was survival.

Harold Hogger had been in the company long enough to know when he was on the horns of a dilemma, and this was a particularly nasty one. For purposes of the change management project, he was now reporting directly to a vicious megalomaniac and yet, at the same time, as the Regional Training and Development Manager, he would report to a pompous twit in an acting capacity. Up to a point, he could now empathise with Melvin.

'There's a kind of irony in the symmetry, don't you agree?' said Harold, after he had updated Melvin on recent events, which included telling him, (in case he hadn't been paying attention) that he had just given him a severe bollocking following orders from the Acting Director of Personnel.

Melvin could see that beneath Harold's display of humour there was an underlying tension. Harold was a much respected figure in the organisation who over the years had conducted himself in such a manner that he was considered by everyone to be a model of independent and fair minded thinking. He was above sleaze and departmental politics, and to split his responsibilities in such a crude manner, was a calculated insult. Notwithstanding the jolt that Nigel's abrupt suspension had given the organisation, and the fact that Clive had no street credibility whatsoever, the thought on everybody's lips was 'if they can treat Harold like this, what the hell are they going to do to the rest of us?'

'Perhaps I should relish the opportunity to refresh my project management skills?' he quipped stoically.

But the damage was done. Melvin also realised that Harold was no longer in a position to influence matters in quite the same way as before and he had little doubt that the dropping of his disciplinary was merely a twisted strand in the Machiavellian plot that Gerald MacNab was now hatching.

The two men walked across the quadrangle of the training college. The sun was low in the sky and a hazy chill was enveloping the countryside. The groundsmen had long since cleared away the last fallen leaves of autumn and everywhere the landscape was a picture of bleakness, of closing down. Somehow it seemed to reflect the culture of the organisation. No one had any hope. Everyone thought in grey negative terms as they scuttled anxiously and furtively about their business.

'Well, do take it easy dear chap,' said Harold, 'nothing is worth getting that steamed up about, especially where work is concerned.'

'Take care yourself too Harold,' replied Melvin, 'and thanks for a great bollocking, next time I shall make sure there aren't any witnesses,' they laughed, 'and if you can prevent the Fat Friar from being re-engaged, I shall be eternally grateful.'

'It may not be my gift to grant,' said Harold, 'but I shall certainly try.'

The two men parted and as Melvin drove through the gates of the college a cloud of depression descended upon him.

Before very long it would be Christmas and if he didn't get his act together there would be a P45 in his stocking.

20

Lunch came and went like a fart in the bath. Mildly enjoyable yet strangely odious. Trying to hold down two jobs was proving to be an impossibility. Ever since Nigel Denmark's suspension, Rupert had become sickeningly smug. Everyone knew he had played a part in Nigel's downfall and were treating him with a mixture of fear and loathing. Rupert considered that he was now destined for greater things and, as a consequence, had endowed himself with executive powers that didn't exist. The problem was that in his snidy, snivelling way, he was playing the Gerald MacNab ticket for all it was worth.

People like Claudia immediately latched on to this new conduit of power and was delighted that he had taken her up on her helpful suggestion that he should present the findings of his payroll investigation direct to Mr Brannigan. Jack Matthews had exploded and Melvin had been summoned to Brannigan's office to defend his payroll staff without even having had sight of the final paper, a fact that the bull brained Brannigan chose to ignore having been well and truly wound up by Claudia's insidious remarks beforehand; 'Rupert told me that Melvin's payroll clerks were worried about any possible backlash on them and the stress was beginning to affect their work and since Melvin had so much on his hands with the change project I thought it best that you were appraised of the situation sooner rather than later'.

Melvin knew that Claudia had been instrumental in accelerating the chain of events but, as he left Brannigan's office in a mixture of frustration and fury, there was something particularly poisonous in her gloating smirk that made him think that worse was afoot. That was confirmed when Lisa told him about the phone call to Troy.

'The fucking fat bitch, it was her, I know it was, nobody else would have the slightest reason to be there except a gluttonous cow like her,' he spat contemptuously, 'and nobody except a fucking, twisted, puke-filled, barrage balloon like her would pull such a sick stunt like that.'

'Troy went absolutely ballistic,' said Lisa, 'I was so afraid.'

'Does he believe it?' Melvin queried.

'I don't think so, but there again, I can't be absolutely sure. He's gone all morose and sulky and he's watching my every move even though he pretends not to.'

'That's all I bloody need,' said Melvin, 'a jealous boyfriend practising grave digging as part of his JCB training.'

'There's no need to be sarcastic about him, anyway, it's not exactly a bed of roses for me either, or hadn't you considered that?'

Melvin felt like sweeping the contents of his desktop on to the floor. Was there no way that he could have a relationship without it being consumed by argument? All he craved for was a simple, trouble free life, one that was capable of appreciating and absorbing pleasure in whatever form it chose to manifest itself but without the debilitating side effects that seemed to typify the one he had got at the moment.

Why on earth did Lisa have to cohabitate with a moron like Troy? You would have thought that someone with the beauty and brains that she had would have chosen someone better. But no, it was not to be. And now there was yet another complication to add to his burgeoning load, in fact, you could say there were three. Claudia, Troy and Lisa.

Claudia was an on-going pain in the arse who had merely chosen to up the stakes, but with their mutual hatred running at such a high level, he knew there would be more to come. As for Troy, well, he always was a potential threat but nothing that a competent piece of shag management couldn't contain. The trouble was, recent developments had made things less straightforward. There was now an unknown factor in the equation, i.e. what would Troy do next?

As for Lisa, it was awful to admit it, but if she would just troll off back to Troy things would be a whole lot better. Unfortunately, she did not view their relationship in quite the same terms. In fact that was the problem with Lisa. She wanted a relationship whereas he did not.

'How was I to know that?' he mumbled to himself as plunged his spoon into the custardy goo of his rhubarb crumble. He was sitting alone in the corner of the staff restaurant where he had escaped to contemplate the tremors of the day. It was understandable that Lisa would be a bit wobbly after an expose like that and, on reflection, she must have done some pretty nifty footwork to convince Troy that it was merely the work of an embittered bitch. What he wasn't too happy about was the promise he had made to accompany her to the Luton office to open the first session of the project - a reminder of the principles of Total Quality.

The fact that Gerald MacNab had taken control of the project had yet to convince most General Managers (Brannigan included) that they should nominate a line manager, or at least somebody with credibility and standing, to perform the role of the local 'Agent of Change'; a title coined by Harold to signify commitment to the process without implying extra responsibilities which would of course immediately nullify the chances of anyone volunteering. Unfortunately, just as Jack Matthews had predicted, General Managers saw absolutely no correlation in Total Quality, or any other mechanism of change, to the real task of running the business and, as a consequence, had nominated their most incompetent or bolshie supervisor as the Agent of Change.

This was no surprise to Melvin but what he couldn't fathom was why Lisa was so reticent about giving the presentation herself. She had done bigger and more complex things than simply address a dozen or so people who would be more than happy to get away from the remorseless demand of the telephones and the bloody customers. Perhaps he hadn't managed to convince her that it was Claudia who was stirring the shit and maybe she really did believe that it was one of her old adversaries who might now be sitting in the front row gloating over her discomfort? The last thing he needed was for Lisa to lose her confidence, so he had agreed to front the session. The niggling worry in the back of his mind, which became ever more real as he peered into the swirling splodge of his rhubarb crumble, was that Luton was Troy's territory and, well, say no more, say no more.

'Have you been sick or have I missed something delicious?'
It was Zelda. Zelda ready as ever with a crazy quip. If only all his relationships could be as good as the one he had with Zelda. Admittedly, it was a strictly platonic working relationship but somehow they always seemed to get on. Even when her constant cheeriness pissed him off it was only for a moment because she had the knack of reading his mood and adjusting instantly, either by pulling him out of it or by focusing on work.

'Well, it smells like urine and has the consistency of quick drying cement, so I think I'll give it a miss,' he replied.

'Looks like a good decision to me, now, shall I get you a coffee and then we can run through your messages before you disappear again?'

'Okay, I'll run with that, thanks.'

Zelda plonked a batch of papers on the table and went across to the serving area; at least you could get a decent cup of filter fresh coffee at lunchtime. He dumped his dish on the tray and pushed it to one side. It was probably best that he didn't eat anything that was likely to make him fart later on. Unless Lisa arrived at Luton before him they would doubtless have to set the room up themselves and a bout of flatulence as one struggled to erect a projector screen was not an ingredient for success.

'What time are you leaving for Luton?' asked Zelda on her return.

'As soon after two as possible, I guess.'

'Is everything okay, Lisa was like a cat on a hot tin roof this morning?'

He knew her concern was genuine but it made him think that perhaps Lisa was more unnerved about things than he had realised.

'She's a bit uptight about having to face the home team and there's quite a few stirrers up there who'll be trying to drop her in it, the usual project implementation stuff, so I thought she deserved a bit of support.'

It occurred to him that he might have over justified his trip unnecessarily but Zelda made no further comment and they proceeded to deal with the business to hand.

'Oh yes, and there were two personal calls,' said Zelda towards the end, 'somebody called Samantha rang, she said you knew her number and please would you ring her as soon as possible, she wouldn't say more than that, and then there was a call from somebody called Shaida, I think I got the name right, she sounded oriental and it was a bit difficult to understand her but she gave her office number, Trans Globe Oil I think she said.'

'Oh, what did she want?'

'She just asked if you could give her ring sometime.'

Melvin was agitated; it was unlike Samantha or Shaida to ring him at work unless something unforeseen had happened. Things were piling up. He could without it.

'How's Outi these days?' said Zelda as they gathered themselves together, 'was she pleased with her life story all lovingly printed and bound?'

It was a perfectly reasonable question but it made his heart miss a beat. Why should she ask that just now? Did she suspect something? As far as he was aware he hadn't mentioned Samantha or Shaida before. Women had this sixth sense though and Zelda in particular. It was becoming increasingly difficult trying to remember to whom he had said about what. Talk about trying to keep a lid on things.

'She's struggling a bit at the moment,' he replied, not failing to miss the irony in a remark that applied more so to himself, 'she was grateful for the typing though and sorry I haven't mentioned that before now.'

'That's okay, you've got a lot on your plate.'

He was grateful that she chose to leave it there.

He was half way up the A1 before using his mobile to put in a call to Shaida. He had been contemplating whom to ring first and had decided that Shaida would probably be the easier to handle, besides which, he had not seen her for a while and was missing her. In the event he got routed to her 'personal voice mail' or whatever damn silly name some companies used nowadays. So he left a simple message.

The prospect of ringing Samantha was not quite so pleasurable. It was a strange thought to have about the woman he had confessed to being in love with but the truth of the matter was he felt uneasy about the way she had been behaving of late, and that was something of an understatement. Bloodshed, she said. Russell's blood. Had he heard her correctly or was he just going mad? As he turned off the main road and began to pick up the congested traffic moving towards Luton he decided to pull into a lay-by to make the call. He sensed it would take all his concentration.

'You better come to the club tonight with one hundred pounds cash,' said Samantha.

'Why, what's the matter, I thought I'd got until the end of the month?'

'Maybe you have, but he's in a funny mood and I just think it would help matters.'

Melvin was on the point of asking precisely what matters she was referring to and then decided he'd rather not know. The line began to break up and he couldn't tell whether it was the interference or whether there really was something peculiar in the tone of her voice. For one awful second the notion that he might be getting into some kind of trap flashed across his mind. It was too ridiculous for words. But then again, if their last conversation was anything to go by, it was not. Everything that had occurred since the start of their affair had gradually dragged him into a murky world that had become more and more frightening at every step.

It was unreal and yet it was there and he was in it.

'Are you okay?' he said.

'. . . Yes, but I think you should talk to Russell.'

'What now?'

'No, tonight, at the club,' there was more static on the line, 'Melvin?'

'I'm still here.'

'Yesterday he wanted to know when we last made love.'

'Christ, that sounds a bit heavy.'

The line faded and crackled, it sounded as if they were going to lose the connection altogether. He yelled her name several times but there was not response. Then he heard her calling him.

'Melvin -'

'Yeah, I'm still here.'

'Just do as I say, get the cash and see him tonight.'

The line went dead before he could reply. He would have said 'yes okay' anyway.

The afternoon session was not a success. He was on edge, Lisa was on edge and everybody else was on edge. It was obvious that nobody cared a toss about the customer supplier relationship, including himself, and so at five o'clock on the dot he said -

'Right, well take it or leave it, it's up to you.'

They all left it. In a way it was a blessed relief. The sheer hypocrisy of his mission was beginning to gag. For all the notice anyone took he might just as well have written 'quality sucks, try dog meat instead' And the last thing he wanted was a string of daft questions.

'We need to talk,' said Lisa.

'It was not my finest hour, was it?'

'I don't mean about that, I mean about us.'

'Look, I can't stay long, I have to get into town.'

Her eyes flashed with hurt and anger.

'Don't do this to me Melvin, we need some time and space together.'

They ended up in a Tesco's car park.

It was dark by the time they arrived but there was little chance of real privacy as everywhere was flooded with light. After Melvin had joined a queue at the cash dispenser they found their way to a spot in the far corner and hoped for the best. Most folks seemed intent on their shopping.

Their conversation went back and forth and round in circles. Melvin made the fatal mistake of saying that he still wanted her and that in turn prompted Lisa to state in no uncertain terms that she wanted him. They agreed that things would be difficult and yes they would ride it out together. And then they locked tongues in a passionate embrace. Even in a big Mercedes Benz there's a limit to what two people can do with an automatic transmission tunnel between them and a brightly lit petrol station across the way. In the end they settled for a mix of saliva and a frustrated grope. By the time Lisa sauntered self-consciously back to her car it was pretty clear that a definite GO situation was now on again.

Melvin swung the Merc alongside the petrol pumps and checked his flies before getting out. His erection had only just subsided. What he failed to notice, as he completed the filling operation as nonchalantly as possible, was a purple Suzuki Vitara with a windscreen flash proclaiming the happy alliance of 'Troy and Lisa'. Nor did he see it fall in behind him as he headed down the motorway towards London.

However, by the time he reached Portland Place a certain uneasiness turned to fear when the Suzuki drew alongside him at the traffic lights and he spotted the flash on the windscreen and a bloke with shoulders like Arnold Schwarzenegger. As the lights turned to green, Troy tried to box him in on the inside lane but Melvin stabbed the accelerator to the floor and the Merc took off like a thoroughbred racehorse. Troy pursued him relentlessly and eventually gained ground as Melvin tried vainly to steer the big car round one corner after another. In blind panic, Melvin screeched into the one cul de sac that he knew might offer a means of escape.

He crunched to a halt, clambered out frantically and leapt across the congealed cake of sick that was the familiar welcoming sight on the pavement outside the Buster Keaton Club. But Troy was now foaming with rage and simply drove the Suzuki up the kerb and straight at him. Melvin dived for cover between two heavy metal commercial garbage bins as Troy's cow bars scythed their way into them. There was a horrendous crash and rumbling like a naval bombardment as the enormous bins keeled over and thundered to the ground. Melvin picked himself up and fled for the entrance only to collide with Russell and Brian on their way out.

'What the fuck!' exclaimed Russell as Melvin cannoned into him.

Troy was already half way across the pavement in hot pursuit.

'This bloody maniac tried to cut me up at the lights!' screamed Melvin, self-preservation fuelling his rhetoric.

'Fuck off mate,' yelled Troy as he moved in for the kill.

But Russell kicked him straight in the groin and Troy collapsed with a sickening thud.

'Oh nice one,' yelled Brian, as he too aimed a booted foot at Troy's ribs. Troy squirmed in agony

'Leave 'im, he's all mine,' shouted Russell.

Melvin, ashen faced and gasping in horror, watched as Russell slipped on a pair of diamond studded knuckle dusters and, grabbing Troy by the throat with one hand, proceeded to smash his face to pulp with the other. When Troy's cries had become a whimper, Russell held him up like a rag doll.

'No one messes wiv me mate Melv, okay?'

Troy gurgled something incomprehensible between a broken jaw and splintered teeth.

'Better let him go now,' said Brian, who was also rather taken aback at the ferocity of Russell's attack, 'I'll get a squad car to pick him up, we'll take him to hospital somewhere else, he won't know the difference.'

Russell released his grip and Troy slumped to the ground in a bloody heap. Melvin remained shaking in the shadows of the doorway.

'Glad you could make it, Melv,' said Russell, oblivious to the human suffering in front of him, 'Sam mentioned you was coming over.'

'Yes,' said Melvin feebly, 'and I've bought your cash.'

21

'You bastard!' shouted Lisa, 'you bloody cowardly bastard!' Instinctively, Melvin knew her reaction signalled the beginning of the end. The day after Troy's beating she did not appear for work, nor did he get a telephone call, instead he received a cryptic fax saying: *Due to a family accident I shall be unable to fulfil my duties for a week.*

Things had not gone too well during the intervening period. The cynicism and negativity that was running rampant throughout the organisation had taken an early toll on the more idealistic of the project team members and most of them were either depressed, turned off or angry. In an attempt to bolster their morale Melvin had chosen one of the oldest tricks in the book; a team briefing followed by a slap up meal with plenty of booze. Harold had declined to attend on the basis that his presence might undermine Melvin's authority, a decision that prompted Melvin to consider that perhaps he didn't have any in the first place and maybe he should use the occasion to create a bit of positive PR.

Much to his delight, Harold had found some money in the college repairs and maintenance budget and obligingly offered a financial code to fund a reasonably excessive beano. This was a relief on two fronts. Firstly, it saved Melvin the bother of looking himself (and he usually got it wrong when he did) and secondly, it blew away a suspicion that perhaps Harold might just be distancing himself from the project for reasons of self-preservation. It was a horrible thought to have about such a close ally and Melvin was glad when it subsided. As Claudia controlled all bookings for the social club it was extremely handy being able to quote a regional personnel code, thus avoiding the usual cross-examination. Zelda steered the dinner request form through the appropriate channels in an inappropriate sequence and even got Fred Brannigan to countersign it in a moment of rare good humour.

'Christ, how did you manage that?' asked Melvin.

'I just put the monthly energy conservation return over the top of it and caught him on the way into the loo.'

Other matters were not so frivolous. Melvin was too scared and ashamed to contact Lisa and left it to one of the team instead.

'She wouldn't really let a domestic issue get in the way of a piss up would she?'

'No, not really, give her bell then.'

And Lisa duly arrived. In spite of the drinks flowing freely it was pretty obvious to everyone except the totally rat-arsed that things were not exactly hunky dory between the two of them but such were the stresses and strains of project work that it would probably blow over eventually wouldn't it? Meanwhile, it made sense to get stuck into the freebies before the company went irrevocably down the pan.

When everyone had vent their bile and then snogged or groped whoever was willing and available, they staggered off into the night leaving the two of them alone together. And that's when Lisa turned on him.

'Oh, I see,' retorted Melvin, 'it was okay for him to crush me to death with his Suzuki but I'm not allowed to defend myself.'

'You call getting two other blokes to beat him up, self defence do you?'

'I didn't know what was going to happen.'

'You didn't try and stop it either.'

'Things just got out of hand, anyway, what was I supposed to do, ask him to calm down so we could discuss things rationally like two mature adults?'

They were going at it like hammer and tongs. Lisa was virtually yelling at the top of her voice.

'Those bloody animals practically killed him.'

'He tried to kill me first.'

'He's got sixty-eight stitches in his face and he's still on a drip feed.'

'I was severely traumatised but don't let that worry you.'

'You bloody bastard,' she screamed, 'you haven't got enough feelings to be traumatised.'

Thus saying, she threw a half empty bottle of Cabernet Sauvignon at his head. It was wildly off the mark and crashed against the opposite wall in a splintering ruby cascade just as the night security guard came through the door.

'Excuse me Mr Powell, but will you be staying put for a while only I've got to lock the main gate whilst I do my site inspection?'

'No, I'm going home now, thank you,' said Melvin, and walked out leaving the guard to do whatever he though best with Lisa. No point overstaying one's welcome.

Back home, which was fast becoming a bit of a tip, he was confronted by Missoo, sitting in the middle of the lounge with the remains of a bird in front of her. Ugly black feathers were scattered all over the place, some of them even hanging in tufts from the curtains. She must have been in a right rage. As a statement of needs it was extremely effective, he had after all been neglecting her, but he did not need to be reminded in such a dramatic fashion. She stared at him angrily.

'This is all very Chekhovian,' he said sternly, 'but somebody has to clear this lot up.' At which point she zig-zagged towards him, miaowing plaintively, until he stroked her chin and fondled her ears and said: 'Okay, point taken, let's go and see what's in the fridge.'

And then she stuck her claws in his thigh before trotting off to the kitchen. It was obvious where the power lay (her small claws were needle sharp) but he was concerned that it should be exercised by the application of pain. These were issues that he was trying to escape from and yet, here in his own living room, they had surfaced to threaten him yet again. His encounter at the Buster Keaton club was an incident he was trying to forget but he was fearful that it was merely an episode in some broader panoply of events over which he had little or no control. He could not even step out of it. It was Wagnerian in its foreboding, but the trumpets were sour and the trombones rasping.

After Brian had scraped Troy off the ground and bundled him unceremoniously into the back of a police car that seemed to materialise out of nowhere, Russell had turned his attentions to Melvin.

'Bloody 'ell, Melv, I thought yer exits were bad enough but now I'm finking it's yer bleedin' entrances that take the biscuit,' he removed his knuckle dusters and replaced them lovingly in his jacket pocket, 'Christ Almighty, let's go inside, I fink we could both do with a large Remy, don't you?'

Melvin was still visibly shaking when Samantha handed him a huge bulbous glass with a deep golden liquid whose cloying bouquet nearly caused him to pass out. She had the strangest of looks on her face and as he poured the fire water down his throat he was aware that her presence was beginning to cause him as much apprehension as Russell's. Things were not how they used to be.

All evening she seemed to be hovering like a bird of prey high up in the sky, seemingly to be unattached to the figures below but every so often making a sharp turn as if spotting a change of events that might allow her that vital second's advantage before striking. But striking for what? Surely there had been enough bloodshed for one evening? When he could separate his thoughts no further he offered Russell the one hundred pounds cash in the hope that it might draw events to a conclusion.

'Oh yes, nah that is a nice thoughtful gesture, innit Sam?' Samantha moved into the table where they were both sitting.

'I said you could trust Melvin,' she replied.

Russell took hold of her arm and she winced as he pulled her roughly into the chair beside him.

'Look at them nice clean notes Sam, go on, count 'em out then, we wouldn't want to embarrass Melv wiv' no misunderstandings nah would we?'

Samantha slowly fingered her way through the notes and then placed them in dishevelled pile in front of him. It was only then that Melvin spotted the pin pricks in her arm and realised she was drugged to the eyeballs. No doubt against her wishes.

'One 'undred smackeroos Melv, and up front and early an' all, now isn't that lovely, we do seem to be getting on like a house on fire, don't we?'

Melvin remained glued to his seat as Russell put his hand round the back of Samantha's neck and slowly forced her into a long embrace. And then, without releasing his grip, he suddenly grabbed Melvin in a similar lock and pulled him towards him until their faces were practically touching.

'Like I said Melv, we've come to a little arrangement, just you, me and Sam.'

Russell forced Melvin's mouth on top of his own and as his tongue began to circle and thrust inside him, Melvin heard Samantha cry out 'Russell, please let go, you're hurting me', where upon, Russell loosened his grip on both of them and pushed their heads backs violently.

'Fire burn and cauldron bubble,' he laughed mockingly, 'what a fucking couple.'

Only the re-emergence of Brian, and Russell's momentarily placed attentions elsewhere, gave Melvin the opportunity to glance at Samantha. She was crying. As the tears rolled down her cheek he saw that her drug filled eyes were full of hate and loathing.

'Do join us, Brian,' said Russell, clearly enjoying the fact that he was calling the shots all round, 'and meet my two lovers.'

'I've met them already,' replied Brian sulkily, and propped himself on a bar stool. Russell stood up and pulled Samantha to her feet.

'Give Brian a drink, Petal, or 'aven't you 'eard of customer care?'

She shot him a crazy defiant look before going behind the bar.

'I s'pose you'll be wanting to push off, eh Melv?' said Russell.

'Well, I have got quite a heavy day tomorrow.'

'Yeah, of course you 'ave,' Russell looked at him with a devilish grin and offered his hand in a formal handshake, 'well, thanks very much for the dosh, much appreciated.'

Melvin thought it best to accept his hand but as he did so, Russell grabbed his wrist and pulled his hand towards him until it was pressed flat against his genitals.

'You don't 'ave to wait until the next payment before seeing me, know what I mean?'

Melvin knew exactly what he meant and remained transfixed to the spot. His hand was now receiving the warmth of Russell's balls so he willed it to remain motionless lest the slightest finger twitch should signal sexual acquiescence. Russell's little teeth sparkled malevolently as he let go his grip and watched Melvin make a bolt for the door.

'Well, fancy that Sam, he never even wished you goodnight.'

But Samantha was not concerned about the absence of a farewell parting; even in her drugged haze she knew that somehow or other she had to rid herself of Russell. But she could not do it alone, Melvin would have to be part of it. There was no alternative.

By the time he got home, Melvin was still in a state of shock and he had only just poured himself a strong black coffee when the telephone rang. It was Shaida.

'Hi, I won't ask you where you been.'

He was relieved that it was not in her nature to cross-examine him anyway.

'I've not been enjoying myself, if that's what you mean - did you get my message?'

'Yuh, I had to leave work and go to the hospital.'

'Oh, has something happened to Dillon?'

'Yuh, him and Outi have gone on a bender and now the hospital say they must leave 'cos they don't accept patients who are drunk.'

Melvin felt his heart sink. Of all the bad news that he could possibly hear, none was as bad as the news that Outi had hit the bottle again. Whatever else might happen he did not want her to lose the battle against that.

'Where are they now?' he asked.

'In some hotel, I don't know where, they just sling their bags in a taxi and tell me to get lost.'

'Where are you now?'

'At home . . . what we do now?'

'I don't really know, sit tight I guess and wait and see what happens in the morning.'

There was an uneasy silence during which the inadequacy of his suggestion piled remorselessly on top of him. After a while he said:

'Will you be alright, tonight?'

'I don't know, I've just lost my husband to your wife.'

Twenty minutes later, Missoo watched him slip out into the dark again. Okay by her. He had just given her a double helping of duck and heart.

22

A state of limbo ensued during which he felt like a court marshalled flying pig grounded for attempting to take off backwards. Nothing was right. Nothing made sense. Everything was wrong. He had lost Outi. Shaida had lost Dillon. Lisa hated him and Samantha had transmogrified into some kind of junkie murderess. Russell was becoming more psychotic and threatening by the minute and any day now, Troy could very well recover from the blood and stitches of his beating to pursue him like Terminator Ten. In short, his life was in chaos.

He looked around to see what guidance and support was available and came to the conclusion that it was a bit thin on the ground. Every time he stuck his head out of the front door, Gladys would appear and natter incessantly about the weather and the price of bleach. Admittedly, she had taken Missoo on board but only on a token basis. When he had spent the week in Norfolk there had been no alternative other than to give her a spare front door key and he was beginning to regret that too. His erratic hours, which seemed to have fallen into a pattern of late nights and stop-overs, justified her holding onto it; he had, after all, a responsibility towards Missoo. They bonded at weekends. Gladys no longer enquired after Outi and he suspected that she had put two and two together and arrived at a disapproving ten. He didn't care a damn for her opinion.

Across the road, Ajit continued to beam magnificently every time he made a purchase. It was not in his interests to comment on the drop in alcoholic consumption since Outi's absence from the local scene, particularly as Melvin's regular weekend order of a bottle of Stolichnaya and a dozen Pils was not to be sneered at. However, you can't get much help from a jolly Sikh with one eye on the till, except perhaps to marvel at the sheer exuberance of his life. Ajit had it sussed.

'How do you do it?' Melvin had once asked.
Ajit's face broke into one of his enormous grins that seemed to reach right up into his turban.

'It's very simple really, every morning I give myself a big smile in the mirror and say how happy I am to be alive, you should try it.'

Ajit's big round face glowed like a Belisha beacon. As a life philosophy statement Melvin thought it was not without merit, indeed, he yearned to apply a similar approach to his own but somehow the reflection in the mirror always told him that happiness was somewhere else today. He observed the lives of others to see how they were coping. If their faces were anything to go by, things were pretty grim. Every so often though, it was possible to spot a happy soul but they were few and far between.

Zelda was always happy.

'How do you do it?' Melvin once asked her.

'Well, the world doesn't owe you a living, so you've just got to get on with it.'

'No, I didn't mean living in that sense, I meant in the general, universal cosmic sense.'

'Well it's the same thing isn't it? What you put in is what you get out.'

'But surely it's not that simple?'

'Look, the universe is big enough to look after itself, so I say love thy neighbour provided he's not throwing bricks at you and just get on with it.'

And basically that summed up Zelda's approach to life and she was very happy with it. In a way he envied her.

Shaida seemed to have some kind of life philosophy too but she had never really articulated it, it just seemed to be her way of doing things. The incident with Dillon and Outi had nevertheless shaken her badly and on the night when he had visited her after she had first broken the news, she had opened the door with tear-stained eyes.

His latest confrontation with Russell had freaked him out and he was too exhausted to do much more than sit quietly with her and talk things over. It was probably just as well. At her suggestion they opened a bottle of wine and considered their position. They had no way of knowing where Outi and Dillon had gone to. The taxi had disappeared round a corner and that was that. It was more of a blow to Shaida than it was to him. He had known for years that his marriage was fatally flawed and that it would only be a question of time before the inevitable separation occurred. Now that it had actually happened though, he did not feel like celebrating. Outi was a woman in a million but he could no longer cope with living with her. He did not want to see her exit from his life completely and yet he knew that everything with Outi could only exist on her terms. All or nothing.

'Is Dillon obsessive?' he asked, realising at that point that he knew next to nothing about the man who had run off with his wife.

'Most of the time he's angry.'

'That's rather ironic, Outi always accused *me* of being angry.'

'Are you saying they won't last?'

'Not if he's angry all the time.'

They filled their glasses and contemplated in silence a variety of scenes that might or might not end in anger. In continuing silence they hoped that it would not last but for different reasons. Shaida wanted Dillon back. It seemed he had been unfaithful but she was prepared to forgive and forget. There was no other man who had touched her heart in the way that he had and she could not accept that their years of happiness, (and there had been many years) counted for nothing.

As for Melvin, it was not quite so cut and dried. Outi was a diamond whose brilliance hurt his eyes and yet he longed to bathe in its radiance. Whilst he had been content to slop along amidst the phlegm and sawdust of life she had set her sights on the chandeliers. He was capable of admiring, and indeed enjoying the higher perspective, but the sheer effort required to heave oneself into the harness of achievement and beauty seemed an endless struggle whose very engagement sucked the life blood in such alarming proportions as to render the body corporate too deflated and depressed to rise the following day in any semblance of strength or inspiration.

Outi had never accepted or even considered defeat. Her vision of what could be achieved was unshakeable. Her confidence in her own ability to attain her goals was as solid as his were pliable. For Outi, decisions were the shortest distance between two points, whereas for Melvin, they were a circumlocutory journey whose en route scenes displayed a perspective on doubts and frustrations that nagged and worried at the fringes of right and wrong, of practicality and whimsicality, of beauty and ugliness, of substance and nothingness. Outi would follow through where he would deviate.

Given that this was so, perhaps that was the reason why there was no longer any harmony in their marriage? If extremes of approaches existed, why had they not found a way of co-existing? Had there really been no compensatory influence in their relationship? Did the absence of ebb and flow in their marriage signify a rigidity in their souls? Was one incapable of recognising the value of the other? Her desires were of this world whereas his lurked in some far off Elysian field. Whatever the answer, and Melvin certainly did not know it, they had chaffed and bulked against the fabric of their lives and now, as the umbilical cord of co-existence was all but severed, there did not appear to be any means of coming together again.

Henceforth, whatever transpired in Outi's life was her responsibility, not his. But then, she would argue that this had always been the case and if only Melvin would stop twittering on about the inessential peripheries of life and stick to the here and now, things would be a whole lot better. And thus it was.

Shaida was grappling with reality and Melvin was trying to plug a hole in the dyke. Together, they had to come to terms with things.

When the wine bottle was empty, Shaida rose and ran her hands across her delicate frame as if to cleanse herself of her anguish and problems. Melvin remained crumpled and confused. He felt an overwhelming urge to take her in his arms and hold her close, saying nothing but offering himself as a conduit for whatever emotion she felt the need to discharge. He wanted to be her protector and confidante. He wanted to be of value to her. He wanted her to recognise his need. Perhaps it would develop in time but for that moment she did not reciprocate beyond a proffered cheek upon which he glanced his lips. He dallied with the moment, savouring its exquisiteness and tenderness. And then, as she said goodnight, she squeezed his hand and inclined her body towards him, touching gently with her breasts and then disengaging to leave him with her lingering fragrances, the essence of her being, so close and yet so far away. He settled for the arms of Morpheus on the sofa. As his head hit the cushion he concluded that tomorrow was another day and he would consider his visage anew when it was upon him.

In the morning she appeared in saffron yellow Judo type silk pyjamas and gave him a smile and a big mug of coffee.
'Hi, bathroom's free.'
He took the mug shakily and propped himself up.
'What time is it?'
'Gone nine o'clock, I work flexi-time, how about you?'
'Yeah, the same, only the company doesn't know it.'
'British manager, huh?' she giggled.
In the bathroom he faced the mirror, took a deep breath, looked dead ahead and with honest and noble determination, forced a big wide grin. It split his lip. 'At least I tried' he muttered to himself as the blood began to spot. He dabbed at it gingerly with loo paper. He looked dreadful.

'You all washed up,' said Shaida, referring not to his ablutions but to his appearance.

'Yeah.'

They sat and munched their way contentedly through toast and marmalade and more mugs of coffee.

'So, what we do now?' she said.

'That's funny, I was just about to say the same thing.'

And indeed he had. In fact, before she had woken him with a mug of coffee, he had come too several hours earlier. Only momentarily, and in a state of dreamy clarity. The thought that struck him was that he needed to get away from it all. Get away as in right out of London, away from the flat, away from work, away from Lisa, Russell, and Samantha. But not from Shaida. As they had chatted through the night and into the early hours of the morning, he had become aware that, in spite of her anguish, Shaida had an inner strength that was not overbearing like Outi's but somehow made him feel that whatever the days ahead would bring, then if she was around, things would not spiral out of control as they usually did. He could not pin point his reasoning but he felt it was basically sound. He had then dropped off to sleep again. Now the thought had re-emerged and he felt he should put it to the test.

'I think we both need a break,' he said, and if he was not unmistaken, he thought he spotted the tiniest flicker of alarm in her eyes, 'I don't mean from each other,' he added, 'I mean from all of this.'

'We can't run away from things, Melvin, we gotta face up to them.'

He liked it when she addressed him by his name like that. He had come to learn that it signified her concern for him and in a funny way he found it rather endearing.

'I know, I'm not suggesting that we pretend that nothing has happened, but I do think we both need to relax a bit, have a change of air, a change of scene, something to give ourselves a chance to, I d'know, just put things into perspective. I mean, when you think about it, we've had nothing but visits to the hospital, Virginia's therapy sessions, work, next door neighbour looking after the cat, rushing about here and there, drinking too much.'

'Affairs,' she interjected, as he tried to avoid completing the list with the single most energy draining factor.

'Well, yes, those too, but, well, d'you see what I mean?'
She thought about it for a while and then shrugged her shoulders as if trying to experience what it would be like to throw off one's problems.

'No, we got no options, we gotta stay put and sort things out.'

'But how? What can we do when we don't know where they are, and what's more, when they don't *want* us to know where they are?'

'I know Dillon, he can't survive without me, no matter how long he was away on business, he always came back.'

'Only because you were there.'

'I was his wife, don't you understand that?' said Shaida, becoming suddenly emotional, 'and I still am. This is just a phase he's going through, deep down he's not really that independent, he'll contact me, I know it.'

Melvin remained silent. It was obvious he didn't understand the real meaning of marriage.

'I'm sorry, I didn't mean to sound insensitive, it's just that right now they're calling all the shots, all we can do is sit tight and hope for the best, I wasn't suggesting we run away from the situation.'

'Yuh, I know,' she said, more calmly now, 'I'm going into work, Dillon often faxes me there, how about you?'

Melvin considered the prospect of work. A vision of chaos, disunity and numerous impending battles did not seem an appealing alternative but he knew that if he didn't hang on in now he would never get to grips with the flailing entrails of his life.

'I'll have glass of water and ring in,' he replied.

'Okay, help yourself.'

She disappeared upstairs and when he had quenched his thirst he put in a call to Zelda to say he would be in after lunch and were there any problems and she had said 'not yet'. He always took her at her word.

By the time he was ready to go, Shaida had changed for work and he was surprised when he realised that this was the first time he had seen her in formal dress. She wore a deep red two-piece suit by Jacques Vert with a cream coloured blouse and a gold necklace with matching bracelets. She looked stunning.

'By the way,' he said, as they stood on the doorstep, 'what exactly *do* you do?'

'I charter oil tankers for Trans Globe Oil.'

'Blimey.'

They pecked each other lightly on the cheek.

'When you gonna ring me again?' she said.

'Tonight?'

She gave him a big smile.

They pecked each other lightly on the cheek but he didn't say anything about the spot of blood he left behind.

23

Days of wine and roses did not follow. In fact in many ways it was a very difficult week. He spoke with Shaida every day. Sometimes he would ring her and sometimes she would ring him. She wanted him to attend Virginia's therapy group but this time he said no. He had already come to the conclusion that he needed major internal repair work and did not need the group to remind him again, thank you very much. Nevertheless, he met Shaida afterwards and she said that everyone had been very sympathetic although the consensus view was to let Dillon and Outi get on with it and just look after herself.

'Did they say anything about me?' he said.

'They asked how you were.'

'What did you tell them?'

'I said you were suffering the same as me.'

It was a pretty good summing up. They had both agreed to check out whatever sources were likely to know where either party was and in his case it meant ringing Christina. He did not relish the task and made the mistake of fortifying himself with liberal measures of vodka before so doing. Not surprisingly, Outi had contacted her and she enjoyed not telling him of her whereabouts.

'Outi has taken me into her confidence and I cannot betray that trust.'

'Bollocks, where the bloody hell are they?'

'I can only say that they have booked into an hotel, they are both alright and I cannot say more than that at the present moment.'

'Oh, I get it, so now I have to contact you for a daily press release about my own wife and her lover.'

'Melvin, I did not say that she and Dillon were lovers, I merely said that they did not wish to be disturbed.'

'Actually you didn't bloody well say that but thanks for the slip.'

'Melvin, I understand that you and Shaida must feel hurt and angry -'

'You've only met Shaida once for Chrissake, so how the bloody hell can you presume to know how the fuck she is feeling -'

'Melvin, please do not use such bad language with me -'

'Bollocks - where the fuck are they?'

'How dare you speak to me like that?'

'I will speak to you how I bloody well like.'

'Excuse me, but you will not.'

'Fuck off you frigid bitch.'

They slammed their phones down simultaneously.

When he recounted the conversation to Shaida he felt his anger rising all over again whereas Shaida concentrated on the information.

'Okay, so we know they still don't want us to know where they are but they not disregard us, it's just a matter of time.'

'We don't even know if they're still in this country.'

'It sounds like Outi is prepared to give some bits of information via Christina, so maybe we'll hear more later on.'

Needless to say they did not and although Shaida refrained from urging him to contact Christina just in case, it was obvious that neither of them enjoyed the uncertainty. As the week dragged by, Melvin's fuse got shorter by the day.

Claudia just happened to sail past his office with a false smile and made a calculated turn at the doorway.

'I hear Lisa is off this week, is everything okay?'

'No, she's stabbed her mother.'

And he slammed the door in her face. He hauled Rupert in and gave him a bollocking for handing the final payroll report directly to Brannigan, When Rupert just sat there with an insidiously smug grin on his face saying nothing, he thumped the desk and shouted angrily:

'Just remember as far as this secondment is concerned you bloody well report to ME on EVERYTHING!'

'The Director of Finance has intimated that I may not be on this secondment much longer.'

'Thank God for that.'

'So before I go, I'd like to know whether you'll be following up on any of my recommendations?'

'Piss off and take this in-tray with you!'

As he sent the in-tray crashing across the desk, Jack Matthews stuck his head through the doorway.

'Is there anything I can do for you, dear boy, like re-writing the principles of Total Quality Management?'

And so the week went by until he bumped into Zelda after he had returned from one of many visits to the loo to peer at his forlorn visage in the mirror and give the Ajit broad smile technique a miss.

'Christina Rangstrom of Ahus Ericsson rang, can you return her call as soon as possible?'

He bit his lip, this could be bad news. Fearing that his face might be a give-away he made a stab at nonchalance.

'Oh cheers, did she by any chance tell you to put an umlaut over the 'o'?'

'Yes, as a matter of fact she did, and she didn't like it when I said I couldn't get through to you.'

'Okay, I'll ring her now.'

'Righto, can you sign these overtime forms before the last messenger collection?'

'Yeah okay.'

Zelda placed a batch of orange forms on his desk before leaving him to it. He was supposed to check all the claims first but he never did because after the first dozen his eyes would glaze as he tried to fathom the real meaning of all the figures in the little black boxes and columns. Jack had told him to budget for a twenty-five percent lie factor and just get rid of them.

Right now his mind was occupied with how to deal with Christina. He could not avoid ringing her because she would have had no other reason to contact him except to give news of Outi. Considering that he had called her a frigid bitch the last time they had spoken, it was a miracle that she had bothered to ring him at all. No doubt she had overcome her contempt for him on the basis that she could enjoy exploiting his anxiety. When he had got up that morning, and as the coffee percolator spluttered, he had pondered over a conversation with Shaida the night before.

'Virginia said that the meaning of your communication was the behaviour you see,' said Shaida.

'What the hell does that mean?'

'Why don't you join the group again?' said Shaida, 'then it would all make sense.'

'Double dutch is double dutch whether it's first or second hand.'

'Melvin, you being obstinate, we all up tight. All Virginia is saying is that other people will react to the way we colour our language. If we behave in anger we can't expect a civil response.'

'Look, I've know Christina for ages, she's a snooty cow who is incapable of perceiving anything other than in black and white.'

'She's still a human being, try showing her some respect.'

'Why? she doesn't show *me* any.'

'Somebody has to break the cycle, please try next time, I'm sure she knows where Outi and Dillon are.'

The annoying thing was that the harder he tried to suppress his dislike of her and think only respectworthy thoughts about her, the more some slimy, leering, boil-dripping, yellow-toothed, devil danced a clutter-bandy jig across his struggling morality and shrieked with evil relish as goodness sank to the floor in confusion. Well, now he was about to put himself to the test again. He dialled Christina's number.

'Good morning, Ahus Ericsson.'

'May I speak to Christina Rangstrom please?'

'Who's calling please?'

'Melvin Powell.'

'One moment please.'

He waited as helpless as Petrushka in the hands of the wicked Blackamoor.

'Good morning, Melvin,' her precise tones made the hairs on the back of his neck stand on end, 'so good of you to return my call.'

In an instant he felt himself rearing, why did the sarcastic cow have to greet him like that? But then he checked himself. Loads of people at work thanked each other for returning their calls, it was a common courtesy, so he would do his best. He had made a sincere promise to himself.

'Sorry I couldn't take your call when you rang, things have gone completely bananas today.'

'I see, well as long as people are not throwing their banana skins on the floor I am sure you are coping.' (was this the Scandinavian concern for the environment speaking or was she implying that he was the possessor of oafish footwork?)

'Well, I have taken a strategic decision to remain in my chair until things settle down.' (so far, so good.)

'How very sensible, well it is probably the best place to be for the moment because I'm afraid I have some news concerning Outi that may not be to your liking.'

'What is that?' he replied.

'Outi has left her hotel and has gone into rented accommodation.'

'Rented accommodation!'

'Yes, why should she not do that?'

He could think of plenty of reasons but all of them would be totally wasted on her biased ears. He clenched the telephone in an effort to remain calm. He didn't want the supercilious bitch to think she had scored one over him.

'I see. Well, thank you for not beating about the bush Christina, now may I ask you a few questions?'

'Of course Melvin, I am a friend to both of you, as you know, although I cannot guarantee that I will be able to give you all the answers you require.'

'Of course not, but I am sure you will try.'

'Yes, I always try to do my best where personal relationships are concerned.'

'Thank you, now could you tell me whether Outi's rented accommodation in any way includes Dillon?'

'I'm afraid that is a personal matter between Outi and Dillon and I cannot comment.'

(bitch cow bitch cow bitch cow)

'I see. So Dillon is no longer staying at the hotel too?'

'Yes, that is correct.'

'Oh good, well we *are making some* progress.' (bitch cow bitch cow bitch cow) 'and where exactly is this rented accommodation?'

'I am afraid I cannot divulge her precise whereabouts at the present moment however I can confirm that she has decided to find her own space in order to consider her options.'

'How nice, well I've always said you can't beat a good plan,' (bloody bitch cow bitch cow bitch cow) 'and am I to presume that Dillon is part of this option considering process?'

'I can only speak for Outi, I cannot speak for Dillon although it would be foolish to ignore the fact that they have been through a close bonding experience.'

'Indeed not, and I am certainly no fool, you fucking bitch cow!'

And he slammed the phone down.

He was still quivering with rage and confusion when it rang again.

'Yes?' he snarled.

'Hey, take it easy Buster,' said Zelda, 'I've got Shaida from Trans Globe Oil on the line.'

'Oh sorry - thanks - put her through would you?'

'Hi, guess what?' said Shaida.

'Surprise me.' said Melvin.

'Dillon's just rung me from the Holiday Inn at Swiss Cottage.'

'Great, how is he?'

'Drunk.'

'Not so good. I bet Outi isn't with him.'

'No, she not, how you know?'

'I've just had a typically unhelpful call from Christina who informs me that Outi has now taken rented accommodation somewhere in the Northern Hemisphere.'

'Oh Melvin, I'm sorry, that not fair.'

'Somehow I don't think fairness comes into the equation, but what about Dillon, is he making any sense?'

'Sort of. He wants to come home. I think he's had some sort of row with Outi.'

'Huh, that's not too difficult. Can you manage him?'

'Yuh.'

'Okay, well best of luck . . . call me whenever.'

'I will.'

There was a moment's silence whilst they both tried to find a way to finish the conversation.

'I'm here if you need me,' said Melvin.

'I know, I won't forget that . . . I'll ring you later.'

'Okay, take care.'

'Yuh . . . byee.'

The suddenness of the call and its relative brevity began to have some kind of shock effect and Melvin made his way to the loo yet again. He doused his face in water and shrieked at the mirror just as Jack came through the door.

'What's up plonker?'

'Oh nothing that six weeks in the Bahamas wouldn't cure.'

'Well piss off home then, it'll still be here tomorrow.'

'Yeah, I think I may do just that.'

Without more ado he returned to his office just as Claudia was placing yet more paperwork in his in-tray.

'Ah Melvin I'm just issuing this month's accounts, and I've marked those items that Mr Brannigan would like an explanation of.'

'I'll pass them to Rupert,' he replied testily, 'he does the financial analysis for me.'

'Well actually, Rupert has gone to Regional Headquarters with Mr Brannigan to see the Director of Finance,' she smiled like a slab of over ripe Brie.

'I'm sure they will all be very happy together, ' he replied curtly, 'and I shall now place this on Rupert's desk to await his return.'

Thus saying he ignored her and made his way downstairs to see Zelda. They crossed paths at the photocopier.

'Outi's leaving hospital tonight,' he blurted spontaneously, 'so I'm baling out now to collect her.'

'Oh that's great, I do hope everything will be fine, will you be attending the Ops Planning meeting tomorrow?'

'I expect so. I'll buzz if not.'

Missoo purred contentedly on his lap as he sat with a large iced vodka watching the television with the sound turned off. He tried to imagine what might be happening between Shaida and Dillon and wished that she might call him to say that Dillon had told her where Outi was. But the evening was full of silence.

When he could stand it no longer, he recharged his glass and slammed on a CD of Prokofiev's second symphony. Missoo's ears twisted angrily as the strident trumpets bounced off the walls and the first violins nattered agitatedly. Melvin thumped the sofa with his fists as the trombones entered with their remorseless chords. Discord just about summed up his current life condition.

Hours later, with the flickering TV screen throwing the only light into the lounge and some shimmering Messian undulating through a heavy vodka haze he thought he heard the voice of his long dead father. 'Come on lad, shake a leg, we haven't got all day'. He must have been about ten years old at the time. But how could he shake a leg when he had just fallen in love with Cheryl Lawrence in Form 3A? She had spurned him cruelly and he had tried to get up front and personal during PE in the school hall but at the parallel bars she had said with mocking contempt - 'Melvin Powell you're going round the wrong way again'. But he found solace in the music of Berlioz whom he had just discovered and so her rejection was subsumed in the ballroom scene from the Symphonie Fantastique. He would hold her in his arms and swirl to the golden harp arpeggios, only to see her disappear as an anguished clarinet sliced his dream in two.

Missoo nudged open the door and slunk off to see if there was anything available to eat. Melvin was lost in his inner world. 'I don't want to go to Sunday school' he heard himself saying, 'the tunes are lousy and Mr Jaycock's got bad breath'. His parents sent him all the same. One wintry day, thoroughly cheesed off with the predictability of Jesus's goodness, he ran out of the church hall but had to dive behind some vaulting arch as he espied the Reverend Vicar caping it down the pathway in the manner of some high church Dracula.

'What are you doing child?' said Dracula.

'Praying' said Melvin.

That piece of divine inspiration brought a clip round the ear and a purple and black escorted re-entry into Sunday school class.

The music of Messian gathered momentum and layer upon layer rose like a gigantic wave of sound before crashing to a tumultuous end. It beat the hallelujah chorus into a cocked hat. But it resolved nothing and the vodka bottle was empty.

So, Outi had taken flight some place to consider her options. He would now consider his.

The Samaritans or Alcoholics Anonymous.

24

If Father Christmas had sat naked on a pair of antlers, the arrival of December could not have been more painful. The turmoil at work was palpable. It pervaded at every level and in every department. From Directors to general clerks, from technical officers to apprentices, there was fear and mistrust of anything even vaguely resembling change. As such, the Change Management project team were treated with almost universal loathing and suspicion. Three of them had gone sick and one of them was Lisa. The message re-laid to Melvin by another team member was that she had got irritable bowel syndrome and couldn't move far from the loo. A pretty shitty excuse whichever way you looked at it. To make matters worse, Harold had rung to say that he had just received a SNOG message from the General Manager at Luton notifying him that several of his staff had made a formal complaint about Melvin's 'take it or leave it' remark at the Total Quality meeting. *'Such comments are unlikely to engender a feeling of trust and respect'* quoth the General Manager, who had chosen to forget that he had blocked Lisa's appointment for the best part of two months.

'Perhaps you should remind him that his bloody admin. services supervisor had refused to provide an OHP and screen because Total Quality did not feature on their poxy so-called Facilities & Equipment Justification Hiring List,' said Melvin, who, in spite of last night's all time low had managed to haul himself into work.

'Well, I don't think there's any need to get too hot under the collar because he said 'may I leave you to sort this matter out as you see fit',' replied Harold.

'And so it's sorted then, is it?'

'I'm sure it was only a slip of the tongue, now tell me, how are things generally?'

'Well actually, I'm full to the brim with the milk of human bileness.'

'Well don't let it give you indigestion,' said Harold, 'and remember, you can always drop by for a cup of Earl Grey, it works wonders.'

'Thanks Harold, I'll talk to you later when if I discover what the project team are doing, they're probably into self immolation by now.'

They rang off as Jack Matthews loped through the doorway.

'Morning, Wankpot.'

'Hello, Turd Face.'

He was relieved to see that Jack had returned to his former state of chumminess as opposed to the cynical swiping of the previous weeks.

'Is it just me, or is it everybody else?' said Jack, throwing himself on a chair, 'but I get the distinct impression that every bugger I've talked to this morning is either going to commit suicide or stick a knife in me, I mean, what gives?'

'Well, I think it's a combination of things,' said Melvin, warming to a shared view of the world (at least Jack remained a friend even if there had been some tensions between them of late), 'firstly, they've just realised that Christmas is round the corner and there's not much goodwill about, secondly, that Clive Pettifer remains the Acting Director of Personnel which means that we'll all be required to go through Assessment Centres and Cognitive Dissonance Testing, and thirdly, that anyone who has not been seriously brown-nosing it during the last twelve months will be shat upon very shortly.'

Before Jack could respond, Claudia appeared and gave them one of her sickly false smiles.

'Good morning guys, Mr Brannigan has postponed the Ops Planning meeting until 2.30 p.m. this afternoon.'

'Thanks Claudia,' said Melvin, with an oodle-full of pleasantness, remembering what Shaida had said about behaviour and communication. So far so good.

'Oh, by the way Melvin,' she beamed, her eyes lighting up like smarties on top of a chocolate Vienetta, 'did you get the message about Lisa not being very well, I do hope she won't be away for too long, especially as she's your key player, isn't she?'

'Yes I got the message thank you, fingers crossed and all that.'

Bitch cow bitch cow bitch cow, he muttered inwardly, as she made her exit like a gigantic mound of pus. Jack remained slumped in the chair.

'That's one person I hope won't get a job in the new world order,' Jack said malevolently.

'She will if Brannigan does.'

'Yeah, I don't doubt it,' replied Jack, 'he's the only one in this organisation that thinks that ton of lard has actually got a brain but has yet to realise that given half a chance she'd photocopy a sheet of used bog paper if she thought there was something on it he should see.'

'Well that payroll report has dropped us in the shit and she made sure he got an advance copy of that.'

'Yeah, but we can ride that one out with a few sacrificial lambs and the odd goat's testicle,' said Jack, as they began to laugh about the sheer absurdity of working for a company that seemed hell bent on eating its own entrails, 'and that reminds me, Brannigan has had one or two meetings at HQ with Gerald MacNab, any idea what that's all about?'

'Pass,' said Melvin.

They were about to enter into discussion when Zelda came in.

'Hi fellas - Melvin, is your phone off the hook? I tried to buzz you just now but I got an out of order signal.'

'See you later,' said Jack exiting, 'I've got a Shop Stewards meeting.'

Melvin checked his phone.

'Everything go okay last night?' enquired Zelda.

Melvin concentrated on the fact that he was about to fabricate Outi's happy homecoming and would no doubt have to sustain the story for some while to come, if not to eternity.

'Yes, fine, I may have to take some time out to help her settle in but I'll see how everything goes first . . . um, any idea how Fat Arse has picked up on Lisa ringing in to say she was off sick?'

'Not a clue, she hasn't rung me, what's up with her, she hasn't been around for quite a while now?'

'Dunno, the runs or something. Any idea why Brannigan is spending time with MacNab?'

'No, but I can find out.'

'Let us know if you can.'

'Okay.'

'Is Rupert the Prick in residence?'

'Yes and looking especially smug this morning.'

'Something's going on I'm sure. The Ops Planning meeting has been postponed until this afternoon and I notice Brannigan's car isn't in.'

'I'll make a few enquiries.'

'Thanks, and can you get Rupert to suss those account items I left on his desk yesterday, I expect Fat Arse will be stirring it before too long.'

'Sure, no probs,'

The telephone rang and Zelda answered it.

'Good morning, Mr Powell's office . . . oh hello Outi, I hear you're out of hospital, how's things?'

Melvin went a paler shade of white.

'Oh I'm so glad, I'll pass you over to Melvin.'

'Thanks,' said Melvin, trying not to drop the receiver as she handed it to him, 'hello, is everything okay?' Zelda made a diplomatic exit, 'what the hell's going on?' he said through gritted teeth when the door was closed.

'Well, if you stop getting angry I'll tell you,' said Outi in a reasoned, sober tone of voice, 'but I'm not going to put up with you ranting and raving anymore.'

He swallowed hard. After the way she had ignored him, did he really have to be ticked off like this?

'Well, I'll try, but I've got every reason to be angry.'

'Maybe, maybe not but I just wanted to let you know where I am, that's all.'

Was that really all she was going to tell him, he wondered? He paused and tried to summon up respectworthy thoughts about her, no doubt she had received the Virginia practical communication package as well.

'Okay, but it may surprise you to know that I've been worried about you.'

'I'm alright now, so you needn't worry any longer,' there was no hint of sarcasm in her voice, 'but I wondered if you could help me get my clothes and things from the flat because I really don't want to bump into Gladys just yet, I couldn't handle the cross examination.'

'So where are you?'

'I'm in Enfield. One of Christina's friends has rented me her flat for six months whilst she works in the States.'

'How nice of Christina to help you.'

'Yes, and perhaps you would help me too by bringing my gear over and then we can talk about things.'

As a stand-alone request he did not think it unreasonable but in the context of the last few weeks, not to say their fifteen-year disintegrating marriage, (still a noble concept) he found her matter of fact approach truly staggering. Which was to say, typically Outi. Nevertheless, their years together had somehow imbued in him the wisdom of not attempting to challenge her single mindedness at a time like this. If he said no she would be just as likely to organise a removal plan with Christina and that he could not stomach. So yes it was.

'You'd better give me the address and telephone then,' he said.

She passed the details over, 'it's not far from this big pub called the Moon Under Water.'

'That's handy.'

'Not any more. I'm going forwards not backwards.'

'That's more than can be said for Dillon by the sound of it,' he replied, at the same time wondering whether he should be stirring things up.

'He hasn't found his higher self yet and I'm not going to be dragged down again by him or anyone else.' Melvin was in two minds as to whether he should expand on the conversation when Outi continued: 'Can you make a note of the things I need?'

'My pen is poised.'

'And can you bring them over this weekend?'

This was clearly vintage Outi. Focused and in high driver mode.

'I'll start packing tonight, I'm not doing anything in particular.'

'Okay thanks. Can you make it on Saturday?'

'Um, I'm not sure,' he thought he may as well give the impression of some sort of life of his own, 'I'll ring you first.'

'Okay, I'll expect your call.'

He didn't know what to say next.

'. . . I'm glad you're in the land of the living again.' Pretty inept.

'So am I. You ring me then?'

'Yes.'

'Okay, bye then.'

'Bye.'

He rang off and found himself trembling as he replaced the receiver. 'Bloody Nora,' he said to himself, 'this has put a whole new perspective on things.'

Missoo was somewhat alarmed at the sight of an open suitcase. She did not relish another week of Gladys and her patronising blather, for that surely was what was on the cards? She chose to sit on top of Outi's clothes until Melvin ticked her off.

'Missoo, for God's sake, things are difficult enough as it is without you getting hold of the wrong end of the stick.'

She slunk off into a corner and much later, when he had finished packing and was slumped on the sofa with a can of

Pils, she climbed on his lap and purred in reconciliation. He settled down with her and tried to contemplate the immediate future. It was like a virulent stinging nettle on a naked limb.

They both started as the telephone rang. Perhaps this would be Shaida?

'Hello?'

The voice on the other end gave him an unsuspecting jolt.

'Where have you been?' said Samantha, 'I've been missing you.'

It took him a little while to mentally adjust before replying. There was no mistaking her voice although it sounded rather slow and fuzzy, not drunk but probably drugged.

'How are you?' he enquired rather awkwardly.

'I miss you,' she said, as if she had not really comprehended his question, and then, after a long pause during which he was unable to think of anything that would allow him to steer a middle course between politeness and concern she said, 'I hear Outi has left hospital.'

'I take it Christina has been talking to you,' he said, trying to conceal his anger and contempt for the bloody woman, 'has she been to the club?'

'Now and again.'

He considered his reply carefully. He had not visited the Buster Keaton for some while now and the mere thought of its rank and dingy passages conjured up an image of fear and suspicion. It signified that part of his life that was unpleasant and poisonous. Samantha's beauty and radiance had been the only attraction.

'Things have got a bit tricky of late,' he heard himself saying, 'you know how it is.'

'I need you,' she said softly, 'will you come to me?'

'It's a bit difficult,' he replied, wondering at both one and the same time how much she actually knew and what his true feelings towards her were, 'I've got rather a lot on my plate at the moment.'

'I need to see you,' she persisted, 'there's something I have to tell you about us.'

He could not imagine, nor could he sense that it was something particularly good.

'What is it?' he asked.

'Come to my flat tonight.'

'Samantha,' he felt himself getting all knotted up inside, 'it's not that I don't want to see you, it's just that I -'

'You have to help me -' there was a desperation in her voice that tugged at his heart strings, '- I need to see you now, tonight.'

His mind was racing. A visit to Samantha's was not on the agenda but he felt himself weakening the more she pleaded.

'Melvin, please.'

She sounded as if she were almost in tears.

'Okay, okay,' he said, 'but I can't stay for long, there's too much going on at the moment.'

As he emerged into the dark cold of a December evening he wondered whether Gladys had overheard their conversation through her beer glass pinned to the wall or perhaps, since of late he had given her carte blanche to enter the flat to feed Missoo, she had bugged the place electronically? It was an absurd thought but somehow the contact with Samantha had sent his mind spiralling in feverish confusion. What something was it that affected them both that she was so anxious to tell him?

He stumbled blindly down the stairs. The staircase lights had blown yet again (no chance of Gladys and her surveillance coming into play there) and the batteries in his pocket torch were long since dead.

He felt no less uneasy by the time he turned a familiar corner in Notting Hill Gate. Every available parking space was taken, forcing him to cruise several blocks away before he found a spot that would permit the big Merc to power ease itself into a slow reverse. With luck he might get out in one go.

A disagreeable sleet began to fall as he made his way towards Samantha's. He put up his collar, shoved his hands in his jacket pockets and walked briskly on. He was damp and shivery by the time he rounded the corner and saw once again the huge Chinese lantern framed in the casement window. It looked so mysterious and still, its subdued globe hanging like a strange solar planet, its gravitational force drawing him inexorably towards it. The sodium streetlights picked out the sleet in murky tranches and bathed the wet pavement with their eerie glow.

The lights in the ground floor apartment were on but the curtains were firmly drawn save for a small triangle at the top. As he mounted the steps and found the intercom, he wondered what dramas of life were being enacted behind those heavy drapes, cocooning the occupants from the outside world. In a way he was glad that he could enter unseen.

He pressed the buzzer.

Hello?' said a far off voice.

'It's me,' said Melvin.

There was no further response and so he pushed open the front door as the automatic lock released with a hornet's angry growl. Up the flights of stairs and then a tap on Samantha's door. It opened slowly and there she was. As always he was enraptured by her beauty and poise but he was taken aback by the changes he saw. The pallor of her skin was dull and where before her eyes had glistened with sensuous vitality they now had a strange haunted look. He felt her body tremble as they engaged in a soft embrace.

'I had to do it,' she whispered, as they held each other in their arms.

'Do what?' he replied, feeling her trembling increase.

She began to sob.

'What is it?' he said, 'what did you have to do?' he felt her body convulse as her sobbing deepened.

She looked at him with tears streaking uncontrollably down her cheeks, 'I love you Melvin - don't leave me - I had to do it.'

It was then that he saw the fear in her eyes.

'It's alright,' he said, holding her close in a comforting embrace, 'I'm here now, you can tell me everything.'

As he tried to console her, his gaze wandered across the dimly lit room to focus on a figure emerging from the darkness of a doorway. He felt his blood run cold.

'Oh yes, now that is very touching,' said Russell, in his usual sardonic way, 'no gettin' away from it, very touching indeed.'

Instinctively, Melvin gripped Samantha harder. He now knew why she was so full of remorse. He had been set up and she had been forced to lure him there. Russell's motives did not leave much to the imagination. He was calling in his dues. Not the payment for the Merc, but Melvin himself.

'Well shut the door Sam and take Melv's coat, or is there something wrong with old fashioned 'ospitality?'

'Can we just cut the crap for once,' said Melvin defiantly. Inwardly he was terrified but since he was cornered it occurred to him that perhaps a show of resistance might surprise Russell long enough for him to think of some other tactic. It was the action of a desperate man.

Russell moved towards them and with one swift grab wrenched Samantha from his arms and threw her across the room with dreadful force. He then kicked the door shut and with a callous laugh, turned up the lights to their fullest intensity. He had the maddest of looks in his eyes and his pupils were fully dilated.

'Take yer anorak off, sunshine, you ain't going nowhere just yet.'

Melvin remained rooted to the spot, his heart thumping madly as tried to assess what best to do next.

'Oh, of course, I was forgetting,' said Russell, 'you only take yer kit off for Sam, don't yer?' Melvin remained silent, 'well, p'raps you need a bit of stimulus, eh?'

With a speed of movement that was extraordinary in a man of such squat muscular frame, Russell suddenly seized Samantha and started to tear her clothes off.

'Leave her alone, you bloody sadistic bastard!' yelled Melvin as Samantha began to scream. But there was no stopping him. He was like an animal. Within seconds he had torn every shred of clothing off her and as she tried to cover her nakedness he pulled her up by her hair and putting his knee at the base of her spine thrust her body forward in a painful arch.

'Take a gander at that Melv, prime pussy what you 'ave fucked.'

'Jesus, you're insane, let go of her for Chrissake, you'll break her back!'

Russell eyes were burning in a manic glare. He suddenly switched positions and, pinning Samantha's arms behind her back, pulled out a Stanley Knife and held the cruel blade against her vagina.

'Time to share yer cock around Melvin, now take yer fucking clothes off or she gets it.'

'Don't hurt her, for God's sake, don't hurt her, please, I'll do it!'

Trembling with fear, Melvin pulled off his anorak. As he pulled his arm free from the second sleeve he thought he perceived a fleeting shift in Russell's grip on Samantha. Without pausing to work out the logistics of his move, or even to consider what action he would follow it with, he whipped his anorak towards Russell's face.

But even before the garment made contact, Russell saw the move and with one sickening yank, plunged the blade into Samantha's crotch and ripped upwards through her stomach to slice viciously across her breasts and throat. As her intestines spilt through the gaping wound she slumped to the floor with a single agonised scream. Oblivious to his own survival, Melvin catapulted himself towards Russell who threw the knife to one side and grasped Melvin's throat with both hands.

'Yeah! yeah! go for it Melv, go for it.'

He was shrieking with laughter and to Melvin's absolute horror, as their two bodies met, he felt the hardened thrust of Russell's erect penis. In blind terror, he jerked his knee up into Russell's crotch with a sickening crunch. Something snapped. Russell gasped, doubled up in agony and dropped to the floor. Seizing his advantage, Melvin lashed out desperately with his foot and Russell gasped again as the blow smashed into his jawbone. Snatching his anorak Melvin leapt over Russell's body and seeing that Samantha was no more than a heap of blood and guts on the carpet, fled from the apartment.

Crashing down the stairs two at a time and practically falling over himself with the force of momentum he made his final leap just as a strange looking lizard, an iguana perhaps, complete with silver collar and chain, came scuttling out of the ground floor apartment door. Unable to alter his trajectory he vaulted over the twisting creature catching its spiny back in the process whereupon it let out a peculiar hissing screech.

'Socrates!' cried a foreign sounding voice from within.

But by that time, Melvin had wrenched open the front door and was racing like a demon possessed away from the scene of the crime.

25

Just as hanging concentrates the mind so fear fuels the power to escape. In Melvin's case, after he had catapulted up the road like snot off a stick, the power came from the Merc which he had leapt into in a state of high distress and had roared off in a vaguely northerly direction to finally swing into a pub somewhere between Crouch End and Hornsey. He sunk two large brandies and a pint of lager before racing off home where, on his arrival, he filled a half pint glass with ice cubes and poured a neat Stolichnaya over the top of it. He continued the process in the vain hope that it might somehow erase the trauma, but it was not to be.

At six o'clock in the morning, having not slept a wink and with a massive hangover, he beat a path down the caffeine trail. Somehow the mere act of consuming liquid provided him with a form of comfort. He was convinced that any moment now a plain clothes detective would appear from nowhere and say 'May I have a word with you, sir' and he would never see the light of day again. Total incarceration with not a jot of quality in sight. Russell would use a false alibi and blackmail every bent copper in the West End network to walk away free.

Only he, Melvin Powell would be behind bars and Russell would come and taunt him during visiting hours - 'ello sunshine, ain't you gettin' it no more, well don't worry 'cos I've got a mate who'll be joining you shortly and naturally I told him you was cockalatrous'. And then that awful cackling laugh.

Having downed six mugs of coffee his brain began to signal that his system had had enough. He stumbled towards the kitchen sink with the intention of running a cold glass of water but instead spewed his guts out in a long heaving wretch. Fortunately there was no crockery within the area of cascade and so he ran the cold tap on full and just hung on to the draining board as the repulsive mess swirled and slid down the plug hole. He drank several glasses of water afterwards and went into the bathroom to clean his teeth. With his head a throbbing burning lump and his legs about to give way any moment, he dragged himself into the bedroom and collapsed in a heap.

Hours later, when a grey wintry daylight had seen off the folds of night, he slowly came too. He thought he saw a hangman in a black hood but gradually, as his vision adjusted, he realised it was Missoo, sitting on her haunches at the edge of the bed observing him with a kind of inquisitive, passive disapproval.

'Get me a new head,' he groaned at her.

She stared green eyed and then yawned before plopping onto the carpet and making her way to the doorway where she turned and observed him once again. As far as she was concerned, he was awake and could set about giving her a spot of breakfast.

There was a knock at the door. God, was this the police? He gradually eased himself into a standing position and moved gingerly along the hallway to answer the front door. May as well get it over and done with.

'Oh good morning, I see you're up and ready to go somewhere.'

It was Gladys with another one of her totally incorrect assumptions.

'Sort of,' he mumbled, as a vague recollection of his assignment with Outi began to filter into his consciousness, 'I'm just about to feed Missoo actually.'

'Oh well that's good isn't it because I wasn't sure whether you were in or not and I sort of thought you were but I couldn't see your nice big car anywhere and so I thought well I'd better knock first just in case, I mean I've still got the key but you never know what's what really do you, I mean anything could happen, if you know what I mean.'

He held on to the side of the door jam. Gladys was wearing her inevitable pink striped nylon house coat and what with her ghastly matching lipstick and gesticulating Marigolds he was beginning to feel visually assaulted and decidedly queasy.

'Everything's okay thanks.'

'Oh well that's good isn't it?' said Gladys, remaining firmly in position, 'and how's Outi then?'

God, he could really do without this. After weeks of silence she chose now to ask awkward questions. He said the first thing that came into his head.

'She's convalescing in Finland actually.'

'Oh, really, I never knew she was better, oh I am glad, when did she go?'

'Last week.'

'Well fancy her going to Finland without taking her clothes, not that I've been nosing about especially or anything like that of course but sometimes when I've been in to feed Missoo she's been curled up on the bed and well, you can't help noticing these things can you?'

'No.'

'I expect you took her one or two things before she went then?'

'No.'

'Oh.'

'I bought her a new wardrobe and a set of suitcases as a present for being so brave and we went straight from the hospital to the airport.'

'Oh. Will you be seeing her soon?'

'Yes, I'll grab a flight when things ease off at work.'

'Oh that'll be nice. Well do let me know when you're going won't you because I'll be only too pleased to look after Missoo.'

'Thank you, I was going to talk to you about it. I'll get loads of tinned food in.'

'Oh righto then. You can leave it in a box in your kitchen or I'll look after it if you like.'

'Good idea.'

He started to close the door. He couldn't take any more and the stripy images were beginning to burn the retina of his eyes.

'So shall I have her food or will you?' said Gladys, scrambling to take advantage of the last diminishing six inches of her conversational opportunity.

'Yes.'

Gladys displayed that look so peculiar to elderly people who are conducting a conversation and yet remain unsure as to what, if anything, it is all about.

'Don't forget to pack your toothbrush then,' she replied valiantly.

'I'm not going anywhere.'

He pushed the door shut and just managed to overcome a wave of nausea. He returned with fragile steps to the kitchen. The telephone rang in the lounge. He moved feebly in its direction. He still felt giddy as he bent over to pick up the handset.

'Hello?'

'It's me,' said Outi.

'Oh yes, I thought so.'

'I just thought I'd give you a ring to see when you were thinking of coming over in case I have to go out.'

Although his brain was not functioning clearly he felt a strange sense of relief at hearing her voice. Outi, who knew his every emotional twist and turn. Outi who was now sober and in control. Outi who he needed to see and talk to.

'I was thinking of setting off shortly, I just need to take a shower.'

'Oh good. You can have some breakfast here if you haven't had any yet.'

That was a bit of a time warp statement. They hadn't had a breakfast together in years, in fact that hadn't had *any* breakfast together in years. It reminded him of their early days when they would nibble on Finnish black bread and thin slices of cheese and follow it with small cups of strong Finnish Presidento coffee. Outi would get a cigarette going and he would puff his way contentedly on one of his duty free Henri Wintermans Senoritas; such a shame that some nerd in their marketing department had decided that they weren't selling enough and had promptly discontinued the brand. The acrid coils of addiction had never been satisfactorily replaced since the airport stocks ran out.

'That would be nice,' he replied with genuine enthusiasm, noticing that the greasy smell of bacon sarnies now rising from the Diamond Cafe below was not doing wonders for his constitution, 'I'll shake a leg and be with you anon.'

He had a vague recollection that somebody had said something similar to him recently but he was buggered if he could remember who or why or when. It was strange though.

'Okay, have you got everything?'
'Yes, I think so.'
'Did you find my lapis lazuli earrings?'
'I found the pair I bought you in Corfu.'
'Yes, those are the ones I mean.'
'Okay, I'll be with you soon.'
'Bye.'

He slopped sardine and trout Whiskas in Missoo's bowl, nearly gagged, went to the bedroom, tore off his crumpled clothes and then got under the shower. The first jet of water was stone cold and the sensation, so contrary to his expectations, sent shock waves through his body pinning him rigidly to the spot like a penguin marooned on a polar ice flow. It cleared his head a treat though. He dressed rather shakily and decided to reconnoitre the lie of the land before emerging with suitcase and plastic bin liners.

He found the Merc down the end of the road, a narrow dog leg of a cul de sac, with one wheel mounted on the pavement. A net curtain fluttered disapprovingly as he reversed the big car off the pavement and drew level with the side entrance of Ascension House. With the engine ticking over he shot up the staircase, grabbed Outi's belongings from the hallway and sped downstairs again. Missoo sat on the brick wall watching him go.

'Where the bloody hell is Enfield?' he muttered to himself as he turned into the main road hoping that he was no longer over the legal limit. He picked up a sign to Enfield at a roundabout near Cockfosters where everybody seemed hell bent on slicing each other's rear ends off, especially the pretty young things who were dashing between hair salons in Daddy's spanking new Land Rover Discovery. Enfield was jammed with pre Christmas shoppers who brought the traffic to a standstill and gave him time to read the road names and not get lost.

He found a space to squeeze into, hauled out the baggage and staggered to Outi's new front doorstep. The effort had set his heart thumping and his head was throbbing badly by the time she opened the door.

'Bit of a hangover, I see,' she said with the slightest hint of irony, 'can you make it up the stairs?'

'Only if you grab some of these.'

They humped the bags up a long straight flight of stairs. The first floor flat was deep and narrow with a mixture of small and spacious rooms. Very moody. Full of potential. The largest room was at the very back of the building and Outi appeared to have made it into some kind of studio. In the middle was an artist's easel and there were several blank canvases propped up against the wall. In one corner a wobbly cheapo decorating table with brushes and paints and in another rolls of paper and a miscellaneous pile of bric-a-brac including a black ebony statuette of a grotesquely thin African woman who looked like she was about to give birth to a hippopotamus.

'Very creative,' commented Melvin.

'It will be when I get properly started,' she replied.

It reminded him that not only was she brilliant at figures but she had considerable artistic talent as well. It ran in the family. Her sister was a successful professional artist although he didn't much care for her fascination in bleeding bodies hanging from meat hooks in deep forest saunas the day after an orgy. Still, there was no accounting for taste and all those long dark winters were bound to make sensitive souls a tad potty. He resisted the urge to ask her what she was going to do for an income; no doubt she had plans for that too.

'You want some breakfast then?' she asked, 'you look as if you could do with something.'

They made their way into another room where she had laid out a continental breakfast. Memories of happier days came flooding back.

'This is very nice,' he commented, as he munched his way through an egg and sill open sandwich.

'So, what have you been up to?' she said, as they supped their coffee.

He did not know where to begin. His frantic fornication with Lisa? A near death by Suzuki? A threatened company disciplinary? His passionate affair with Samantha? Or his witness to her brutal murder by a drug crazed bisexual psychopath to whom he owed money for a stolen Mercedes Benz?

'Well, you know me,' he said, prising a small fish bone from his teeth, 'not much really.'

Outi said nothing. She drew on her cigarette and exhaled long and silently. He avoided her eyes and clenched his coffee cup. He began to feel himself shake. It started imperceptibly and gradually took hold of him. He broke into a cold sweat and began to hyperventilate. He tried to suppress his rising emotion but he could do nothing to stem the tide of guilt and remorse that flooded over him.

'Just try and take long, deep breaths,' said Outi reassuringly, 'it's just some kind of panic attack but you'll be alright in a minute.'

'I'm in such deep shit,' he whispered hoarsely, when he had regained his composure, 'this may be the last time you see me.'

Outi drew deeply on her cigarette again. 'You'd better tell me all about it.'

He buried his head in his hands, unable to find the words to begin.

'Just start at the beginning and go through to the end,' she said, in a tone that was both level and compassionate, 'there's no point bottling things up.'

It was easier said than done but somehow he was able to take a deep breath and launch himself into it. He did not mention Lisa or the growing intensity of his feelings towards Shaida. Surely, his relationship with Samantha and last night's traumatic event was confession enough? At the end of it, he asked for a glass of water and sank exhausted in the chair. When Outi returned with a long glass, obligingly topped with ice and lemon, they sat in silence for a while before she said:

'I knew about your affair with Samantha.'

He grimaced, 'Christina of course.'

'Not only her but also Karel.'

He recalled Christina's beleaguered boyfriend who'd confessed a life of misery over a bottle of Finnish vodka. He thought he was an okay guy but obviously living with Christina had finally buggered him up.

'You mean she sent him spying on me?'

'No, he saw you leaving Samantha's flat on several occasions.'

'Huh, I suppose he just happened to be walking the dog or looking for a new art gallery or something?'

'No, it wasn't like that at all, his business partner Janek Kapolka owns the ground floor flat below Samantha's.'

'Bloody typical, he doesn't have a pet lizard by any chance?'

'Yes, he's a bit of a weirdo but very observant. He's heard Samantha getting beaten up on several occasions and seen Russell coming and going.'

'Well why didn't he bloody well report it?'

'That sort of thing goes on all the time, it was none of his business.'

'Christ, I don't know what the world's coming to,' said Melvin, burying his head in his hands, 'maybe he knows all about last night, I practically squashed his lizard into the carpet.'

'I don't know but I think you should go the police.'

'Jesus Christ.'

'The longer you leave it the worse it will become.'

Melvin buried his head again. It was no good pretending he wasn't scared shitless. He looked at Outi. There was something different about her. Maybe it was all to do with finding this higher self that she mentioned. She seemed to have lost quite a bit of weight and although it made her rather gaunt, her Slavic cheekbones were seriously attractive. Her complexion was still pale but her eyes no longer had that glazed and bleary film. They were clear, steady and alert.

'You must despise me,' he said, shamefacedly.

'No, I don't despise you,' she replied, taking hold of his hand, 'but I no longer love you either . . . but that doesn't mean to say I want to see you suffer, you're a victim of your own selfish impulses and there's no way anyone other than yourself can take responsibility for that.'

'I know . . . I know ...'

Her pale green eyes held him steadily as he choked back his tears.

'I've had to face up to myself as I really am, now you must do likewise.'

He knew she was right, but how much more did he have to endure before he could break the cycle of events? He knew he had been reckless and stupid but he wasn't evil for God's sake. Everything seemed so unfair. He was about to lapse into self-pity when he realised that what Outi had just said resonated exactly with the explanation Agit had once given him about cause and effect. According to Agit, it was a law of life that could not be altered. Whatever causes you made in this life, or the next, or indeed had made in the past, the effects would exactly reflect them. It was inescapable. The same causes repeated life after life became one's deep seated karma. Only sustained good causes would lead to everlasting peace and happiness.

He finished his glass of water and saw the nadir of his life beckoning through the sodden centre of the ring of lemon. Redemption seemed like a cocktail that was out of stock. He could see the ingredients but they remained stubbornly sealed inside a line of bottles all jeering at him from the top of an unreachable shelf. The scale of the challenge was daunting.

'I think you should lie down for a bit,' said Outi, 'you look dreadful.'

'I can't switch my mind off what's happened and I don't know which way to turn or what to do.'

'I've got some sleeping tablets, they're a mild form of tranquilliser too, it won't hurt to take a couple of those.'

'Okay,' he said, hopelessly, 'maybe you're right.'

Minutes later, under the soft folds of a duvet, he began to drift off.

He was in deep sleep by the time Outi went to the telephone and began dialling a number

26

    Legends are born of heroes whereas cowards are eventually forgotten. Melvin knew nothing of this as he slumbered deeply on. Night had fallen by the time he awoke and gradually, as his senses came into play, he remembered where he was. He thought he saw the sword of Damocles above his head until his eyes adjusted to the light and he discerned the tell tale signs of water ingress on the plastered ceiling. That was not his problem. He had enough to contend with as it was.

    He eased himself out of bed swaying unsteadily on his legs. From another room he became aware of the rich reverberations of a male baritone voice that seemed vaguely familiar but which he could not place just yet. He emerged cautiously into the landing and headed for what looked like the bathroom. It was, and there was the toilet too. He sat on the pan and relieved himself, his first proper bowel movement in days. He washed his hands and splashed water on his face. Am I lucky to be alive, he wondered? He gave the Ajit smile a miss. Well, it could become habit forming and there were enough funny goings on in public lavatories as it was without building up an alternative repertoire in the private sector.

Feeling better now that he'd had a good rest, Melvin moved toward the source of voices. His aural memory was just beginning to scan when Outi saw him on the threshold.

'How are you feeling?'

'So, so.'

'I've got somebody here who can help you.'

He entered the small dining room and there, sitting at the table in the midst of tea cups and a burgeoning ash tray was the shambolic frame of Brian the bent copper.

'Hello Melvin,' said Brian quietly.

'Christ!'

'Well, not exactly,' he replied, with a kind of slow half chuckle.

As Melvin moved closer he saw a blood stained surgical dressing down one side of his face.

'What happened to you?'

'I had a disagreement with Russell,' he said gruffly.

The mere mention of Russell made Melvin feel uneasy.

'D'you want a cup of tea?' said Outi, 'this one's still reasonable.'

'Yes please.'

Nobody said anything whilst Outi poured him a cup and he supped the strong over brewed liquid.

'So, what's going on?' he said, feeling grateful for the tranquillising effects of the sleeping tablets.

Brian lit up another cigarette and offered one to Outi.

'You're lucky to be alive, d'you know that?' said Brian, sending clouds of smoke to join the already towering mass above them.

'Yeah, but how do I stay that way?'

'Turn him in,' said Brian bluntly.

Melvin had difficulty in comprehending that statement, particularly as it had been uttered by Russell's closest sidekick and someone for whom the honour of the Metropolitan Police Force was a matter of utter contempt.

'*You're* telling *me*?' said Melvin incredulously.

'I've finished with him,' said Brian, 'finished with him for good.'

'Somehow I find that difficult to believe.'

Brian's big nicotined stained fingers fidgeted with his cigarette.

'Alright, I don't blame you for questioning me, but he did this to me last night when I refused to - ' he hesitated for a moment, 'well, clear up Samantha.' The big man was clearly uncomfortable and took deep drags on his cigarette, 'the odd bit of merchandise is one thing, but cold blooded murder is another. I told him I'd drawn a line at that and if I hadn't moved fast enough he would've Stanley'd me bloody eyes out. He's gone too far this time.'

'So where is he now? I don't exactly feel safe.'

'You fractured his pelvis and he forced one of the others to take him to a doctor.'

'What about Samantha?'

'I don't know, she's not on my patch.'

Melvin gulped on his tea. The images and sensations of last night began flooding back. Outi was right. It was only a matter of time and what kind of defence did he have? And what exactly was Brian proposing?

'I'll come with you to the local nick,' said Brian, as if reading his thoughts, 'tell them everything that went on and I'll make a statement about everything that I know.'

'But you weren't there, it's his word against mine.'

'Forensic will nail him, besides there's other things I can spill the beans on.'

'But what if Samantha isn't there any longer?' he felt a wave of nausea at the very thought of what such an action would entail.

'None of the boys are playing ball on this one, we need to move fast though, he's got the constitution of an ox, a fractured pelvis won't immobilise him for that long.'

Melvin could hardly believe what was going on. He worked in an office with people who were normal to the point of boringness, this was unreal, it wasn't happening surely? He looked at Brian intently. He seemed real enough and Outi certainly wasn't a figment of his imagination.

'I've spoken to Janek,' said Outi, sensing his anguish and confusion, 'he saw Russell before you arrived and he saw him leave after you, he's prepared to make a statement.'

'The Police won't detain you,' said Brian, 'they'll probably keep an eye on you, maybe even follow you, but I'll make bloody sure they bang that psycho-nutter up good and proper, and refuse bail. I'm on the inside remember and I've got enough on the bastard to send him down for a good few years.'

'It's up to you, Melvin,' said Outi quietly, 'you know I'll stand by you.'

More clouds of billowing blue smoke filled the room like a ghost scene in a pantomime.

'The Force and I had it years ago,' said Brian, matter-of-factly, 'still, there's loads of security jobs for blokes like me when it all blows over.'

Half an hour later, the three of them were heading towards central west London.

27

Dawn broke like blood in glass of Alka-Seltzer but Melvin did not see it. The fact that the skies were clear did not become apparent until midday when he awoke from a long, sleeping tablet induced slumber with not a nightmarish remnant in sight.

He rose and put on a silk kimono that he had discovered at the bottom of the wardrobe when packing Outi's suitcase. With his hair a dishevelled mess, he looked like an up-market Worzel Gummage. He tried an Ajit life affirming grin. 'The crow has landed,' he said to himself. Missoo, usually quite silent, gave an uncomprehending miaow. Something in the air said it was a fresh start of sorts.

A long, sudsy bath followed. He did not sing but neither did he shake. Provided Gladys didn't knock on the door this might very well be the overture to Life Part Two. The interview and statement to the Police went exactly as Brian had predicted. In a funny sort of way he was rather miffed by their apparent indifference. Definitely not in the manner of Prime Suspect. Surely, if they got off their butts and visited the scene of the crime he would at least get to see Helen Mirren? However, he was reminded of the gravity of his situation when they had returned to Enfield and Brian said:

'They've been tailing us all the way.'

In spite of everything, he rose from his steaming bath with a sense of relief. Clean on the outside, clean on the inside.

'Cathartic,' he said to Missoo, as she tucked into her chicken and liver, 'that's what it was.'

Later on, watched by Gladys from her dining room window, he ambled across the road and bought a newspaper. He half expected to see some gory headline in the tabloids but, as usual, the scoop of the day went to some moronic footballer whose girlfriend had discovered him balls akimbo between the silicon implants of a Bay Watch look-alike. Was their *any* human relationship for whom familiarity did not breed contempt?

'Step forward all ye who have reached the Golden Gate in total purity,' he declared, stepping out into the oncoming path of a customised Ford Capri whose two dozen spotlights lit up the sky whilst triple air horns blasted away like the '1812' was going out of fashion.

'I was here, I was here!' he yelled, stabbing at the zebra crossing like Dustin Hoffman as Ritzo Ratzo in Midnight Cowboy. The young punk driver with a Nazi haircut and diamond studded nostrils stuck his finger crudely in the air and roared off in a cloud of burning rubber. No doubt he would be joining his fellow pagans in their ritualistic Sunday lunchtime Valhalla-von-Arnos-Grove-Tattoo. Spunk hungry Tracy's and four-packs of Special Brew being the Neber-yob's alternative to meat and two veg at six ninety-nine.

Safely back inside the flat, Melvin flicked through the pages that declared the measures that New Labour would introduce to make everyone, except the socially deviant, happy and contented, nay smug. The filthy rich were given notice that they were about to be shafted and the millennium voter would awake to the realisation that dropping off the week's about-to-be recycled empty plonk bottles in the jolly old turbo-diesel was soon to become a taxable indiscretion. Bring back child labour and vote for the Donkey Sanctuary Bill. Somewhere there must be figures to support it? The spluttering classes of

Kensington and Chelsea would repair to their Queen Anne writing terminals to remind the proles that whilst the routed Tories might know the price of everything and the value of nothing, the present government could identify the value of everything except the specific gravity of the nearest banana skin. So yah boo sucks. Happiness, it seemed, was once again to be forged in the laundered knickers of self interest whose clammy folds would spew forth donations of such moral rectitude that even Jesus himself, acutely aware of his diminishing congregation, would recommend as a share offer worthy of instant take up. Or perhaps divine intervention would somehow assuage the furious memory of the Fat Cat handouts?

The telephone rang just as Melvin was contemplating whether the art of fence sitting had yet again become a raw buttocked proclivity peculiar to all but the reviled legions of Benefit soakers and the misunderstood dispossessed.

'Hi, how you been?' said Shaida, bringing an Eros thwarted pulse to his heart beat.

'I'm coping in spite of some colourful moments,' said Melvin honestly, 'how about you?'

'Dillon say he want to go back into hospital but Virginia say give it forty-eight hours to test his resolution.'

'She's probably right. Is he sober now?'

'Yuh.'

'Good, so's Outi.'

'You heard from her?'

'Yes, and what's more I've been to see her in her rented flat in Enfield.'

'Oh Melvin, I so glad things are moving forward for you too.'

'It's touch and go but she's doing all the going and I'm just touching, but quite what I don't know.'

'You reaching the parts you never reached before?'

'You're crazy Shaida, but I think you're probably right.'

They contemplated the current state of their existences. Outlook promising if not fully understood.

'D'you think you might rejoin Virginia's group therapy classes?'

He considered the question carefully. His re-union with Outi had been more civil than expected but he had still to get to grips with their separation. She had offered him tremendous support so far and had not even shown the slightest hint of revenge over his affair with Samantha. He knew he needed something and he knew that he should begin to develop a life of his own. Dillon's return to hospital would impact on his relationship with Shaida and if he managed to kick the habit then it was probable that they would never see each other again. Their closeness would be at an end. He did not relish the thought but neither did the idea of attending group therapy as a way of seeing her again.

'If Dillon remains sober, when d'you think he will go back in?'

'Not before Tuesday.'

'Maybe I can see you after then?'

'Yuh, I'd like that - I'll ring you.'

They met in the Nag's Head plastic grot pub Tuesday night and he told her about Samantha and how Outi had contacted Brian and Janek and his visit to the Police station. He told her everything, just like he'd always done.

'My God, Melvin, something somewhere is protecting you, this is not just a lucky break.'

'Maybe you're right, I d'know. Even Brian rang me to say that Russell had been arrested and bail had been refused just like he said it would.'

'And Outi still want to see you, it's kinda spooky like you got Gods of protection on your side.'

'Yeah, I'm counting my blessings.'

It was true, he was beginning to do just that. As the days went by, it was apparent that a reconciliation of sorts with Outi had been achieved and although it looked probable that they would remain apart, they continued to see each other in a growing atmosphere of mutual understanding and respect. Outi had launched herself into her painting with tremendous gusto and some of the results were quite startling and beautiful.

'Can you make me a sort of wooden frame to hold all my canvasses in?' she said one day, 'it will have to be free standing because I can't drill holes in somebody else's flat.'

Melvin set about the task with relish. It reminded him of the days when he had created coat racks and hat stands and even now they had not fallen apart. Soon, his visits to Outi became more regular. He would knock up various bits and pieces positioning his Workmate bench on the concrete veranda of Ascension House and Missoo would sit on the brick wall and watch him. Inevitably, Gladys would find an excuse to walk past him and say 'another job I see' and he would counter that with 'yes indeed, these evening class projects are coming thick and fast'. The big boot of the Merc would swallow them up and she would never see them again. His rudimentary carpentry was proving to be a pleasurable relief from the chaos that still reigned at work.

Christmas was practically upon them and everyone was becoming more stressed out and unmanageable. Joy usually took the form of revelling in someone else's misfortune and cynical sweepstakes were taken as to whether their latest cock up was liable to put them out of the job race altogether. But nothing fuelled the grapevine as intensely as the news that Jack burst into Melvin's office with early one morning. He was practically dancing.

'Sit down wanker and get a load of this, you'll love it, you'll absolutely love it - guess what?'

'Well I don't bloody know, tell me for Chissake.'

'Nigel Denmark has been sacked.'

'No!'

'Yes! yes! the puke filled bastard has been shafted good and proper, tee hee hee!'

'Great, oh bloody great.'

'Yeah, bloody yippee,' the two of them whooped and thumped the floor, 'and rumour has it that the Chairman gave Denmark the shove personally because he couldn't trust Clive Pettifer to do it properly.'

'Oh, I love it, I love it - and I bet Gerald MacNab is like a dog with two tails.'

'Two dicks more like it, now listen, I've got something else to tell you and I've got to get it in quick before Brannigan calls you, so shut up and listen, maybe you won't like this so much, on the other hand I expect you probably won't care a toss.'

'Try me.'

'HQ have published the re-organisation structure, all the General Managers have a copy and they've been told to hand it out to their management teams tomorrow morning and organise a cascade briefing to every single employee. They're going to merge Administration with Customer Service and create a new management position to handle the lot, so you and I will effectively have to re-apply for our jobs and go through Assessment Centres and all that bloody clap trap.'

'Not before Christmas surely?'

'No, you prick, of course not, but obviously they're hoping that some of us will get major ring piece twitter during Christmas and pull out of the running.'

The telephone rang. It was Claudia.

'Melvin, Mr Brannigan would like to see you right away in his office, it's very important, so please come quickly.'

'Yeah sure, I'll pop right along.'

'Fat Arse?'

'On the dot.'

'Right, don't let on you know this but Brannigan has asked me to take over your lot as well as mine as a holding arrangement to stop things falling apart because Rupert the Prick is going back to Audit and Brannigan's done a deal with MacNab to offer you a twelve month secondment as Regional Change Manager whilst they kick arses in and out of place. I think there's another grade on the table which is good for the old severance package'

'Jesus, how do you know all this?'

'I'll tell you afterwards, now don't keep him waiting and for Chrissake act surprised.'

'I am, why me?'

'No other fucker wants it.'

'But I'm making one bloody cock up after another.'

'Nobody cares and apparently Harold has put in a good word for you, now get going, I'll see you afterwards.'

And so he did.

Brannigan was his usual blunt self and yet, surprisingly, showed some glimmer of understanding about the realities of keeping the Service Centre functioning satisfactorily.

'It's too much to expect any manger to handle a big project and run a separate administrative operation simultaneously, Jack has more Senior Officers he can delegate to and I don't think our friend Rupert Selwyn-Smythe has quite got the common touch.'

'Zelda was beginning to mould him though,' replied Melvin, making sure she got a mention in dispatches.

'It's alright, I know they don't come better than that and I shall support any recommendation you put forward in the way of staff bonuses.'

'Oh thanks.'

'Now I want you to make your mind up by the end of the week so we all know where we stand before Christmas.'

'I can't believe in the current climate that HQ are prepared to offer *two* grades higher than the one I've got already.'

'There has to be some incentive for a job like that. Come and see me eight o'clock Friday morning.'

As things transpired, Melvin discussed the issues with Outi the night before. He had been working on a surprise woodworking project for her and the timing was spot on.

'I thought you could store your brushes in it,' he said proudly, as she inspected the giant piece of bamboo cane which he had Araldited to a block of walnut, 'it's nearly six inches in diameter and solid as a rock.'

'You're telling me, it could almost double up as a door stop,' then she noticed that he was a little hurt by her playful remark, the aesthetics of form being something that he could never quite get the hang of in practical terms, 'no seriously, it's very nice, I may even varnish it.'

'Okay, so what about this job then, I don't know what to do for the best.'

She lit her umpteenth cigarette and considered everything he had told her. He topped up their coffee and waited for her reply.

'It strikes me that you'll be swapping one lot of aggro for another so you might as well go for the higher rate of pay, especially if it means you can get out and about a bit, besides you don't really want to spend the rest of your days in an organisation like that, do you?'

'I'd go tomorrow if they offered me the money.'

'Well there you are then, it probably won't even last six months.'

And so that was another decision arrived at. They chatted amiably for another hour or so until come eleven o'clock he decided it was time to go.

The night air was cold and miserable and as he paused on the doorstep trying to remember where he'd parked the car she surprised him by saying:

'You look washed out, I think you need a break, I'm spending Christmas in Finland, if you fancy coming I can probably get another ticket.'

The thought of frozen forests and pure white snow had a certain appeal, especially as the alternative would probably be to haul up the drawbridge and get canned in desperate isolation.

'Hmm, that sounds rather nice, it seems ages since we last went.'

'I'll see what I can do then.'

'Okay, thanks.'

As he walked past the Moon Under Water pub, he realised that this was the first December in fifteen years that he had missed their traditional lighting of the Finnish Independence Day candle.

28

Christmas is always revealing. Knickers come down as the divorce rate goes up (battered children and starving pets being largely ignored until the New Year's press).

At British Energy Services Limited, the run up to the Yuletide festivities saw a string of departmental shin-digs culminating in the pagan ritual of the Service Centre Christmas lunch. As the great primordial shovel-in got under way, the catering manager's voice rose by about three octaves. Most of the supervisors who were supposed to be providing operational cover were drunk at their posts.

It was traditional for the management team to get up and sing a Christmas carol, this usually being the signal to pelt them with half eaten bread rolls and anything else that could be lobbed through the air without actually causing grievous bodily harm. Grabbing a catering size potato scoop as a pseudo microphone Melvin led the troops with Hark the Herald Ages Sing. The robustness of his diminished seventh was not appreciated. Boos, jeers and catcalls followed. He sank, in no small relief, beside Zelda and the girls, looking as inane as everybody else amidst the shreds of Christmas crackers and lopsided party hats. The celebrations had reached the point where most folks began to collide with the furniture or stick their tongues down each other's throats. Still, it was friendlier than a stab in the back.

'Merry Christmas,' said Zelda, giving him a big hug and a kiss, 'don't be late for your plane.'

'No, I may as well bale out now, I'm pretty superfluous to the remaining events.'

They hugged again.

'Thanks for everything you've done, Zelda, I couldn't have managed without you.'

'Does this mean we won't be seeing you again?' said the girls. News of Melvin's appointment had spread through the grapevine like a champers cork from a well-shaken bottle.

'I'll send you all personal SNOG messages from Headquarters,' he replied.

'Rather have a real snog now,' said one of them, knocking her wine glass into a plate of congealing brandy sauce. It was clearly time to go.

The air outside was damp but refreshing as Melvin climbed into the Merc and headed straight for Enfield. It was a tight schedule but he had packed the night before and given Gladys her Christmas present when handing over a box with Missoo's cat food.

'Ooh, how lovely,' said Gladys, in genuine delight at the triangular shaped parcel, 'what on earth is it?'

'Well, it's not a Balalaika, I can tell you that much.'

'Ooh, I'm so excited, can I open it now?'

'No, wait until Christmas day,' he replied.

He didn't want the embarrassment of seeing her unwrap a long handled dustpan and brush.

As he coasted towards the outskirts of Enfield, the big Merc coughed and spluttered and came to a halt. The petrol gauge registered empty.

'Shit!' he exclaimed.

No spare can of petrol and no mobile telephone. He knew there was a garage about a mile further along and since there was no alternative, he gritted his teeth and set off at a thunderous pace, cursing and swearing between rasping breaths.

'Twenty-four pounds fifty,' said the cashier, indifferent to his suffering.

'Bloody rip off,' replied Melvin, clutching a bright plastic petrol container complete with a separate shrink-wrapped tapir shaped spout and multi-lingual pouring instructions.

'EC regulations mate, nothing to do wiv' me.'

He paid up and crossed the road to a BT phone box. The handset had been torn out and lay in pieces on the floor. An aerosol arsehole had given vent with the simple message - 'BT Sux' By the time Melvin returned to his car he was in a kind of compressed rage that did not lend itself to freeing a petrol spout from a hermetically sealed package. In the end, he attacked it savagely with his teeth.

'Where the hell have you been?' said Outi angrily when he eventually arrived at her doorstep stinking of petrol and with his fingernails torn. The atmosphere was no better by the time they pulled away from a second garage, having endured a long queue at the checkout whilst the tattooed driver of a black BMW Series 3, changed his mind about a special offer CD and grabbed half a dozen bags of glacier mints instead.

As airports go, Luton had really got its act together, unfortunately, the same could not be said for all the approach roads. Add to that the fact that nobody was prepared to give way to anybody else because they all just wanted to get the hell out of it, everything soon ground to a fairly impressive halt. Outi was now virtually chain-smoking as they inched their way forward through a mass of mud splattered road cones that stretched in all directions as far as the eye could see. Outi remained tight lipped and silent, exhaling clouds of smoke through dragon flared nostrils. As mass frustration became palpable, drivers resorted to extreme measures in an attempt to escape the gridlock. Some tried U turns in the face of oncoming vehicles which caused yet more swathes of rage and the flashing of lights. Emergency sirens could be heard in the distance.

'What's happening?' yelled Melvin to a lorry driver who had been forced to jam on his brakes and come to hissing halt alongside him.

'Some bloody contractor has ripped up a gas main and there's also water shooting up like a fucking fountain in the middle of it.'

'Jesus Christ, it's absolute chaos,' said Melvin, pressing the window button as the lorry revved up.

'Well do something,' snapped Outi, 'or do you really want to spend the entire Christmas stuck in this hell hole.'

'What am I supposed to do, fly out of it?'

'Try following that driver, he looks like he knows where he's going.'

Outi pointed to a Range Rover that had crossed the verge and was climbing steadily up a muddy embankment. It had a Chilterns Radio sticker on the back of it.

'He's got permanent four wheel drive, I can't do that sort of thing in this.'

'You'll have permanent brain damage if you just sit here doing nothing, just take a bloody run at it.'

This was the point where rational thinking ceased to play a part in things. Stabbing the accelerator to the floor, he swung the nose of the big car towards the embankment and roared up its incline in a shower of mud and detritus. Nearing the top it suddenly lost its traction and started to slip and slither down a gully on the other side. Melvin grappled wildly with the steering wheel, keeping the car revving madly in the hope that it might heave itself out of the next mountain of rubble that they were now crashing into. The huge car bucked and reared violently as it vaulted miraculously over the top of it. Thundering down the other side, they spun out of control sending a gang of contractors diving for cover as they crashed through a group of dumper trucks and assorted vehicles.

'Keep going!' yelled Outi, as they slewed to a halt in front of a JCB. As Melvin searched frantically to find a way out of the no-man's land he recognised the face of the driver in the JCB. To his absolute horror it was Troy, his face contorted with scars yet alight with the fuel of revenge. The arm of the scoop swung dangerously towards them.

'What's that maniac trying to do?' screamed Outi.

'Trying to kill me - now hang on!'

He yanked the gear lever into low drive and stamped his foot on the accelerator. The Merc shot forward twisting madly from side to side in a cascade of mud and water. The rear wheels lost their grip again, spinning and burning as the big engine screamed at maximum revs. Behind them, Troy clattered inexorably forward in the smoke belching JCB, the jaws of its huge scoop raised malevolently like the head of Tyrannosaurus Rex. It loped and thundered towards them. The wheels of the Merc suddenly bit again and they rocketed forward with the force of an elephant's fart ignited with nitro glycerine. Troy was left behind to wallow and plunge in fury.

They reached the airport check-in just as the flight was closing.

'Your luggage will have to go on a later flight,' said the check-in clerk, 'I'll try ringing boarding control, it's your only hope now and I'm afraid you won't be able to sit together.'

'That doesn't matter,' snapped Outi, 'we're separated anyway.'

When they arrived flushed and breathless at the threshold, the air stewardess managed one of those smiles that only those who have toiled at the cutting edge of public service could truly appreciate. The passengers seethed and tut-tutted as Outi and Melvin dropped their sweaty bodies at opposite ends of the cabin. Within minutes the big jet was surging down the runway.

'Would you like something to drink, sir?' enquired the stewardess pleasantly, when they were thirty thousand feet above the North Sea. Melvin had no idea what Outi was doing, so as far as he was concerned, he may as well suit himself.

'Thank you, I'd like four double vodkas with a separate tumbler of ice.'

Surprisingly, he got what he asked for. He sat back in his seat and contemplated their narrow escape. What if they had remained stuck in the mud? Would Troy have killed them both? Would Lisa have forgiven him then? And where was Russell now? And what about poor Samantha? He had done his best to save her, hadn't he? God, it was awful. Suddenly his insides began churning, so he leapt into the aisle and made a dash for the toilet. Mercifully, it was vacant. He spewed his guts up and looked in the mirror. The pallor of his skin matched the burnished aluminium of the toilet pan, the blue of his eyes like the chemical disinfectant still dribbling from the rim.

'Soon be landing, sir,' said the blonde stewardess helpfully as he returned falteringly to his seat. He gazed through the porthole at the icy panoply of the Finnish horizon, watching spellbound as it turned from golden red to deep tinted indigo, and finally, as the plane began its descent, the blue remembered twilight of a Nordic evening. The captain announced that the temperature was minus twenty-two degrees centigrade and hoped that everyone had packed their thermal underwear. Ho ho ho, very waggish. A stint as Father Christmas in Oxford Street would soon knock that on the head.

Outi was in much better spirits as they walked together across the carpeted arrival lounge. Her sister was there to greet them and he watched fascinated as the two women embraced each other lovingly and began chatting away merrily in their native language. It sounded like machine gun fire under bath water.

By the time they reached the car it was snowing. A perfect crystal floated down to rest in the palm of his hand. It remained there, unmelting in the dry cold air. He gazed in wonderment at its faultless symmetry. A precious jewel of nature. And then Outi caught his eye and smiled. It was a smile as big and round as a sunflower, its radiance beaming from cheek to cheek. He returned her smile with joy in his heart.

The moment had come to have an affair with life itself.

oooOOOooo

Other novels by Martin Pilcher
Visit the author's storefront for direct on-line purchase.
www.lulu.com/aadvarkzap

Up a Yum Bum Tree

Freddie is a missile scientist with a mad idea. When the British Government rejects his plan, he signs up with Boris Blodvrinsky, a mega-rich Russian Mafia boss. But nobody could envisage the effects of the mysterious Yum Bum tree which grows to become an icon of peace for the 21st Century, visited by world leaders desperate for good publicity. When its sap is discovered to contain a volatile compound for rocket fuel, as well as being a fantastic body cream - greed, ambition, lust and loathing all combine to produce a human drama that climaxes in front of the world's media.

Beyond the S-Bend

Ambrose is a politician who believes he has achieved spiritual enlightenment. The truth is, he's a smug, right-wing, muddle-headed control freak. Nevertheless, he convinces the nation that he will fulfil his manifesto promise 'to put the dignity of human beings above all else'. He becomes Tory Prime Minister in a landslide victory. But, within months of taking office he announces plans to build six new mega-sized prisons and introduce national identity cards. It is all part of his personal vision known as The Great Thrust Forward which includes doubling the police force, immigration service, customs & excise and the national coast guard. When he begins an affair with Helga, a mysterious civil service secretary, with fascist tendencies, everything starts to go pear-shaped. His enemies mount a leadership challenge, but not everything runs smoothly in politics. A tale of political incompetence and human delusion.

www.ingramcontent.com/pod-product-compliance
Ingram Content Group UK Ltd.
Pitfield, Milton Keynes, MK11 3LW, UK
UKHW021318180426
11947UKWH00015B/1305